MURDER AT NASA

LUKE RYDER
BOOK 2

JOHN G. BLUCK

ROUGH
EDGES
PRESS

MURDER AT NASA

ONE

BATHED in the eerie light of the waning crescent moon, a masked figure in black slipped through a back entrance of a NASA building, part of a facility that occupied eleven acres. The rear door's dead bolt had been taped over to stop it from locking.

Called the Unitary Wind Tunnel Complex, the huge research area was the very place where the Apollo moon rocket and space shuttle models had undergone critical tests decades ago. The building had a 1960s look and feel.

This evening, at the heart of the mammoth structure, in a large room four stories high, Dr. Scarlet Hauk sat alone. She perched on a metal chair next to two workbenches and a drill press, yearning for the company of her fiancé, Nigel Worth, who also worked at NASA. Her mind wandered, and she reviewed previous relationships she'd had with men.

She sat close to the impressive 9-by-7-foot Supersonic Wind Tunnel that stretched the length of the sizable room. The tunnel's massive steel body resembled a small grain silo lying on its side. Through one of the tunnel's optical glass portholes, Scarlet gazed at a scale model of the X-909 Space Plane.

Pungent marijuana smoke wafted from Scarlet's lips. Weed reduced her anxiety. Her job as the space plane project test manager came with a full dose of pressure.

Fifteen minutes ago, Scarlet's team had completed the second of three wind tunnel tests of the model that had been slated for that evening. Turning the tunnel's huge fans to blow air around the model used enough power to serve a big city neighborhood. Her team ran tests in the wee morning hours when electricity rates were the lowest. But most importantly, fewer people were aware of the wind tunnel experiments. Though the effort to produce the space plane was well known to the public, many details of the program were top secret.

A wisp of cool air soothed Scarlet's face. She crushed her reefer on the floor, picked up the butt, and put it in a metal bandage box in her briefcase. She snapped the case shut, stood, and stretched.

Why had she agreed to stay with the model when the rest of her crew had left to eat at Ralph's, an all-night diner, during their meal break? After all, a guard stood duty at the front door, though she considered him unreliable. The more she thought about it, though, she admitted to herself that she remained in the tunnel to avoid unwanted attention from a couple of the male members of her team. Then again, she also did it to prevent arguments about who would stay behind to monitor the test setup.

A loud pop from a breaker switch echoed. The room's lights went out. The huge space was now inky dark. Scarlet felt a chill. "Hey, guys, quit the funny stuff," she yelled in her German accent. There was silence, save for the padding of soft footfalls. "Stop screwing around."

A sound, like mud hitting high up on the wall, startled Scarlet. Splat. Jitters cascaded down her back. In the gloom, there was no way she might've seen someone shoot a paintball at the lens of one of two security cameras. A second wet-sounding plop echoed farther along the wall.

Scarlet huffed. "Okay, the joke's over."

Clearing her throat, Scarlet stepped toward a door that led to the front foyer. A hand grabbed her long blond hair from behind. The hand yanked her head backward. A serrated blade sliced her neck. Blood spurted. Her weak scream halted the instant her voice box was cut. Acute pain jolted her. She fell. In fifty seconds, she died, her life evaporating like a fleeting dream.

* * *

AFTER RIPPING Scarlet's watch from her wrist, the killer stuffed the timepiece in a pocket. The assailant snatched her briefcase, opened it, and removed documents. A camera flash fired five times in the darkness. The killer put the documents back into the valise, closed it, and wiped its brass lock and handle with a clean handkerchief.

The murderer in black neared the wind tunnel, peered at the space plane model through the glass porthole, and then left the large room. Minutes later, the intruder removed the tape from the back door's lock and fled. The rent-a-cop guard who sat on a chair just inside the front door snored. Evil had prevailed.

TWO

IN EASTERN KENTUCKY, Deputy Sheriff Luke Ryder sat at his desk, relaxed. He realized he had become accustomed to his new job, although it had taken quite a few months to do so.

Previously, he'd been a Kentucky game warden, and as a warden, he'd had law enforcement powers, which he'd occasionally had to use. But now, law enforcement was his everyday duty.

He glanced across his desktop and smiled when he noticed the portrait of his live-in girlfriend, Layla Taylor, and her young daughter, Angela. Six months ago, he'd rescued Layla, the most beautiful woman he'd ever seen, from the abusive owner of an escort service, who later proved to be a serial killer.

But his smile gradually turned into a frown when his thoughts traveled to his ex-wife, who had become an incurable drug addict. Since his divorce, he'd felt emotionally numb, and sex had become his drug of choice. Now he believed something was changing inside him. He certainly cared for Layla. He wondered if he truly was beginning to love her, or if she simply was a passing fancy. Did she love him?

All of a sudden, a pesky fly buzzed in circles and then landed on the wall. Ryder grabbed a newspaper and swatted the insect. It fell dead onto the floor just as Ryder's tan desk phone rang.

"Luke here."

"Luke, this is your cousin, Nigel."

Six-foot-two Ryder—of half-English and half-Italian descent—stretched his long body and lifted his brown leather boot on top of an open desk drawer. "Nigel, I ain't heard from you in a coon's age. What's goin' on?"

Ryder pictured his cousin Nigel Worth, a big-boned man, an ambitious achiever, now working in California at NASA as the chief of external affairs. Nigel lived in a world alien to Ryder, who was at home in the Kentucky woods, but not comfortable in any city. It had been more than a year since they had spoken, and Nigel had lost most of his Southern drawl.

Nigel said, "I'll get to the point. It's been two years since Scarlet was killed, and the FBI task force to find her killer might disband soon if they can't make progress." He coughed. "I wonder if you can come out here and help."

Ryder rubbed his black mustache and remembered that Nigel's fiancée, a NASA engineer, had died on NASA property, her throat cut. A native of Germany, she'd come to NASA from the European Space Agency to assist in joint space plane research and development. "I'd be willin' to ask for time off, but is the FBI gonna say it's okay for me to butt in?"

"If you decide you want to help, it's already been set up." Nigel paused. His voice faltered. "I hope this won't irritate you, but I called Jim Pike without consulting you first. The FBI called him, too. He said helping them would be a feather in your cap, and he'll support it." Sheriff Jim Pike had been a boyhood friend of both Ryder and Nigel. Pike was also Ryder's boss.

"When do you need me to leave?"

"Soon. I'll e-mail you the contact info for the FBI travel office. They'll set up and pay for the trip."

"I'll call 'em."

Ryder was puzzled. It wasn't like the FBI to invite an inexperienced lawman into their fold. His cousin, Nigel, must've become quite influential in the last two years.

Ryder looked out his window. He studied beech and linden trees waving in the breeze and the very green landscape, teeming with plants and animals. He remembered watching deer outside his office at dusk as they feasted on tree and shrub leaves and on the shoots of vines and woody plants.

He wondered what California was like, how it was different. He was aware of its mind-numbing traffic jams, dry heat, fires, and earthquakes. He'd also heard of the redwoods, the giant sequoias, Big Sur, and Yosemite. Layla's little Angela hadn't stopped talking about Disneyland ever since her best friend had recently visited there. He didn't know how far away it was from Northern California. He'd find out more about the Golden State in the days to come.

THREE

WARM AFTERNOON Californian sunshine calmed Ryder as he sat in a black iron garden chair on the patio of his rented backyard in-law suite. It was a garage-sized building with one bedroom, a sitting room, a bathroom, and a kitchen. The freshly cut grass had a sharp, sweet smell.

The FBI had leased this place in Sunnyvale, near NASA, for him and Blackie, his young bloodhound. The dog lay at his feet. Its ears perked up at the sound of a wren.

An enterprising FBI agent had decided Ryder would bring the hound to NASA as a service dog. The person must've seen the recent picture of Blackie and Ryder in a Lexington, Kentucky, newspaper after the sociable canine had led Ryder to a murder suspect.

Ryder's FBI-provided cover story noted that he'd served in the Army during the Congo Conflict and suffered from post-traumatic stress disorder—PTSD. Of course, he'd never been in the armed forces. He didn't like to lie, but to fool a killer, Ryder would do so.

Ryder rubbed his scalp. Self-doubt plagued him. How in the hell had the FBI decided he was qualified to work undercover on a murder that had gone as cold as the North

Pole in January? The Bureau seldom worked with outsiders. Besides that, he'd been a deputy sheriff for less than a year.

Ryder yawned. He hadn't slept well lately. He'd been under pressure from the moment he'd disconnected from his cousin's phone call. The week had been hectic. He had needed to find someone to help his girlfriend, Layla, take care of the farm he rented. He'd worked with the FBI travel office to get Blackie on his flight and to find a rental place with a dog door that exited to a fenced yard. The detached in-law suite had proved to be perfect. The homeowner/landlord had been told NASA required temporary housing for a recently hired contractor.

Something else bothered Ryder. Why had the FBI sent him merely basic information about the case? If the Bureau had provided him with a special application for his phone, it would have enabled him to decode sensitive material.

Tomorrow, Monday, would be his first day undercover at NASA. He'd walk onto NASA grounds knowing not much more than his cousin, Nigel, had told him two years ago after Scarlet's death. He sighed. It was like attending the first day of school, which had always made him nervous. Now in his late thirties, he thought he shouldn't worry like a pimply-faced teenager.

Ryder stood and decided one way to get rid of his beginner's jitters would be to explore the neighborhood. "Blackie, let's take a walk."

Blackie's ears wiggled. The excited dog trotted toward a metal patio chair from which his leash drooped. Wagging his tail, the hound carried the leather strap to Ryder.

Two minutes later, Ryder strolled along city sidewalks and surveyed stucco ranch houses and bungalows. An ex-Kentucky game warden, this trek through a town was unusual for him. He was more at home in the wilderness.

Ryder noticed a stunning young woman of Asian descent.

She stared down the block and called out, "Max. Max."

When Ryder stepped closer to her, he noticed her

distressed expression. A broken collar attached to a blue leash was in her hand.

"Ma'am, did your dog run away?"

The woman nodded. Her dark eyes were liquid, ready to leak tears onto her flawless skin. "He run after squirrel," she said with a foreign accent.

Ryder smiled. "If you'd like, I'll help you find him."

"I would be thankful."

Ryder pointed to his hound. "My dog, Blackie, is a tracker. If you'll hand me Max's collar, Blackie can sniff it. There's a chance he can find your dog by following his scent."

The woman gave Ryder the broken collar and leash. Her long black hair draped over her bare arms as she bowed and said, "Thank you."

Ryder held Max's collar near Blackie's nose. "Track."

The hound sniffed the sidewalk and pulled his leash. Ryder walked briskly behind the animal as the dog's nose locked on to a scent.

The young woman followed Ryder and the bloodhound. "How come he knows to do this?"

Ryder glanced over his shoulder. "I trained him to track deer back in Kentucky, where I'm from."

"The dog good at it."

High in an elm tree at the end of the block, a squirrel flashed its tail. The diminutive creature screeched an alarm call.

Ryder pointed. "See that tree? Perhaps that varmint is the one Max chased."

Blackie led Ryder and the woman toward a garden shed next to a short, white picket fence. A medium-sized terrier poked his head around the corner of the storage building. Ryder pointed.

"Is that your dog?"

The woman smiled. "Come here, Max."

The dog raced toward them, jumped up and down, and panted. The woman picked him up and held him tightly.

Ryder smiled. "He's frisky."

The woman bowed a trifle. "Thank you, sir." She paused. "You live 'round here?"

"I recently moved into the neighborhood. My first day at a new job is tomorrow." Ryder thought he should practice his cover story. "I was hired to work as a contractor at NASA under an Army program called Project Transition. It's for GIs who finished their service."

"You work for NASA. How exciting." She inspected Ryder. "You still soldier?"

Ryder felt guilt course through his body. "Not anymore. I decided not to re-up after the Congo Conflict ended."

"You seem like soldier. Tall, strong. Why NASA hire you?"

"To write press releases and articles. They told me my first one's gonna be about a space plane. I'll be in the Public Affairs Office."

The woman smiled broadly. "I know man who work there. He Josh Sable, news chief."

"I'll meet him tomorrow."

Still holding Max, the woman shifted, reached into her purse, and fished out a business card. "Here. I work with business partner in flower store. It not far. If you need flowers, come by. I give you deal." She handed the card to Ryder.

It read, "Ms. Kang Hyo-Ru—call me Candie." The card also named her business, Simply Flowers, and listed its address and phone number.

Candie fluttered her eyelashes, "What your name? I mention you to Mr. Josh Sable when he next visit shop."

"Luke Ryder." He extended his hand.

She shook it with a gentle grip. "May I have card back for minute? I write something." She set Max on the lush grass near the sidewalk and put her foot on his leash. He sat quietly. She removed a pen from her handbag.

Ryder handed the card to Candie.

She scribbled on its back. "That my cell number. Call me any time to learn about this area."

"Thank you, Candie." Ryder glanced at the number and stuck the card in his shirt pocket. "It was nice to meet you."

"The same here, Mr. Luke Ryder." She picked up Max. "Don't forget call sometime."

"I'll call 'cuz I'll need flowers to send to Kentucky."

"Bye, bye." She waved, her palm facing Ryder.

"See ya later," Ryder said.

She turned and walked back the way she had come. Ryder watched her until she turned the corner.

Walking back toward his new apartment, Ryder thought his stroll had been successful, and he felt relaxed. Candie was friendly. He would find time to visit her shop and have a dozen roses shipped to Layla, his live-in girlfriend. He yearned for her and wished he wouldn't have left her to take on his undercover assignment.

After he walked a half block, thoughts of his upcoming first day at NASA again invaded his brain.

FOUR

RYDER STARTED out early to commute to NASA in his rented electric pickup truck. He liked the heavy-duty black vehicle because he sat high enough to see the traffic all around him.

The four-lane city road in a Sunnyvale commercial district was crowded during rush hour. A large paper cup of coffee sat in the holder next to his seat. The steam from the hot brew smelled good. It was a friendly, familiar odor, and it relaxed him. Blackie was in the back seat with his head sticking out of the window. He sucked in the smoky smells of the city.

Ryder stayed in the right lane, taking his time, though he kept up with traffic. He reduced his speed for a slow-moving, gray, late-model luxury sedan in front of him. It had extensive rear-end damage. Four young men rode in the gray sedan, two of them black, one hispanic, and one white.

The white man turned his head and stared out of the rear window, catching Ryder's eyes.

Ryder glanced at the left lane. He noticed an older, red, gas-powered sedan closely following a purple sports car, which was traveling alongside his truck. Ryder was boxed in, unable to pass the sluggish car in front of him, which further reduced its speed.

Ryder resisted his urge to tailgate the gray sedan. He cut his speed again and saw a large brown car parked at the curb. It had a two-way radio antenna protruding from its roof. Ryder thought the vehicle might be an unmarked police car. Two men sat inside.

Ryder's truck was traveling twenty miles per hour in the forty-five mile per hour zone.

The purple sports car moved forward and now was side by side with the slow sedan.

At the same time, the red-beater maneuvered next to Ryder, preventing him from moving into the left lane. The red car's driver, dressed in ratty clothes, grinned and nodded at the occupants of the slow-moving sedan.

All of a sudden, the driver of the purple car jammed down his accelerator. The vehicle's tires squealed, and the pungent smell of burning rubber entered Ryder's truck.

The purple car immediately swerved in front of the slow sedan and stopped abruptly.

The sedan's driver screeched to a halt.

At the same instant, Ryder smashed his brake pedal to the floor. His truck swerved right. It slid into a driveway, narrowly avoiding the sedan.

The purple sports car and the beat-up red sedan sped away.

Heavy traffic funneled into the left lane to move around the stopped gray sedan and Ryder's truck.

Ryder shook his head and let out a breath. "That was close, Blackie."

Ryder figured it was an attempted intentional crash to suck him into an insurance fraud scheme. He remembered police back in Kentucky called it a "swoop and squat" maneuver.

The four men stepped out of the gray sedan. The Hispanic driver walked toward Ryder's truck. He had a beer belly and appeared to be six-foot-two.

"Hey, you. You hit my car in the back." He pointed his tattooed arm at the rear of the gray sedan.

Ryder backed his truck into the street.

"I didn't hit you. You and I both know it's a scam."

"You're full of shit, mister. Me and my passengers got whiplash, too."

Ryder put his truck in gear, but the Hispanic man stepped in front of Ryder's vehicle.

"We gotta exchange insurance information."

"There was no damage," Ryder said.

"See the back of my car?" the Hispanic man asked.

"That's old damage," Ryder said as he exited his truck. Blackie hopped out, too.

A young woman dressed in a floral top and blue jeans walked up to the Hispanic man.

"I saw it all. The black truck hit the back of the gray car. I'll be your witness."

The sedan's three passengers approached. Ryder thought they were gang members.

From another angle, two unshaven men in work clothes walked at a quick clip from the sidewalk toward Ryder's truck. One was Asian American with shoulder-length hair, and the second was a black man with dreadlocks.

The two men displayed their badges.

"Police. Everybody stay where you are."

The Asian policeman said, "I need everybody but the driver of the black truck to sit on the curb." He caught the attention of the woman who had claimed to witness the "accident."

"That includes you, ma'am."

The white man nodded at his companions.

At once, the four men who'd occupied the sedan and the woman ran in different directions.

The Asian cop pursued the white passenger.

The black policeman sprinted after the Hispanic man and tackled him. The obese, olive-skinned Hispanic rolled aside, kneeled, and pulled a short wooden club from his back pocket. He struck the lawman on the head when he began to stand. The peace officer fell like a bag of concrete.

Ryder rushed toward the injured policeman.

The Hispanic man raised his club, about to strike again.

As Ryder dove at the hoodlum, he used his left hand to grab the man's right hand, which held the club. An instant later, Ryder's clenched right fist smashed into the Hispanic's jaw, jolting it like an electric shock.

Blackie latched onto the thug's leg, drawing blood.

Ryder slugged the man twice more.

The short wooden club fell from the fat Hispanic's hand and hit the pavement. It sounded like a mop handle dropping on a basement floor.

Bleeding from his mouth and nose, the Hispanic collapsed backward to the street's surface, unconscious.

Ryder said, "Let go, Blackie."

The dog obeyed.

The arm of Ryder's brand-new sports coat flapped loose, ripped.

"Damn," Ryder said. Hearing footsteps behind him, he turned around.

The Asian policeman had reappeared. He cuffed the Hispanic man.

The black lawman came to, shook his head, and rubbed it. He studied his blood-covered hand. "Hurts."

The Asian policeman said, "Hang in there, Ollie." He pulled a handie-talkie two-way radio from its holster and radioed for backup and an ambulance.

The black policeman began to stand but hesitated. "You certain I need an ambulance, Frank?"

"He hit you hard." Frank turned to Ryder. "Thanks for helping. If he'd connected with the second swing, Ollie would be at heaven's gates talking to Saint Peter."

"Sorry I wasn't faster."

The distant sound of sirens became louder, piercing Ryder's ears. An ambulance slid to a halt next to his black truck.

Ollie again tried to stand. "What happened?"

Frank touched Ollie's back. "Don't try to get up." He pointed to Ryder. "This man saved you."

Ollie focused his eyes on Ryder and said, "Thanks, mister. I'll get in touch with you soon."

Emergency medical technicians rolled a stretcher to Ollie and helped him onto it. In seconds, the ambulance raced away.

Frank turned to Ryder. "We videoed the incident. You're not at fault, but we need a statement from you. Please let me see your driver's license, registration, and proof of insurance."

Ryder nodded. He opened his truck's front passenger door, and Blackie jumped in the vehicle. Ryder took out his paperwork, including his contract job offer on NASA letterhead. He felt fortunate the FBI had provided him with a substitute driver's license and credit cards and had created new supporting information about him, which also was posted on the Internet and elsewhere.

"You're from Kentucky?"

"Yes, Officer." Ryder remembered his FBI instructions were to maintain his cover unless otherwise instructed by the FBI agent in charge of the task force. Normally, government employees are not supposed to buy private rental car insurance because the federal government is self-insured. The FBI had required Ryder to buy insurance for his truck rental because he was working undercover as a government contractor.

"I'm on my way to my new job at NASA. I hope I won't be late." He examined his ripped sports coat.

Frank said, "I'll buy you a replacement."

Ryder smiled. "Thanks, but you don't have to."

"I insist." Frank turned his head as two patrol cars arrived. "You can leave after we take pictures. I'll give you a call later to tie up loose ends. I need the address where you're staying. What's your cell number?"

Ryder told him his address and phone number. "Will I have to testify?"

"These guys committed a felony. They're members of an

organized criminal ring. Let's see what the district attorney says."

"Okay."

"We staked out this stretch of road because it's where three staged accidents have occurred. This is a high-priority case."

Ryder nodded.

A second ambulance arrived, and EMTs used smelling salts to revive the cuffed Hispanic man.

Frank motioned to a patrolman and pointed at the restrained man. "Place him under arrest for assault on a police officer, section 204C, and for staging a car accident, penal code 550PC. Go with him to the hospital."

"Yes, sir."

A man wearing a crime scene technician vest took pictures of the area. An investigator measured Ryder's skid marks and photographed his truck's undamaged front bumper.

Frank squinted at Ryder. "I know you need to report to your job at NASA. Either I or the DA will call you if we need your help with this case. You're free to go." Frank handed Ryder a business card.

Ryder glanced at the card. "Thanks, Officer Chen."

Ryder entered his truck and resumed his drive to NASA. He realized he'd been lucky the incident hadn't interfered with his undercover assignment before it had even started.

FIVE

RYDER SAT near Nigel Worth's desk. A single tear ran down Nigel's face. He wiped it away, though his chin quivered. Then he fingered a well-worn photographic portrait of Scarlet Hauk.

Ryder's mind's eye flashed back to a gruesome crime scene picture the FBI had sent him. The poor young woman's throat had been cut, and her blond head rested in a puddle of blood on the NASA wind tunnel's cold, concrete floor.

Nigel wiped his cheek and fixed his gaze on Ryder. "Sorry." He cleared his throat. "I still love her."

"I understand." Ryder nodded. "Ain't you dated anyone else yet? It's been two years."

Nigel sighed. "After we set the wedding date, I felt married."

Ryder reached across his cousin's gray government-issue desk and patted his arm. "We'll git whoever did it." He let out a breath.

Blackie sat near Ryder's ankles and watched Nigel with intelligent canine eyes.

Ryder figured the animal sensed most, if not all, human emotions. Did the dog absorb and understand Nigel's sadness and loneliness?

Nigel dipped his head, inhaled, and stood. "Let's get over to Building N-204 and meet your civil servant boss, Josh Sable. He's a senior public affairs specialist, a GS-14, but we call him the news chief."

"What's he like?"

"Two or three years ago, he was okay. Then he became a prick. Treats his crew like peons. They hate him."

Ryder wondered if he'd pass for a professional writer. "I hope this cover works. I wrote for the Bluegrass Community College newspaper, but that was years ago. And I took journalism classes, but—"

Nigel held up his hand. "Don't worry. Send your news stories and articles to me at my personal e-mail address. I'll edit them if needed."

The men followed the highly polished hallway that smelled like it had been waxed and buffed recently. Ryder held Blackie's leash, and the dog's claws clicked and slipped along the floor. Ryder said in a soft voice, "I would've preferred an alias."

Nigel began to descend a staircase. He used a quiet voice. "Mike Lobo, our chief of counterintelligence, and most everybody on the FBI task force debated what name you should use. Their story that you served in the army during the Congo Conflict was genius. It works well with Project Transition because a lot of soldiers are getting out of the Army. And I don't care if anybody finds out we're related. That makes your cover story realistic."

"You don't care if people say it's nepotism?"

"That's illegal. Nobody would guess you're in law enforcement." Nigel glanced at Blackie. "The story that Blackie is your PTSD dog is clever, too."

Ryder took his time going down the steps. "I hope I don't run into any Congo vets who wanna swap stories."

Nigel smiled. "It's all going to be fine. Just me, Mike, the FBI, the chief of Ames Security, and your contract boss, the owner of Sullivan Logistics, know you're undercover. Sullivan's sworn to secrecy." He paused. "Before anybody else tells you, the FBI created false records that say you were fired from both your game warden and deputy sheriff jobs. That's in case anyone hears you worked in law enforcement."

Ryder turned his gaze toward the building's exit. "Sounds like the FBI covered the bases." He paused. "You positive it was acceptable to tell Sullivan about this investigation?"

"No problem. Mr. Sullivan has a contract with the FBI in San Francisco."

As the two cousins left the administration building for the short walk to the public affairs offices, Ryder glanced at nearby older structures, many of which had sturdy concrete walls. He also spotted a myriad of newer buildings.

There were shade trees planted along many of the roads and sidewalks that crisscrossed the research center, which had been founded in 1939. Since then, at least three billion dollars had been invested in its physical assets. By 2030 Ames had more than three thousand employees.

Most of the trees Ryder saw had been planted in the latter half of the twentieth century, thanks to the insistence of a previous center director. The foliage, the grass, and the many buildings gave the campus the appearance and atmosphere of a major university.

While Ryder walked, he heard the powerful sound of air rushing through a wind tunnel. His whole body sensed the power of it. He spoke loudly. "This is a huge campus."

Nigel spoke with a strong voice. "Have your map?"

Ryder tapped his dress shirt's breast pocket. "Yep."

The sun was bright. The California sky was blue and almost cloudless. The air was fresh, but Ryder wondered if he should have accepted this undercover assignment. As a recently sworn-in deputy sheriff, he'd never envisioned himself needing a cover, pretending to be someone he wasn't.

SIX

IT WAS a hundred-yard walk to Building N-204, which housed the Public Affairs Office as well as the Office of the Inspector General on the second floor. Nigel turned his head toward Ryder as they walked. "The FBI agent in charge will call you to set up a meeting off-base tonight to bring you up to speed."

"Good. They sent me case file highlights. But I need to go over all of the evidence."

Nigel stopped. "I'll fess up. I wasn't the one who suggested you join the task force. The agent in charge, Rita Reynolds, did."

Ryder halted, too. "Rita Reynolds, the skinny girl that was two years behind us at Boone High?"

"Yeah, but now she's a charming and influential woman. Ambitious, too. Her life is the FBI. She never married."

"That's how the FBI knew about me?"

"She said she's been in touch with people in the holler for years." Nigel rubbed a foot on the mat outside Building N-204. "When she came to me with the idea that you should be on the task force, I was surprised. After she explained her reasons, I agreed she had a great idea. She didn't want to tell you she thought of it. She believed I'd have the best chance of convincing you to come out here."

Ryder took a deep breath. "No matter how it happened, I'm here. I'll do my best."

"I know you will, and I'm pleased you've come." Nigel pulled open the sturdy aluminum and glass door to Building N-204.

The two men and Blackie climbed the steps to the second floor. The sparkling building smelled fresh, as if it had been cleaned that morning.

Nigel kneeled to pet Blackie when the men paused at the top of the stairwell. The dog licked Nigel's hand, making a smacking sound with its lips and tongue.

Nigel focused his eyes on Ryder and whispered, "Josh's office is at the end of the hall." He wiped his hand on his trouser leg.

Offices were on both sides of the light-tan corridor. Nigel guided Ryder and his dog down the hallway, their footfalls echoing. Men and women, members of the public affairs staff, glanced at them from their desks.

After Ryder and Nigel passed an open area with cubicles about halfway down the hall, Nigel pointed through an open doorway at an empty desk. "That'll be your office. You'll share it with Lucinda Lu."

Ryder nodded. He noticed a petite, young Asian woman with waist-length hair sitting at a writing table across the room from his empty desk. "First-class office," he said in a low voice.

The two men and the dog reached the end of the hallway. Nigel tapped on Josh Sable's open office door. Josh—a short, stocky man with a face to match—peered up from his desk. He seemed sour, as if he were irritated. He held the nub of a pencil in his left hand. He'd been editing a typewritten sheet. Staring at Ryder, Josh cleared his throat. "Hello, Nigel. I'm guessing this is Luke Ryder."

Nigel stepped into the office. "Yes, sir. Fresh out of the Army, together with his service dog, Blackie. Project Transition is a godsend. It's hard to get money to hire extra help. We got lucky when the politicians decided to create and fund the project to help vets."

Josh's pale blue eyes grabbed Ryder's attention. "It's a pleasure to welcome you to the office, Mr. Ryder." He paused. "This is your service dog?"

"Yes, sir." Ryder blinked and cleared his throat. "He helps with my PTSD."

Josh rose and held out his hand to Ryder. "Thank you for your service."

Nigel smiled. "Like we discussed earlier, Luke will concentrate on the X-909 program. But you can use him for other duties, too, such as the *Astrogram*." He turned to Ryder. "Be certain you also write articles for the *Astrogram*. It's the employee newspaper."

Ryder nodded.

Josh frowned. "We're shorthanded, and there are too many stories to cover. We'll keep you busy."

Ryder realized even if he didn't feel confident going into this undercover role as a writer, he must appear self-assured. It's what police call "command presence." He stood tall, made eye contact with Josh, and mustered a smile. "Thanks for the opportunity, Mr. Sable. It's going to be exciting." Ryder's eyes drifted to a large picture frame covered in glass that displayed a dozen poker chips branded with different casino logos.

Josh glanced aside at the large display. "My collection of poker chips. I like the colors and designs."

Nigel pointed at the chips. "Josh travels to Vegas every year to play in an annual poker tournament. He's quite a player."

Ryder analyzed Josh's unblinking blue eyes. "It must be fun."

"It has its ups and downs. You have to learn to play the odds." Josh paused. He pointed down the hall. "I've asked our secretary, Lucinda Lu, to introduce you to the staff. She'll set you up with office supplies. We'll have a staff meeting today promptly at 1:00 PM. Basic rules of our office are to meet all story deadlines and be on time for our meetings."

Ryder cocked his head. "Yes, sir."

As Ryder left, Josh turned to Nigel. "Please stay and close the door."

SEVEN

NIGEL CLOSED the heavy maple office door, sat in the chair next to Josh's desk, and straightened his tie. "What's up, Josh?"

Josh sat behind his desk and wrinkled his brow. "I've scrutinized Mr. Ryder's resume. To be blunt, I'm not impressed."

Nigel leaned forward. "Beggars can't be choosers. We're lucky we acquired anybody from Project Transition plus the money to fund his slot for a year."

"Yeah, but the guy has no real experience except for his community college newspaper. He isn't a university graduate. We need professional people, like a guy who worked as an Army public information officer."

"Luke has served his country, and we owe him. He's smart. Talk with him. You'll see."

Josh drummed his pencil on his desktop. "Why mandate that he cover the X-909 program? I'd prefer he cover easier stories, do employee human interest features for the *Astrogram* to get experience."

Nigel took a deep breath. "The higher-ups agreed they

would give me the money and a contractor slot for the X-909 program, which needs positive publicity."

Josh bit his lip and then said, "The space plane public affairs duties are too important and sensitive for an inexperienced person to handle properly. If he messes it up, I'll be in your office demanding we switch him to easier assignments. If the directors learn he's blown it, it'll be hard to keep him employed."

"Give him a chance, Josh. If you're worried, offer advice. Review what he writes, and do what you do best, edit."

"Let's pray he works out. By the way, is he going to have that mutt with him? What if he craps on the floor?"

"The man was in hairy situations in the Congo. It's a service dog, and yes, it'll be with him because of his PTSD. It's well-trained and gentle."

An artery in Josh's throat pulsed, a bead of sweat rolled down his temple, and his forehead reddened. "I'm keeping an eye on Luke."

"I'm certain you will. You're a perfectionist. But after he's been here a while, he'll know the *Associated Press Stylebook* as well as anybody." Nigel stood. "I'm late for a meeting with the directors."

EIGHT

RYDER SAT on the swivel chair behind his empty, gray metal desk.

Blackie rested on the floor.

The dog perked his ears and stood when Lucinda Lu entered the office, carrying an armful of office supplies. She was a young, short woman with long, black hair.

She smiled and plopped pencils, pens, legal pads, and manila folders onto the ink blotter on Ryder's desk. She brushed her dark hair aside. "Hello, Mr. Ryder. I'm Lucinda Lu." She spoke fast, like she was high on caffeine. "Josh told me you'd start today. When I saw you go by, I decided to raid the supply cabinet."

She kneeled and petted Blackie. "Who's this guy?"

Ryder pushed himself up from his seat. "Blackie's his name. And you can call me Luke." He glanced at the pile of office essentials on his desk. "Thanks for the supplies."

"I'm here to help the staff with typing, copying, and computers." She stood and offered her thin hand.

Ryder grasped it. "If you're not busy, do you mind givin' me a rundown on my computer?" He pointed at the modern machine on his desk.

Her eyes sparkling, Lucinda cocked her head. "Glad to." She rolled her chair next to his, making a clattering sound. She sat and turned on his machine. "Programs such as word processing and e-mail are on top here. I wrote your NASA e-mail address, your direct line, and the general office number on this index card."

She slid the card across the ink blotter and then fingered the computer mouse. "We use Leaf Word processing and View Graph Generator for presentation slides. And then there's CPA Pro for spreadsheets…"

Ryder sat down. "Will I need all of them?"

"They'll be there if you require them later. If some of the programs are unfamiliar, I can help. One I enjoy is the Fantastic Artist program. I use it to create computer artwork for presentation graphics."

As Ryder's eyes wandered past Lucinda, he was captivated by paintings and graphic prints on the wall behind her desk. They were an interesting combination of classical Oriental and modern art. "Are those your work?"

She colored. "Yes. Thanks for noticing. Most people don't because they're always rushing around."

Ryder stood and stepped closer to the artwork. "They're outstanding." He paused and turned to her. "Is it possible for you to tell me about the people in public affairs? If they're in such a hurry, it might be hard to get to know 'em."

She waved him back to his chair and then leaned toward him. "I plan to take you around to meet everyone after the one o'clock staff meeting." She lowered her voice. "If you don't say who told you, I can give you the lowdown on everybody."

"I'd like that, and I can keep a secret."

She moved closer to Ryder. "If you tell me something about yourself, I'll tell you about me before our tour of the office."

"You go first."

"My grandparents came from China. I grew up in Chinatown in San Francisco, and I speak Mandarin."

Ryder took a breath. "My mother was born in Naples,

Italy. My dad was from the valley in Kentucky, where I was born. They've both passed on."

Lucinda widened her eyes. "You have such a distinctive Southern accent. I wouldn't have guessed you have Italian roots. Do you feel like I do? Like an outsider?"

"My maw had an Italian accent, and she was a Roman Catholic. Even though I was born in the holler, I was kind of an outsider. But still, I got close friends there."

Lucinda shifted in her chair. "What's the holler?"

"A narrow valley between hills or mountains."

"A rural location?"

"Uh-huh. Now, how about the folks in this office?"

Lucinda touched her cheek with her forefinger and peered upward as if she were trying to compose answers in her head. "Let's start at the top, with the guy you must watch like a fox—our fearless news chief, Josh Sable." She paused. "Don't tell anyone where you heard this."

Ryder studied her. "My lips are sealed."

"Josh was an upstanding guy three or four years ago, but he was flighty. Down in the dumps one minute and a short time later, high as a kite." She paused. "Now he's mean."

"Is he divorced?"

Lucinda shook her head, her raven-black bangs swaying across her forehead. "He never married. But something must've happened. A couple of years ago, he sold his hot sports car and bought a used clunker."

"He was gruff when I met him."

"A superb way to describe him. When he's off the job, he might be different. I wonder if a girlfriend rejected him. I can identify with that. I've had breakups. They mess with your head."

Ryder nodded. "A crummy love life can make a person bitter."

"Josh is bitter, and he takes it out on the rest of us. Such as, everybody has to arrive at the weekly staff meeting on the dot. If you're ten seconds late, Josh will make a check in his green notebook next to your name. If you get three or four checks a year, he'll reduce your evaluation by one step if you're a civil servant. If you're a contractor, he'll write a complaint to your company supervisor." She frowned.

Ryder sighed. "I hope this job works out. I've got to cover the X-909 Space Plane tests."

Lucinda arched her back. "The X-909's very important. They must think a lot of you to take Leon Turk off that beat." She peeked out of the open office door and then returned her gaze to Ryder. "Leon's peeved."

Ryder bit his lip. His first day on the job, and already people were upset with him. The office clock read 11:50 AM. "Sorry to interrupt, but is there any chance of you givin' me directions to the cafeteria? My stomach's growling."

Lucinda stood and rolled her chair back to her desk. "I'll take you there. I'll tell you about strange stuff that happened in the X-909 program, too. That is, if you want company."

"Thank you. Let's go when you're ready." A solid meal would make him feel better, and Lucinda seemed to be a fine information resource.

NINE

CARRYING HER TRAY, Lucinda led Ryder toward a far corner of the Ames cafeteria. "Let's sit where it's not crowded. I want to speak normally without anyone else listening." The large eatery was packed with people enjoying lunch.

Ryder balanced his tray while he led Blackie on his leash. The dog's nose was busy taking in a plethora of food scents.

Diners glanced at Blackie as he trotted by their tables, his claws clicking on the vinyl tiles.

Lucinda set her tray down and pulled out a chair while Blackie scavenged a fragment of bread from the floor.

Ryder said, "I'm most interested in the X-909 project 'cuz it's the main reason I was hired." Ryder's coffee was bitter and tasted like it had been made with a powder.

Lucinda spread and smoothed a napkin across her lap. "The first thing that comes to mind about the space plane is something dreadful."

Ryder furrowed his brow. "What do you mean?"

"A woman was murdered two years ago after midnight in the high bay area of the supersonic tunnel. She headed the X-909 test project."

"Terrible."

"According to rumor, Dr. Scarlet Hauk—the person who was killed—slept around. She must've done something to tee off whoever did her in." Lucinda shook her head. "They never caught anyone."

"How do you know she slept around?"

Lucinda blinked and sighed. "My boyfriend at the time told me. I think he might've had firsthand knowledge." She looked down for a moment. "I thought he was going to marry me. I was sad when he dumped me, so I dated several men on the rebound. I'm not in a permanent relationship now, although I'd like to find Mr. Right." She paused. "I'm already thirty-one, and I want to have children."

"You don't seem to be older than twenty-three."

Lucinda smiled but teared up. "Thanks."

Ryder took a bite of his sandwich. He hoped to give Lucinda time to regain her composure. He listened to the chatter of the noontime crowd and the sound of cool air flowing from a vent. As he peered through the picture windows that wound around the perimeter of the cafeteria, he noticed a large wind tunnel not far away, its gray, solid steel structure impressive against the blue sky.

He put down his sandwich. "What about that public affairs officer, Leon Turk, the guy you said used to cover the X-909? You told me he's annoyed they gave me that beat."

Lucinda directed her eyes at a table in the middle of the cafeteria. "See the muscular guy with the red plaid shirt, wearing expensive cowboy boots?"

Ryder caught sight of the tall, blond man with the body of an NFL player. He appeared to weigh roughly two hundred twenty pounds.

"He's Leon. A pushy guy. Wants to be in charge. Reminds me of a strutting rooster."

"You don't like him?"

"He's a rat. He's spread word you're a country bumpkin who's not qualified to cover the X-909, and you're bound to fail."

"Feels like I'm walking onto the set of a soap opera."

Lucinda tittered. "Perfect portrayal."

Ryder slid his chair closer to the table. "I heard the X-909 test manager's now Bill Little."

Lucinda nodded. "Everybody knows Bill was passed over to give Scarlet the space plane test manager job. I'm all for breaking the glass ceiling, but I hate to say she wasn't as qualified as Bill. I can't blame him for being upset."

"Was Bill as irritated with Scarlet as Leon Turk is with me?"

Lucinda took a sip of cola. "Yeah, but now word has it he's mad at Leon because Leon wants to stage elaborate media events to build backing for the space plane, but Bill wants the tests to be low-key. I bet that's why they hired you."

Ryder finished his sandwich. "Why wouldn't Bill want publicity?"

"On occasion, engineers think fancy PR campaigns take too much time away from tests and slow down research. Also, Bill realizes political appointees at NASA Headquarters in Washington, DC, might cancel Leon's publicity if they think it might adversely affect the administration. Then it would be a total waste of time to do the public affairs work."

"That so?"

Lucinda frowned. "Didn't they tell you all the news items you write, except *Astrogram* employee newspaper stories, must be cleared in DC? Guess who's in control there? Party hacks. Each president appoints campaign workers and donors they trust to be part of the bureaucracy. They determine what's released."

"Why bother to have public affairs?"

"The Space Act of 1958 that created NASA says the agency must inform the public about what it's doing and the results of its research. I'm told it's the only—or maybe one of the few parts of the government—ordered by law to publicize itself."

"Seems complicated." Ryder lowered his chin and said, "'Cuz the law says we must do publicity. If I write what Bill likes, it should be okay, correct?"

Lucinda's body language showed skepticism. "When you submit something to headquarters, even if Bill likes the write-up, it's just as if you're shooting it toward a black hole. You don't know if it'll be kicked back as okay or if it'll be swallowed, never to be seen again."

"That's depressing."

"Yes, and…" Lucinda scanned the cafeteria tables behind her as if she wanted to be certain no one was listening. "I had to type a document for Josh's boss, the guy who brought you to the office this morning, Nigel Worth." She leaned closer to Ryder. "There was plenty of technical stuff, but I noticed the X-909 is also being developed for the Space Force, not just NASA."

"Why does it matter?"

Lucinda whispered, "Because the document said the X-909 can fly to any place on Earth in an hour. It could drop a bomb, shoot rockets or bullets, and fly back undetected."

"It's a weapon?"

"I don't know. I just type stuff." Lucinda stood. "We better get going. It's close to one o'clock, and I don't want Josh to put a red check next to my name for being late to the staff meeting."

Ryder noticed Leon Turk swagger at a quick pace as he moved toward the cafeteria's exit in a rush to arrive at the meeting on time.

TEN

LUCINDA CHECKED her watch as she power walked from the cafeteria toward the building that housed the public affairs offices. Two sparrows in a bush next to the sidewalk chirped and flew away as she rushed by.

"Come on, Luke." She glanced at Ryder. "I don't want to be late."

Ryder quickened his stride.

Blackie's tongue dripped saliva as he trotted behind Lucinda and pulled Ryder with his leash.

When Ryder held Building N-204's aluminum and glass door open for Lucinda, he glanced at his watch. The time was 12:56 PM. "I need to visit the men's room." He stared upward at the restroom door on the second floor near the stairwell.

"Better be fast," Lucinda said. She trotted up the stairway. "The meeting's in the conference room."

Ryder took care of business as fast as he could. When he entered the conference room, the wall clock read 1:01 PM.

Josh sat at the head of a heavy, elongated wooden table. Showing signs of being uncomfortable, public affairs staff members filled the seats at its edges.

After he opened his green notebook, Josh made a check in it. "I see our new man has arrived, but tardy."

"Sorry," Ryder said. He eased onto a chair near the conference room wall next to Lucinda's chair. Blackie lay at his feet. Office members who didn't fit around the large conference table had taken chairs beside the walls.

Josh wrinkled his forehead. "After the meeting, let's have a word in my office, Mr. Ryder."

"Yes, sir."

Josh addressed the group. "Mr. Luke Ryder has joined our office by means of the Army's Project Transition, which eases soldiers back into civilian life." Josh glanced at his notes, which he'd written in black ink with a fountain pen. "Mr. Ryder is from Eastern Kentucky, where he obtained his associate degree in journalism from Bluegrass Community College. He wrote for the student newspaper. Later, he joined the Army and took part in the Congo Conflict, according to Department of Defense documents." Josh fixed his eyes on Ryder. "Thank you for your service."

Ryder nodded. He felt heat flood his face. All of it was true except his fictitious military service.

Josh scanned his staff. "I expect all of you to help Luke gain experience during his stint in our office. Perhaps after that, he can become a permanent member of public affairs or, if he wants, find a related job in private industry." Josh tapped his pen on his notes for two seconds while the restless staff watched. "Luke will take the X-909 beat as directed by upper management."

Staff members traded glances. Leon blinked and then gazed at Ryder.

Josh took a deep breath. "He'll also be available for additional duties as assigned. Employee *Astrogram* stories, for example. If any of you need help covering your beats, let me know. I'll decide if Luke can lend a hand."

Blackie fixed his eyes on Lucinda and wagged his tail, hitting her leg with it. She petted him and said, "Excuse me, Josh, but I'd like to introduce Blackie, Luke's service dog. He's friendly."

Josh relaxed and sat back. "Thank you, Lucinda." He glanced at Leon Turk, who scratched the left shoulder of his plaid, red cowboy shirt. "Leon, as we discussed—take Luke over to meet Bill Little, the man in charge of the X-909 model tests, after the meeting."

Leon nodded. "I've set a meeting for later today." He turned to face Ryder and rolled his eyes. "If Luke needs help, I'll assist."

Ryder frowned. Leon's body language signaled he wouldn't be of much assistance.

Josh said, "Thanks, Leon. Now, let's make brief reports on your beats, starting with Susan and life sciences."

As staff members reported, Ryder lost track of what they said. He knew he must keep Leon's high-and-mighty attitude from psyching him out and interfering with the investigation. Would things get better after he became acquainted with Leon?

After the last person spoke, Josh stood. "Thank you. I'll see you next Monday at 1:00 PM sharp."

Leon approached Ryder. "I set the X-909 meeting for you with Bill Little at his office in the Unitary building at two-thirty."

Ryder rose and grasped Blackie's leather leash. "Thanks. That saves me time."

Leon rolled a shoulder. "Happy to help."

When Leon took a step forward, Blackie retreated behind Ryder's trousers.

Leon concentrated on the dog's fluid eyes. "Sensitive, isn't he?"

Ryder petted Blackie's head. "He's still a pup and bashful."

The hound wagged his tail, panted, and then sniffed and licked Ryder's hand.

Leon slapped Ryder on the back. "It's not a long walk to the Unitary. I'll be at my desk after you meet with Josh. Gotta watch him. You're already behind the eight ball."

Ryder forced a smile. "See you soon." He led Blackie toward Josh's office.

ELEVEN

JOSH SABLE'S office door was ajar when Ryder tapped on it.

"Come in. Sit."

Ryder entered the office. Blackie trailed behind him, and Ryder eased into a chair. "You wanted to see me?"

"Yes. I wish I wouldn't need to enlighten you again about promptness and deadlines. Most of my public affairs officers have experience as reporters working for newspapers, magazines, TV, radio, and web-based outlets." He took a breath. "Meeting deadlines is an absolutely vital requirement. You were late to the staff meeting. That shows me you also may not meet story deadlines. I suppose people may already have told you about my checks system. I made a check next to your name in my notebook because you were late. Get too many checks, and I'll write a letter to your contract supervisor. I'll demand you improve or be fired. Is that clear?"

Ryder bit his lip. "Yes."

Josh sat back in his chair. "Now for your first real assignment. You will write a fact sheet about the X-909 wind tunnel test program for release on the web and as a brochure for trade shows, educational use, and a news media handout. You will have it double-checked and initialed for technical accuracy by X-909 test management. You will contact the imaging department and have photos taken. This package is due on my desk by Monday morning at 9 AM sharp."

"Yes, sir."

"Now you and your mutt get the hell out of here."

Ryder nodded and left. He took deep breaths as he headed for Leon's office. He hoped the extra air would calm him and reduce his heart rate and blood pressure. If his undercover assignment wasn't about the murder of his cousin's fiancée, he'd tell the FBI to shove it. His cell rang.

"Hello?"

"Hi, Luke Ryder," a female voice said in a Southern inflection. "I'm Special Agent Rita Reynolds, in charge of the task force. Don't remember me, do you?"

Ryder paused. Would she care that Nigel had told him about her? "You're the Rita from Boone High who was two years behind me and Nigel?" She had to be thirty-six years old.

"I'm that Rita."

Ryder stared at a floor tile and then said, "Nigel confessed he didn't think of getting me out here. That was you."

"Yeah." She paused a moment. "I'm pleased he convinced you to join us."

Ryder remembered she was so smart she'd been placed in the junior class after her freshman year.

He walked to Leon's office and pointed to his phone.

Leon nodded.

Ryder approached the stairwell and descended the steps. "Just a sec, Rita. I'm going outside so I can talk without whisperin'."

"That's fine."

Ryder sat on a concrete and wooden park bench thirty feet from the building's entrance. Blackie lay on the cool, shaded sidewalk. "I can talk now."

"I was alerted Sunnyvale police ran your driver's license. What happened?"

"On the way to NASA, gang members tried to blame me for a faked accident, a swoop and squat."

Rita mumbled, "Jesus Christ."

"Police had staked out a stretch of road and filmed the whole thing. I didn't hit the car the perps wanted me to hit."

"Good."

"An undercover detective, Ollie, was about to have his head clubbed, so I knocked out the perp."

Rita sighed.

Ryder continued, "A Lieutenant Frank Chen said I could go because they had video of the incident, but the DA might call me."

"You have contact info?"

"Yep." Ryder read her Chen's number.

"I know the DA. I'll check it out immediately. After I'm done, I don't think Chen or the DA will call you, but if they do, text me."

"Okay." Ryder breathed in cool air and then said, "I wouldn't have guessed you'd go into law enforcement."

"It's complicated. I'll fill you in tonight if you can have a quick meeting with me."

"Where?"

"The Ten Kegs Bar in Mountain View at eight-thirty."

She was silent and then said, "Don't worry. You don't have to drink. I know about your AA—I mean LifeRing— meetings. I'll buy you a ginger ale, but I'll need to have a glass of red wine."

Ryder sighed. "You know I'm a recovering alcoholic?"

"Yeah. My best friend is Carol Cuddy. We talk once a week."

Carol was Ryder's ex-girlfriend. Now he had a live-in girlfriend—Layla Taylor—a black woman who also had a young daughter. He exhaled. "You know everything about me?"

"The ugly and the good. There's lots of good. See you tonight."

"You gotta tell me how you got me on this assignment."
Ryder stroked Blackie's head.

"I will."

Ryder re-entered the building and headed for Leon's office.

TWELVE

RYDER STEPPED into Leon Turk's office, and Blackie reclined at Ryder's feet. "Leon, ready to go see Bill Little?"

Leon sat with his feet propped up on his messy desktop. He slid his fancy cowboy boots off the desk onto the floor with a click, and a paper flittered to the floor. Leon ignored the document. "Yes. We can take our time walking over to the Unitary."

The men trotted down the steps to the building's exit.

"Could you tell me about the X-909 on the way over?" Ryder asked as he held the door for Leon.

Leon swaggered ahead and then stopped for Ryder to catch up. "The X-909 is supposed to fly anywhere in the world within an hour. They say its suborbital top speed would be nine thousand miles per hour, and a lot faster if it'd go into orbit."

The two men walked abreast, following the tree-shaded sidewalk. Ryder raised his eyebrows. "Can they get it to go that fast?"

"Who knows?" Leon stopped and turned left to face the thirteen-story-high air intake edge of a huge wind tunnel across the street. "That's one part of the NFAC, the biggest wind tunnel complex in the world."

Ryder could hear the loud, steady sound of air flowing through the gigantic complex that occupied at least three city blocks. He felt its power. "What's NFAC stand for?"

Leon surveyed the cloudless blue sky and then said, "It's one of those multi-word names the government's famous for. It's officially called the National Full-Scale Aerodynamics Complex."

"That's a mouthful."

"In one section, they can test aircraft the length and width of commuter airliners—real airplanes, not models." He pointed at a building tucked beneath the massive tunnel's exterior steel framework. "That's the part of the complex where there are offices. The fitness center is also inside. You might be interested in it because you're tense, Luke. Physical activity would loosen you up."

"Sometimes I train," Ryder said.

Leon lit a cigarette, and the odor of lighter fluid and burning tobacco lingered in the air. After blowing smoke out of his mouth, he added, "The center opens at 6 AM."

Again, Leon sucked on the cigarette, and his lips made a puckering noise. "Besides exercise equipment, there's an undersized ring for wrestlers and sparring." More smoke leaked from his lips.

Ryder caught Leon's eyes. "For boxing?"

"Uh-huh. I like to hit the bag to work up a sweat." Leon took a drag on his fag and exhaled a cloud of smoke. "You wanna go a couple of rounds sometime? I'll go easy on you."

Ryder concluded Leon was trying to intimidate him. "Someday, we could spar, but I'm not a trained boxer. The fightin' I've done was in bar-room brawls." Ryder didn't want to mention he'd boxed when he was a member of the Police Boys Club during high school, and he had won most of his bouts.

Leon held his cigarette near his trouser leg and flicked ashes away. Smoke drifted toward Blackie, and the animal recoiled. Leon started to walk again and sucked on his cigarette. "I thought a vet like you would've been in the ring sometime." He glanced sideways at Ryder. "What outfit were you in during your Congo deployment?"

"The 75th Rangers." Ryder thought, *That's a real whopper.* He didn't like to lie as part of his cover story, even if the FBI task force had invented it.

Leon said, "Years ago, when I was in the DRC—true, I was a simple grunt—I never heard the 75th Rangers were there."

Ryder halted. Blackie peed on the grass near the edge of the walkway. Ryder focused on Leon's eyes. "It was classified. You didn't have a need to know."

Leon flicked his spent cigarette into the grass where Blackie had urinated. The butt hissed. Ryder could smell warm dog urine.

A sleek, olive-drab Army attack helicopter made whup-whup sounds as it circled over a runway. The airfield was adjacent to the NASA Ames campus and its hundreds of buildings and test facilities. Ryder stared at the chopper as it made a steep descent. "What are they up to?"

Leon gestured at the airborne killing machine. "It's a test of a heads-up display or advanced radar."

"There must be a lot of military work going on here."

Leon took out his pack of cigarettes and pulled one out. "Yeah, but there's lots of stuff besides airplane and space-craft tests going on here. Remote sensing of the earth, much of it to monitor climate change. Rocket engine tests. The search for life in the universe. Psychological research on astronauts and pilots. Heat shield tests. Asteroid impact simulations. Satellite construction. The list goes on and on."

"Any of it classified?"

"Like you said, you have to have a need to know to get the real lowdown." Leon lit his cigarette.

The men and dog picked up their pace and were silent. They had reached the end of the huge NFAC wind tunnel complex. There was still a block to go to reach the Unitary wind tunnels where the X-909 tests took place. Ryder said,

"Lucinda told me a woman was murdered where the space plane is being tested. Is it true?"

Leon slowed down. "Yes. Her name was Scarlet Hauk. It happened two years ago." He stopped walking and turned to Ryder. "I dated her twice and dumped her. She was prissy."

Ryder guessed Scarlet Hauk had learned fast that Leon sought to control her and everybody else. He was delusional about his supposed superiority. Ryder figured Scarlet had discarded Leon rather than the other way around. "What do you mean by prissy?"

"She was too proper. Didn't like it when I kissed her." Leon exhaled. "But she didn't always act Puritan. They say she was sleeping around. In fact, our ultimate boss, Nigel Worth, was engaged to her just before she died. Rumor has it she was pregnant with his baby."

Ryder wondered why Nigel hadn't mentioned that Scarlet was pregnant. Or was her pregnancy merely a rumor? Was Leon jealous of Nigel?

Leon broke Ryder's train of thought. "Speaking of sleeping around, let me warn you about your office-mate, Lucinda. She'll try to hook you. An unknown guy made her pregnant, and he refused to marry her. She had an abortion."

At the next corner, the men turned to walk east on Boyd Road toward the front entrance of the 9-by-7-foot Supersonic Wind Tunnel. Ryder observed Leon. "What's Bill Little like?"

"The guy's a typical engineer, a nerd with his nose in books or studying test results. He never goes to a bar or a party to let his hair down. He can be abrasive. Won't listen to me when I suggest public affairs strategies."

"You must be happy I'm taking over the beat."

Leon stopped, set his jaw, and then said, "It's a significant program. You won't be here three weeks, and you'll be gone. I'll be reassigned to it. Bill doesn't know squat about how to get media coverage. I do. Management knows it."

Ryder decided to change the flow of the conversation when he and Leon started to walk again. "How does Bill compare to Dr. Scarlet Hauk? I heard he took over as the head of the X-909 testing after she died."

The men halted near the wind tunnel complex's front door. The building's middle section appeared to have a stone or concrete exterior and was three stories high. Office windows ran the length of each level.

Leon stared at Ryder. "Why do you care about Scarlet versus Bill?"

Ryder reached down to pet Blackie. "It isn't often there's a murder at NASA."

"True. Scarlet was easygoing compared to Bill. She was careful not to make waves, and she was wishy-washy. People said she put things off too much while she listened to everybody on her team. She was too young and inexperienced to be in charge of an important test program."

Ryder wondered if it wasn't better to listen to everybody on that kind of a team. Then he asked, "Does Bill Little have much experience doing wind tunnel tests?"

"Yeah. He was upset she was promoted above him."

Ryder consulted his watch. "It's almost two-thirty. Guess I'll find out about him soon."

THIRTEEN

LEON LED Ryder and Blackie down the supersonic wind tunnel building's dim, first-floor hallway to Bill Little's office.

Ryder peered through the open doorway. The workspace was inadequate and drab compared to the public affairs offices.

Pencil in hand, Bill sat at his desk. He glanced up from a drawing similar to that of a Buck Rogers spaceship. His shirt sleeves were rolled up, exposing his hairy arms. His clothes were not in fashion, and Ryder wondered if Bill had bought them at a secondhand store.

Without knocking, Leon stepped up to Bill's desk. "I wouldn't have thought a NASA engineer would still use a pencil and a ruler to do a drawing when there's plenty of software that can do the job faster and better." He smiled derisively.

Bill said, "Shows what you know about engineering." He stood, his wrinkled trousers suggesting he might have worn them for a week. A cup of steaming coffee was on the far corner of his desktop. He turned to face Ryder and looked him up and down. "Is this our freshly assigned PR man?"

Leon nodded. "Yes. Luke Ryder."

Bill blinked and then shook Ryder's hand.

Ryder noticed his strong grip. "I'm ready to get to work, Mr. Little."

Bill squatted and petted Blackie. "I heard about your dog." He smiled. Blackie licked Bill's hand and continued to do so as the canine wagged his tail.

Ryder was struck with how fast word spread at Ames. He caught the dog's attention. "Blackie, don't overdo it."

Leon said, "Since I've already briefed you about Luke the last time we met, I'll leave so you two can get acquainted." He started to exit the office but then turned to face Bill. "If you need help, I can assist. Just call."

"Duly noted," Bill said.

Leon was on his way in seconds.

Bill pointed at an uncomfortable government-issue, gray metal chair. "Have a seat, Luke. Want coffee?"

"Thanks. Black is fine." Ryder felt relaxed after Leon left. Ryder now knew why Bill disliked the brash and egotistical Leon.

Bill set a chipped mug of coffee on his desk near Ryder. "What would you like to know about the X-909 test program?"

"I've been assigned to write an updated space plane fact sheet that also would be printed as a brochure. It's due Monday at 9 AM. I'm supposed to get pictures shot, too."

Bill rubbed his forehead. "Why the rush? We've been doing tests for two years on and off. We're not at the next milestone yet."

Ryder figured Josh wanted to use a poorly written fact sheet as a reason to pull him off the X-909 beat. Ryder took his time to answer. "The news chief, Josh Sable, wants me to get my feet wet without delay."

"I'll give his boss a call, Nigel Worth. I need time to do a technical approval, and I have a lot of things to do. Plus, we already have a fact sheet." He paused. "Sorry. I don't mean to unload on you. I'm tired of public affairs pushing me to put out news about the tests. But I'll be willing to talk with you so you can update the fact sheet."

Ryder took a gulp of coffee while he figured out how he was going to work in questions about the murder. "I can make it quick today…if you have written material you can share."

Bill opened a battered file cabinet next to a heavy-duty safe and withdrew a glossy pamphlet. "Here's the old fact sheet the prior test director had ginned up. She had lots of pictures taken. They're in the photo lab's archives. Nothing's changed over the previous couple of years that the public would be interested in."

Ryder skimmed the pamphlet. Lucinda Lu had already given him a copy. "I have questions."

"Shoot."

"Wouldn't it cost a lot for a ticket to fly from here to London in an hour?"

Bill bit his lip. "I'm not the one who figured out the economics of this. There's an important reason to make this space plane work. You're a military man. Should be obvious."

Ryder examined the space plane artwork on the brochure. The craft had a sharp, slender, needle nose and resembled a large fighter jet. "Could it carry a bomb to any place on Earth in an hour?"

"If we can get it to work, yes," Bill said. "Here's the thing. Remember Mr. Wise Guy—your colleague, Leon—said we don't need to use a pencil because a computer can draw a picture easier and faster?"

"Yep."

"He's wrong. A computer can't spit out all the answers. Engineers use supercomputers to help with the initial design of spacecraft. But in the real world, there are things a computer can't simulate. During the high-speed climb to earth orbit, unpredictable low-frequency forces and turbulence hammer space probes and can destroy them."

Ryder took his cell phone from his pocket. "Okay if I record this?"

"That's fine." Bill patted his computer. "Because computers can't predict everything, we use the supersonic wind tunnel and various tools to better forecast what may happen in the real world."

"Wasn't the Space Shuttle tested in the Unitary?"

"Yes."

"Why can't you use the shuttle plans to come up with a space plane design?"

"Many things affect a spacecraft—its size, the material it's made of, the kind of rockets and engines it has, the fuel, the heat shield. Alter one thing, and it can affect multiple things. Conditions change as you accelerate toward orbit. There's extreme friction when air rubs on the spacecraft at high speeds. Without a proper heat shield, the craft would burn up when reentering the atmosphere. This tunnel isn't the only place we conduct tests. For instance, heat shields are tested in an arc jet at high temperatures and high speeds."

"Y'all do tests elsewhere?"

"Yes. Different facilities test a multitude of conditions. Here, in the nine-by-seven, we do tests from about Mach one point five to Mach two point five. The speed of sound is Mach one, about 760 miles per hour. Because the X-909 would fly into orbit, it's also tested in the three-point five-foot hypersonic tunnel at Mach five, about 3,500 miles per hour, and at higher speeds. To reach low earth orbit, it'd have to go 17,600 miles per hour and even faster to enter a higher orbit or to go to the Moon."

"This is complicated. It has to be simplified for the public."

Bill retrieved an airplane wing model from the shelves behind his desk. The wing was bumble-gum pink. "Here's something simple the public can understand." He handed the wing shape to Ryder.

"Was this used in a wind tunnel test?"

"Yes. The pink paint on the wing shape is pressure sensitive. It changes color as the pressure on the wing changes when the wind blows around it. These color changes show us the effects of different wind speeds and pressures."

"Is your X-909 space plane model pink, too?"

"Yes." He opened a closet door and rummaged on a top shelf. "Here's an earlier version." He set an X-909 model on his desk.

"Did the pink paint tell you the older X-909 shape needed improvement?"

Bill smiled. "You're catching on. If the plane would've been built in this shape and launched, it would've shaken itself into pieces."

"Did they test that model before you took over after the lady engineer was killed?"

"It was tested twice the night she died. It's unfortunate she didn't get to see how we changed the shape to get rid of about half of the vibration problems."

Ryder slid forward in his chair. "Must make you feel edgy working in the same place where that woman was killed. I heard it was gruesome. And they never caught whoever murdered her."

Bill sighed. "People don't think about it much. It's been two years."

"Who would've been angry enough to kill the woman?"

Bill shrugged. "I'm speculating, but it could've been a love triangle."

Ryder took a sip of coffee. It was now lukewarm. "People can get jealous and do crazy things." He swished the coffee around in his cup.

Bill fingered the X-909 model. "She was going to be married. Maybe some ex-boyfriend did it."

"Was she well-liked?"

"People didn't like her management style."

"How's that?"

Bill tapped the space plane model with a fingernail. "We might've discovered design problems earlier, but she was a recent addition to our group. She was conservative, wanted to keep the peace instead of listening to opposing arguments."

Ryder nodded. "That could've frustrated people." Ryder

remembered that Leon had told him the opposite—that Scarlet Hauk had listened to everyone.

Bill glanced at Ryder's phone. "You still recording?"

Ryder nodded.

"The latest stuff's personal. Could you erase that part?"

"Yep." Ryder stopped his phone's audio recorder. "Is any of the technical stuff confidential?"

"No. I wouldn't tell you anything secret." Bill slapped the side of his heavy safe. "If there were anything like that, it'd be locked up."

"It's a solid safe." Ryder smiled. The safe was as tall as a normal filing cabinet, but it had thick steel walls.

"You're okay, Luke. I don't often eat at the cafeteria, but if you want, we can meet at lunch one of these days to finish the fact sheet. I could call you when time on my schedule opens up. I'll contact Director Nigel and have the fact sheet delayed."

"Thanks, Bill," Ryder said.

Bill stood. "Sorry, but I need to go to a design review."

* * *

AFTER RYDER WALKED BACK to his office, he decided to learn more about the Unitary Wind Tunnel Complex.

Lucinda was typing when Ryder sat down at his desk.

"Lucinda, sorry to interrupt, but I was wonderin' if we have historic information about the Unitary wind tunnels."

"There's a book that has great background," she answered as she rose from her chair and took a volume from a shelf. "Here's a history book about Ames." She handed the book to Ryder.

He looked in the index and turned to the relevant sections in the tome. He learned that a proposal to construct the Unitary had been submitted to Congress in the late 1940s and that President Truman had signed the plan into law in October 1949.

Ryder found out a few of the wind tunnel system parts

were enormous. Its four electric motors were the largest of their kind ever built at the time of the facility's construction in the early 1950s. They powered the tunnel's air compressors. The Unitary also included two diversion valves—twenty and twenty-four feet in diameter—with a combined weight of five hundred tons.

All new US military and many civilian aircraft, as well as all manned NASA spacecraft, were tested in the Unitary. Now, during the twenty-first century, this wind tunnel complex was still a vital national treasure. It was a hell of a lot more important than he'd first believed.

Ryder thought about his upcoming meeting that evening with FBI Special Agent Rita Reynolds at the Ten Kegs Bar. Would she reveal whether or not the task force had investigated possible murder motives related to national security? After all, the Unitary continued to be a national asset dedicated in part to improving weapons of war.

FOURTEEN

THE BLACK SKY was punctuated with millions of bright stars and was lit by a waxing crescent moon.

Ryder guided his rental truck into the parking lot next to the Ten Kegs Bar. When he exited his vehicle, a chilly wind was gusting from ten to twenty miles per hour. He thrust his hands in his pockets as he neared the neon lights of the large drinking establishment. He guessed it had once been a sizable restaurant. Through large picture windows, he saw five brightly lit stainless steel brewing tanks and many drinkers seated around dining tables.

He pulled open a heavy glass door, and he spotted a hostess. "Could you tell me where Rita Reynolds is sittin'?"

"You're Mr. Ryder?"

"Yes."

"She's expecting you. Please follow me." The hostess led him past the bright stainless steel beer fermentation tanks in the center of the spacious room to a table in the far corner of the building, away from occupied tables.

Rita rose from her seat and offered Ryder her hand. She wasn't the wispy girl he remembered. Now in her late thirties, she was of medium height and curvaceous. She still had shiny brown hair that matched her brown eyes.

Ryder's face flushed while he focused on her face. "You've certainly grown up since I last saw you." He felt her hand loosen.

She sat. "You haven't changed much. You're still the tall, dark, handsome guy I remember from high school."

Ryder pulled out a chair. "I'm positive Carol Cuddy told you I'm divorced, and my drinking's been a problem." He viewed numerous people across the room holding mugs of craft beer. "I wonder how you convinced the FBI to let me join the task force."

"I was given freedom of choice. I need you because I heard how you solved murders back home." She stared at Ryder. "Folks in the holler say you have a sixth sense. That's the kind of magic we need to solve this crime."

"I was lucky. It wasn't magic."

"Whatever it was, it worked. I persuaded Nigel and Sheriff Pike to encourage you to join the task force."

She smoothed her hair. "I talk with Carol every week, and you come up in our conversations. She told me how you solved the Jenkins murder when you were still a game warden. She said it was the talk of the holler how you saved two hookers when a serial killer shot at them through a café window. Now that you're a deputy, you used your blood-hound to crack a case a month ago."

Ryder didn't want to tell Rita that one of the hookers had left prostitution and was now his girlfriend. Or did Rita already know? Most likely, she did.

The muffled sound of a blaring car alarm brought Ryder out of his reverie. "I hope I can help."

Rita took a sip of red wine and set her glass down. "I have total confidence in you, especially after the DA told me how you helped Sunnyvale Detective Chen and his partner bust the insurance fraud gang. Chen gave the DA a hundred dollars to pass on to you for a replacement sports coat. The DA said Ollie suffered a concussion, but he'll be okay. You don't have to testify. There are plenty of witnesses and lots of video."

Ryder smiled and relaxed. "Good." He toyed with a fork and shoved his napkin so it was square to the edge of the checkered tablecloth. "How important is the Scarlet Hauk murder case?"

"It's significant, but about to go cold unless we come up with fresh leads. I'll be candid. They put me in charge to give me experience. We have a short time before the task force can be disbanded. That's why we're reinterviewing people and going over the evidence again. You're our sole under-cover guy at Ames."

"I'm your shot in the dark?"

"You and Blackie." Rita paused. "Where's he now? I was hoping to meet him."

"He's in the rental house the FBI travel office got for me in Sunnyvale. There's a flapping dog door that opens to the fenced backyard."

"I'm pleased the dog has a secure place to stay." She leaned forward on her elbow. "How'd you train that puppy to be a tracker so fast? Carol said you bought him weeks before you solved the latest case."

Ryder glanced at the ceiling, then down again. "I bought him for Layla, my girlfriend. I rented Ford's farm to share-crop after old man Ford died. We're growin' hemp. There's lots of room for a dog. I decided to train him to track deer. I started by having him practice by sniffing two farmhands. He's a quick learner. Found the two men fast, even after they crossed the creek. That's how Blackie learned to find people. The rest, you know."

A portly waitress came to the table. "Anything I can get you, sir?"

Ryder rubbed his chin. "Ginger ale, please."

She waddled away.

Ryder said, "What else can you tell me about the case? I wish I'd had a chance to see the whole file earlier."

Rita smiled. "I have a package in my briefcase. Normally

I keep it locked up in a house I rented for the task force in Sunnyvale."

"Okay."

"I'd like to show you the house, our command center. We can review the package there tonight." She reached into her purse. "Here's a house key you can keep."

He took the key and dropped it into his pocket.

"We'll leave after..." She glanced away from Ryder toward a man who approached. He walked rapidly, his short, dark ponytail bobbing behind him. She waved. "It's Mike Lobo. I asked him to meet us here. It wouldn't be wise for you to visit his Ames office."

Ryder nodded.

Mike, a short man, sat in a chair near Rita. He pulled it closer to the table with a scraping sound.

Rita gestured toward Mike. "Luke, this is Mike Lobo, Ames chief of counterintelligence. Mike, this is Deputy Sheriff Luke Ryder, the man I've told you about."

The men shook hands.

Rita said, "We were talking about the case. What should Luke know about it from your viewpoint?"

"At the moment, we don't think Scarlet's death is related to espionage, either corporate or involving foreign actors." Mike seemed to study Ryder.

Ryder leaned forward. "How can you be confident espionage isn't likely?"

Mike caught Rita's eyes. "Can I?"

"Tell him."

Mike's eyes drilled into Ryder's. "The X-909 tests conducted the night Scarlet died showed the vehicle would've shaken itself apart in flight if it had been built. Sources in industry, and in our embassies who are in positions to hear about such things, report they heard nothing about it."

Ryder shifted his shoulders. "If a spy would've found out something, it would've been useless?"

"Yep, except they'd learn not to use that design."

"What if a spy killed Scarlet to get info, and the spook

later learned it was no good?" He paused as the waitress neared their table. She set a glass of ginger ale in front of Ryder.

Mike addressed the server. "Could you bring me a peach pale ale?" He waited until the woman was out of earshot, and he answered Ryder's question. "I agree we can't totally rule out espionage, but the evidence suggests a love triangle is the more likely motive for her murder. Of course, if new details pop up, they could change our thinking. Have you had a chance to review the case file?"

Rita said, "No, he hasn't. That's my fault. We'll review it tonight."

Mike cleared his throat. "Then you don't know Scarlet Hauk was pregnant. We don't know who the father was, even though we have DNA from the fetus."

Ryder raised his eyebrows. "Y'all think it was a crime of passion? Did you ask Nigel for DNA?"

Rita set down her wine glass. "Nigel was at a meeting in London three days before and after the killing. We asked him for DNA. He complied." She sighed. "He isn't the father. We didn't tell him because we want to hold that close to our vests. We suspect whoever got her pregnant might've killed her."

Ryder said, "I hate to say this about my own cousin, but couldn't he have hired someone to do the deed?"

Rita pursed her lips. "A hitman would've had to get past the Ames guards at night. It would've been easier to kill her someplace else. Nigel's not a suspect."

The waitress returned, set a glass of ale by Mike, and left.

Mike took a sip. "We've been trying to track down Scarlet's lover by searching for his DNA, grabbing discarded drinks and things from men who work at Ames. We've had no luck."

Ryder rubbed his chin. "What if I get a chance to snatch DNA?"

Mike smiled. "Do so. I'll provide a list of men from whom we've acquired samples. Rita can give you evidence bags." Mike chugged his ale. "I hate to run, but I have to pick up my daughter from her school play rehearsal."

Rita said, "I'll put the ale on my tab."

"Thanks. I'll get yours next time."

Rita finished her wine and said, "I have a gut feeling things will move fast with you on the job." She picked up her purse. "Let's leave for the command center."

Ryder drank the rest of his ginger ale and stood. "I'll follow you."

FIFTEEN

RYDER FOLLOWED RITA REYNOLDS' black sport utility vehicle. They drove on dimly lit, bumpy roads that led to the FBI command post.

Rita pulled to the curb near an ordinary, middle-class, white stucco house on a side street.

Ryder parked behind her and stepped out of his truck as a cool wind blew across his face.

Turning to Ryder, Rita said, "An elderly couple is renting this place to us. They'll be in Greece for two months." As she started toward the home's front porch, a streetlight silhouetted her, and an owl began to hoot.

Ryder followed her and asked, "What about the neighbors?"

"I told the couple we'd use the house for company meetings and mentioned this option is inexpensive. I'm sure they spread the news to their neighbors."

"What's the name of the phony company?"

"Innovation Computers." Rita unlocked the front door.

As they entered the front room of the four-bedroom home, Ryder noticed a whiteboard facing a worn mauve couch as well as five stuffed chairs upholstered in pink and yellow floral patterns. The heavy white drapes were closed. The burgundy area rug felt extra thick as they walked on it, but a faint, musty smell pervaded the house.

"Do y'all use this place a lot?"

"Yes. Tomorrow night we'll meet at seven-thirty. I'll introduce you to our team, which includes Mike, me, you, and Henry Dunbar, an experienced agent."

Ryder sat on the soft couch near a walnut coffee table with a glass top. "This house has a calming effect."

Rita opened her cheap, government-issue briefcase and pulled out a fat folder. "It's quieter here than at the San Jose office. I get a lot done in this place." She joined Ryder on the couch and plopped the hefty dossier on the coffee table.

"That package is thick," Ryder said.

"It has background on Scarlet's associates, relatives, friends, but not much evidence." Rita cleared her throat. "Agent Henry Dunbar and I are reinterviewing people who worked late the night Ms. Hauk was killed. But there's a problem."

"What?"

"Except for the computer buildings that have card readers to log comings and goings, Ames doesn't normally keep track of employees entering and leaving base. They show their badges to the guards and drive through the main gate. When employees leave, guards don't check IDs. We only know who worked late from workers' testimony."

Ryder opened the folder. He saw tabs for Nigel Worth, Lucinda Lu, and a Walter Fuldheim. "Who's Fuldheim?"

"Scarlet's ex-boyfriend and chief of a robotics development group. She dumped him to hook up with your cousin."

"Did y'all get his DNA?"

Rita shifted her position on the couch. "Not yet."

Ryder said, "Today, I heard Scarlet also had gone out with Leon Turk."

Rita appeared puzzled. "I didn't know that."

Ryder set the folder on the coffee table. "It's like we're dealing with a real Peyton Place." He stretched his legs under the table and knocked his knee against the heavy glass top. "I also found out something today about Lucinda Lu you might not have heard."

Rita's eyes widened. "Yeah?"

"Scarlet may have slept with Lucinda's old boyfriend, according to Lucinda, but she didn't say who the guy was."

"He could have been Nigel, Fuldheim, Leon, or someone else."

Ryder placed his fingers on his forehead. "Let's say Lucinda's boyfriend was Nigel. Lucinda could've been jealous and killed Scarlet. A separate possibility is Scarlet was pregnant by an unknown man, who killed her because she broke off their relationship."

Rita moved to the whiteboard and added Lucinda Lu's name to a list of persons of interest. Rita said, "Scarlet slept around. The father-to-be may not have known she was with child. It could've been a one-night stand. She was six weeks pregnant."

Ryder let out a breath. "Also, Leon Turk told me it's common knowledge Lucinda had an abortion. He heard that Lucinda's boyfriend didn't want to marry her. Leon didn't know who he was."

"We didn't know that stuff about Lucinda." Rita touched her chin with her index finger. "Hmm."

"What are you thinkin'?"

"I have a hunch Lucinda likes you. She has her ear to the ground. Knows the gossip. Get closer to her. Ask her out for dinner or coffee. She could incriminate herself or somebody else."

"If it's part of the job, okay."

"Don't take it too far."

Ryder felt embarrassed. "I wouldn't." He paused. "What physical evidence do you have?"

"Besides the fetus DNA, we have Scarlet's briefcase that was near her body. No fingerprints were on the brass latch or handle. Someone wiped them clean. There were papers inside the case, information about the X-909 model that's also on the Internet."

Ryder nodded.

Rita said, "An important fact is the latest space plane model is faulty. They're doing tests to find out what's wrong." She sat back on the couch.

"What about this picture of a knife?"

"It's the murder weapon, a serrated butcher knife. It came from the Unitary building's break room. The knife was clean, except for Scarlet's blood."

Ryder glanced in the folder. "I see you checked out Bill Little, the guy who landed Scarlet's test manager job after she died. Got his DNA yet?"

"No. He's a person of interest, but not by much. I don't believe he's the type to kill somebody. But he was jealous of Scarlet getting promoted over him."

Ryder rubbed his forehead. "What if a random guy got her pregnant but didn't know it? He'd have no motive to kill her 'cuz of her pregnancy. Y'all say espionage isn't in play, but it's possible."

"Espionage is conceivable, but we don't think so." She caught his eyes. "Did you see the picture of the black cloth strap with a buckle?"

Ryder thumbed through the folder and pulled out the photo. "What's it for?"

"It's from a black trench coat. The strap's used to tighten the sleeves around the wrists. We think the killer might've dropped it near the rear door of the Unitary complex." Rita pursed her lips. "I bet Blackie might like to sniff it."

Ryder stroked his stubble. "Where's the strap?"

"We sent it to a lab out East for special DNA analysis. We'll get it back soon."

"Blackie might be able to help us," Ryder said. "It depends on how the strap was stored."

"Is it realistic to think Blackie can still pick up an odor?"

"If it was in a sealed container, yes." Ryder shifted his shoulders. "Durin' the Cold War, the East German secret police collected thousands of pieces of evidence and stored them in sealed jars. Bloodhounds sniffed the items and could trail people even after two years."

"Impressive."

Ryder flipped through the case file. "Is there anything else?"

Rita tapped her forehead with her fingers. "Oh, yeah. Agent Dunbar learned Scarlet had a large student loan debt, and three months before her death, her Corvette was repossessed."

Ryder yawned.

Rita stood. "It's late. I'll take a shower and call it a day."

Ryder stood. "You stay here?"

"I keep clothes here. You're welcome to stay to read documents. Lock the front door when you go."

"Okay."

For the next few minutes, Ryder could hear the shower running while he read. He learned two security camera lenses had been covered in paint. The FBI had analyzed it and found it had been shot from a paintball gun. Where the paint had come from was a mystery.

Rita stepped into the living room, clad in a pink sateen pajama top and shorts.

Ryder noticed her legs. He felt his body temperature rise.

"Good night, Luke. I'm fortunate to have you on the case. Don't stay up too late." She went into a bedroom and closed the door.

Ryder left. He needed to call his girlfriend, Layla, in Kentucky, even if it was late. He had to hear Layla's voice. A lump formed in his throat as he thought about her. He sure as hell missed her comforting presence now.

SIXTEEN

RYDER UNLOCKED his backyard in-law suite. He'd left the lights on. Blackie was asleep and snoring near his food and water bowls on a throw rug in the kitchen. Back in Kentucky, Ryder's girlfriend, Layla Taylor, was watching over the Ford farm. She had told him to call her even if it was past midnight her time.

He texted her.

You still up?

Yes, hon. Call me.

Ryder felt his heartbeat increase as he pictured Layla's smile. He could almost feel her warm lips against his. He settled in an easy chair, and his finger shook as it hovered over Layla's name on his cell phone's contact list. It was after 1:00 AM in Kentucky when he tapped "Layla" on the mobile screen.

"Hello, Luke. I was wondering when you'd call."

"I almost didn't, being it's real late. You gotta be tired staying up for my call."

"I couldn't sleep. I was thinking of you. I want you now. I haven't felt like this for years."

Ryder sighed. "Truth be told, I feel like a teenage boy all agog over a pretty woman. You're on my mind a lot, too. It's hard for me to describe exactly what's happened to me. I thought I'd never feel like this again after I divorced Emma."

Layla took a deep breath. "Being apart from you, Luke, has shown me how much I care for you. I was crushed by love once a long time ago, too. When I'm up to it, I'll tell you all about it, but for now I'm just going to say you make me feel alive again."

Ryder felt tears form in his eyes. "Layla, I think we have a lot in common. You're my soulmate."

Layla cleared her throat. "I'm going to tell you the truth, Luke, because I owe it to you. When I first made love with you, I did it just to thank you. Eventually, as I came to know you better, I realized what a wonderful man you are. I never thought I'd love again, and I feel like I can't live without you. I love you so much."

Ryder's heart seemed to soar. "I'm so glad you said that. What's better than two people who are in love? Before you, I felt dead to the world." Ryder could hear Layla choke up. A tear dribbled down his face.

Layla made a kissing sound. "You hear that, dear?"

"Yep. I wish I could feel your lips, too."

Layla sighed. "I want you to come home soon." She paused three long seconds. "How are you doing with the job, honey?"

"I'm thinkin' I got myself in over my head."

"What do you mean?"

"There's an unfriendly work atmosphere 'cuz of the news chief who's my supervisor. And one coworker's hostile."

"You'll get through it."

Ryder leaned back in his chair. Its cushion relaxed his muscles. "This investigation will end soon. The FBI will shut down the task force unless we make progress."

"The bed's cold without you in it. I hope there aren't tempting women crossing your path."

"I can resist 'em if they get too close."

"I sense I have competition."

Ryder paused. "One thing surprised me."

"What?"

"Rita Reynolds, a girl who was two years behind me in high school, heads the FBI task force. My cousin, Nigel, didn't ask for me to be on the task force. It was Rita."

"Now I'm worried. I hope she's a tough, ugly lady."

"She's not ugly. But I think she's so dedicated to her job she'll never marry."

Ryder could hear Layla exhale. He said, "After this wraps up, I'll fly you out here. I talked to my sister. She'll watch Angela. We'll take a cruise to Alaska."

"Now you're talking. Who's going to watch the farm?"

"I asked Tom Hartsfield to take care of it. Pike will stop in every so often, too."

"You set it up before you left for the West Coast?"

"I planned it before I had a clue about NASA and the murder case."

"Sneaky." She paused. "Keep yourself out of trouble with the womenfolk, hear?"

"Yes, ma'am."

"Better get to sleep, honey."

"Yep. I need to get up at the crack of dawn. I'll call tomorrow. Love you."

"Goodbye. I'll dream of you, my love." She hung up.

He pictured her classic ebony face and sighed.

Ryder lay down in bed, but his mind was busy. He wondered how the hell he'd handle Josh and Leon and still conduct an undercover investigation. He couldn't sleep.

He arose while Blackie snored. Ryder decided to work off a bit of steam. He'd jog in the park near the FBI house, which was two blocks from his rental.

He put on a pair of shorts and running shoes. After stretching, he slipped outside into the night. A cool westerly breeze awakened his senses, though his body was tired. The perfume of flowers and the smell of plant life brought visions of precious Kentucky woods to him. He had always relished his time alone walking among the trees of his holler, which calmed him.

Drawing sweet-scented air into his lungs, he began to jog on the sidewalk. He needed to push himself, so he broke into a run and then settled into an even pace.

The park was surrounded by a sidewalk. As if on autopilot, his feet guided him into the park's grass. Streetlights dimly lit the sidewalk that was now to his left. He ran clockwise around the perimeter of the park twice and began to sweat, though the night was cool.

After slowing near a grove of trees, he halted. He walked back and forth on the lawn, and his breathing returned to normal.

He returned to the sidewalk and began a leisurely jog back to his apartment. As he moved forward, he thought of Josh, Leon, Lucinda, and Rita. They were simply people who were living their separate, finite lives. They were now a part of his life, and he'd deal with them all in due course.

In five minutes, he was in bed, but his brain was still active, and he thought, *Tomorrow, I gotta write the X-909 fact sheet. And I need to get a date with Lucinda Lu, too.*

SEVENTEEN

RYDER ARRIVED at the Public Affairs Office and began to review background information about the X-909 test program. He was reading the old space plane brochure at his desk when a young redhead clad in a flowery cotton dress entered the room.

Blackie concentrated on the woman and sniffed the air.

The woman approached Lucinda. "Hi, Lucinda. Do you have pictures I can hand out to fifth graders? I'm giving a talk to them about astrobiology on Friday. My sister's son is in the class. There are twenty-five kids."

Lucinda stood. "It's marvelous you're getting out to give a talk, Phoebe." Lucinda stepped to a tan file cabinet. "We have color lithographs." She opened the top drawer.

Phoebe grinned.

Lucinda rummaged through a folder, pulled out twenty-five copies of the most popular lithographic pictures, handed Phoebe a manila envelope, and said, "They'll be protected in this."

Phoebe's bright smile emphasized her red lipstick. "Thanks." She turned her gaze to Ryder. "I see you have a new office-mate."

Lucinda nodded. "Yes, this is Luke Ryder and his service dog, Blackie."

Phoebe stepped to Ryder's desk and held out her hand. "I'm Phoebe Tillus."

Ryder could smell her expensive perfume when he grasped her hand and gently shook it.

She held Ryder's hand for a bit after their handshake ended. "Since you're new to the office, may I ask, what's your role?"

"I'm coverin' the X-909 space plane beat. I'll write press and public information material. I'll also be writing articles for the *Astrogram*."

Phoebe shifted on her high heels. "In that case, you should come over to the Space Biosciences Division. I'm the secretary there, and I can show you around. I'm positive there are plenty of excellent stories you can write concerning the search for life in the universe."

"Sounds interesting."

"Give me a call. My number's in the Ames phone book."

"I'll do that."

Phoebe caught Ryder's eyes for a moment, blinked, and then left, her high heels click-clacking in the hallway outside Ryder's office.

Ryder pushed aside his X-909 brochure. "She's friendly."

Lucinda glanced toward the doorway. She whispered, "Like I did yesterday, I'll tell you something you didn't hear from me, okay?"

Ryder nodded.

"Stay clear of her except for purely business reasons." Lucinda bent forward and spoke in a loud whisper. "They say she'll sleep with practically any man." She paused. "Some have even said she's a nymphomaniac."

Ryder straightened his back. "I'll keep that in mind."

Lucinda exhaled. "It's said her current boyfriend is the Space Biosciences Division Chief, Peter Adams."

"Hmm. Really?"

"Yes. Before settling on him, she and Scarlet Hauk were

rivals, always hitting on the same men. I'm pretty sure Peter Adams went out with Scarlet a long time ago."

Ryder figured he'd better visit Phoebe soon to determine if she could be a suspect. "Seems lots of people may have disliked Scarlet."

Lucinda furrowed her brow. "I've often wondered who may have killed her and why."

Ryder nodded and then glanced down at the X-909 brochure on his desk. "I'm gonna start updating the space plane fact sheet. Do we happen to have details about the space plane in our files?"

"We do." Lucinda stood and opened a second file cabinet. "I know just where to search. The public affairs officer who worked here before Leon Turk took notes and had lots of background literature."

"That'll help. I figure I can revise this and get it over to X-909 management before lunch."

EIGHTEEN

RYDER SCANNED the space plane information Lucinda had found in her file cabinet. If he could get his revised fact sheet approved by next Monday, he might get on News Chief Josh Sable's good side. If so, it wouldn't matter whether or not Bill Little had delayed the document. Chances are, after Nigel edited the updated version, Josh would like it.

Ryder believed the old fact sheet was too complex for the average Joe to understand.

He took stock of Lucinda, who wore a boutique dress that fit her artistic personality. She was clacking away on her keyboard.

Ryder tapped her shoulder. "Okay if I ask you questions about the space plane when you get tired of typing?"

"I'm always up for an excuse to take a break. Ask away." She dug into a box of chocolates and ate two.

Ryder stared at an X-909 document. "I'm trying to find out what folks should know but don't." He paused. "What's the difference between a space plane and a rocket?"

"A space plane is smaller and can't carry as much fuel as a rocket."

Ryder held up the document. "According to this, designing a plane that can fly from Earth up into space can be like a vicious circle. You have to go so fast that you need additional fuel, which is heavy. The more fuel you carry, the larger the plane you need. That's why it's hard to design a space plane that can fly into orbit."

Lucinda shrugged. "Then how can they make the space plane work?"

"They'll reduce the plane's weight as much as possible, and they're also workin' on magnetic levitation."

"What?"

"You know how two magnets repel each other when their two south poles come close?"

"Yeah."

"That's how a train can float over its rails, levitate. The space plane would sit on top of a carrier, floatin' over a long track. Electricity would shoot the carrier the length of the rails, and the carrier would fling the plane at great speed up into the sky before the rocket engine would fire at full force. That would save fuel and weight."

Lucinda said, "I never heard of that before." She turned to her keyboard. "I better finish this typing for Josh before he has a fit."

* * *

AFTER A HALF HOUR, Ryder had written an improved fact sheet in pencil and had begun to type it with two fingers.

Lucinda touched his shoulder. "Stop struggling." She cocked her head and brushed her draped hair aside. "I'll type it, and I'll format it both as a fact sheet and as a brochure since it'll be a dual-use publication."

She picked up his penciled rough draft. "Your handwriting's clear. Relax and get a soda from the machine. I'll be done by the time you get back."

Ryder felt relieved. "Want one, too?"

"Anything diet would be fine." She carried Ryder's draft to her desk. "Okay if I add things?"

"Absolutely."

Ryder returned with the drinks.

Lucinda caught his attention. "Be done in a minute." She stopped typing. "I like how you say the plane would shake itself apart if it's not properly designed."

Ryder sat in the chair near Lucinda's desk. He thought she was fun to be around and friendly, like a younger sister might be. He wondered why she'd had trouble keeping a boyfriend. Then his mind flashed back to the present, and he said, "Wish I could add pictures."

"No problem. I love to fool around with art and photography."

Ryder studied her artwork on the wall above her desk. "That's right. You're quite the artist."

Within ten minutes, she'd added pictures and printed a dummy fact sheet and brochure.

Ryder reviewed the color printout. "I like it."

"I just e-mailed it to you."

Ryder sat at his computer. "I'll forward it for approval." He sent it to Nigel's private smartphone e-mail and then dialed Nigel's number. "It's me. Can you check my draft X-909 fact sheet?"

Nigel jostled his phone. "I received a call from Bill, and he asked me to delay it. I told Josh it was put off by the X-909 front office."

"But if I get it done now, it'll be out of my hair."

"I'll read it right away."

In five minutes, Ryder received a text message from Nigel.

It's great. Let's meet tonight at five at Joe Brown's Coffee Shop in Mountain View.

Lucinda grabbed Ryder's attention. "I'm leaving to pick up clothes at the dry cleaners. See you after lunch."

Ryder forwarded the draft to Bill Little to ask for his technical review and then eased back in his chair and sipped his soda.

His computer chimed, and he saw Bill's reply.

Superb. I have no changes. Your fact sheet is technically approved.

Ryder took a breath, and the air smelled better, as if he were suddenly outside in the leafy woods. He mumbled, "This is easier than I thought," and then he forwarded the fact sheet to Josh, noting Bill had approved it. Would Josh like it?

NINETEEN

NEWS CHIEF JOSH SABLE burst into Ryder's office. "This fact sheet needs extensive work." A dozen minutes had passed since Ryder had submitted the space plane draft to Josh. "There's nothing new here. It's overly simplified and omits basic facts."

Ryder stood. "I'll contact Bill Little and rework it."

Josh's face was red. He tossed a printout on Ryder's desk. "I made suggestions, but I gave up a quarter of the way through."

Ryder said, "Bill told me he was busy and put off the deadline through the management chain of command. I took a crack at rewriting it so I could show him something. I was real surprised he okayed it so fast." Ryder picked up the printout and saw that blue pencil marks littered the first pages.

Josh scoffed. "He didn't review it because he doesn't like being bothered by the Public Affairs Office." Josh sighed. "You need to work on your writing. I'd like you to concentrate on writing features for the *Astrogram* about employee activities such as clubs and whatnot. Report to me when you line up a story."

"I'll get on it."

Josh started to leave but stopped, turned, and zeroed in on Ryder's eyes. "Improve, or I'll ask for an alternate candidate, even if I irritate Nigel Worth." Josh stamped back into his office and slammed his door.

At first, Ryder felt angry, but he knew he had to quit stewing about petty stuff when the investigation had to proceed fast—like Usain Bolt running the hundred-meter dash. Working on employee newspaper articles would allow Ryder to suggest stories involving persons of interest. He began to think of people he'd like to interview.

TWENTY

A NAME POPPED into Ryder's mind—Walter Fuldheim, Scarlet's ex-boyfriend, the man she'd dated before she dumped him for Nigel. The task force needed to get Fuldheim's DNA to find out if he was the father of Scarlet's unborn child.

Ryder faced his computer and opened the *Astrogram*'s online portal. He searched the newspaper's past issues for "Fuldheim." There was one article about him and his robot group. But the majority of references to him were scores from the Ames Golf Club tournaments. Ryder saw an opportunity. Fuldheim had won the March tournament, which was held at the Moffett Field Golf Course, but there was no article about his win.

Ryder pulled the Ames map from his breast pocket. The golf course was on Ames territory across the airfield. The course was eighteen holes and covered in drought-resistant kikuyu grass that had been introduced to California from Africa in the 1930s, according to the course's website. It also noted that anyone with a driver's license from any state in the US was allowed to play golf at Moffett.

If he could convince Fuldheim to meet him there, Ryder

could work Scarlet into the conversation in an offhand fashion. He could say he needed to take a picture of Fuldheim with his clubs on the first tee.

After buying Fuldheim a soft drink, a beer, or a cup of coffee, maybe Ryder could snag the man's DNA. But how could Ryder get the discarded container? He would have to wear gloves and put the sample into a paper evidence bag. He could not do that in front of the suspect. Ryder needed help, so he decided to call Rita. She could book a tee time without arousing suspicion. She or a partner could properly pick up the sample, place it in a bag, seal it with evidence tape, then date, identify, and initial it.

A chain of custody had to be maintained. Each person who would touch the evidence bag would need to log it with his or her name and the times he or she had it. If the chain were broken, the evidence could not be used in court.

Ryder liked the plan. But would Josh like the golf feature idea? Ryder resisted the temptation to head at once for Josh's office to propose the article.

Instead, Ryder left for the cafeteria. He pulled out his mobile phone and touched Rita's name on his contact list. He needed help.

TWENTY-ONE

FBI AGENT RITA REYNOLDS answered on the first ring. "Luke?"

Ryder kicked a pebble as he walked toward the cafeteria. The stone skittered into the lush grass. "I got an idea on how I can interview Walter Fuldheim and get his DNA. For the DNA part, I need your help. I can't pick up his drink container when he's with me."

"I'd help, but there's a problem. Except for Mike and you, our task force members shouldn't go on base unless we're going to collar someone. Our presence could arouse suspicion. I don't think Mike would like to be seen picking up a can, either."

"My plan will work anyway. Fuldheim won a golf tournament. I'll ask him to meet me at the Moffett Field Golf Course for an employee newspaper interview. The course is across the airfield from NASA, and it's open to anybody who shows a driver's license. I'll buy him a drink. After he tosses the empty, that's where you or somebody else comes in."

"That'll work." Rita paused for a beat. "I've played

Moffett, and Henry Dunbar often goes with me. I'll ask him to help."

"Could you and Henry stand near the first tee like you're going to play and wait 'til Fuldheim throws his drink container away?"

"Of course. Afterward, I might play two or three holes or hit a bucket of balls. When can we do it?"

"First, I need an okay from Josh Sable, the news chief, to do the article. Then I'll ask Fuldheim for an interview. The best-case scenario is he'll meet me on the course late this afternoon. But it also could be in the next day or two."

Rita took a breath. "Henry and I can be at the course this afternoon. Set it up for today, but if you can't, make it ASAP."

Ryder needed to talk to Josh right after lunch.

TWENTY-TWO

IT WAS JUST after the lunch hour, and Josh was following the public affairs hallway toward his office.

When Ryder caught sight of the stocky man, he noticed Josh walked in a fluid gait, seemingly less tense than he normally was.

Less than a minute later, Ryder stood next to Josh's office, knocked on its steel doorframe, and peered into the room.

Josh appeared happy, satisfied by a sizable lunch. Unmarried, the midday fare was his main meal of the day. "Come in, Luke. Have an idea for a feature article yet?" Josh's voice was friendly in contrast to his angry mood merely two hours before.

"Yes, sir. That's why I'm here." Ryder stepped into the office and stopped by Josh's desk. "Walter Fuldheim won the Ames Golf Club tournament in March. I noticed no article about the win was in the *Astrogram*. I'd like to ask him for an interview."

"Give it a go." Josh paused. "Take notes. Write a captivating lead, put the best quote in the third sentence, and then add details."

"Yes, sir."

"Let me see a draft when it's ready."

Josh reached for a cup of coffee and dropped three sugar cubes in it. He shoved four pills in his mouth and washed them down with a gulp of sweet coffee.

Ryder left. He didn't want to give Josh a chance to set a deadline. He wondered if Josh's sudden mood swings suggested the man had bipolar disorder, but Ryder didn't have time to ponder this. Instead, he needed to call Fuldheim at once to keep the investigation moving forward full steam ahead.

TWENTY-THREE

RYDER HELD his ear to his desk phone's handset and heard its ringtone chime three times.

"Walt Fuldheim here."

"This is Luke Ryder with public affairs. I noticed you won the last Ames Golf Club tournament, so I'd like to interview you about your win for the *Astrogram*. I'd also like to take a picture of you with your clubs at the Moffett Golf Course's first tee."

"Sounds like fun." Fuldheim paused. "Luke Ryder, correct?"

"Yes. I recently joined PAO, the Public Affairs Office."

"When would you like to meet?" The sound of paper flipping came through the phone's handset. "I'm checking my calendar. If you can fit it in, I could meet you late this afternoon at the first tee. How about three-fifty?"

"That's fine."

"Since you've just started at PAO, after meeting at the course, I could show you our robotics lab. I bet an article about robots would be of great interest."

"I could work it in another day."

Fuldheim said, "Good. Meanwhile, I'll see you shortly at the first tee."

"Thanks, Walt."

Ryder extracted his mobile phone from his hip pocket. He selected Rita's number. "Hi, Rita. It's a go for this afternoon at the Moffett Field Golf Course."

"When?"

"Three-fifty."

"Henry will be with me."

TWENTY-FOUR

LUCINDA TOSSED her long hair backward and handed the public affairs point-and-shoot digital camera to Ryder. "Have fun with your first *Astrogram* article, even though it's about golf."

He nodded.

"Could you take close-ups of Fuldheim's clubs, too? I'll make a graphic to perk up the article."

"Okay."

* * *

WHEN HE PULLED into the Moffett Field Golf Course parking lot, Ryder saw a man taking a bag of clubs from a car trunk. As Ryder drove closer, he recognized Walter Fuldheim from a snapshot in the FBI case file.

Ryder parked next to Fuldheim's car. "You must be Walt Fuldheim." Ryder extended his hand.

When Ryder opened his truck's rear door, Blackie hopped out.

Fuldheim gestured at the dog. "Somebody told me about your service dog."

Ryder smiled. "Word gets around fast at Ames."

Fuldheim hefted his heavy golf bag and placed its wide strap over his right shoulder. "Ames is like a village. News and rumors spread as fast as a gasoline fire."

The men passed a building that included a pro shop and bar. Fuldheim glanced at a vending machine that stood under a veranda and started to reach into his pocket.

Ryder put a five-dollar bill into the machine. "I'm buyin' this time. Punch the button for what you want."

Fuldheim chose root beer. "When you visit the robotics group, it'll be my treat." He balanced his bag on the concrete walk.

Ryder withdrew a can of ginger ale, sipped the drink, and wished it contained real ale. He hadn't had an alcoholic beverage in many months.

Ryder glanced inside the pro shop and saw Rita buying a bucket of balls. Her golf outfit enhanced her figure and revealed her shapely legs. The man behind the cash register tried not to stare at her, but he failed. Rita also wore golf gloves that were the same turquoise color as nitrile crime scene gloves. A barrel-chested black man, obviously Henry Dunbar, stood next to her.

Fuldheim took a swig of root beer. "Let's mosey over to the first tee. We can shoot the pix there."

Ryder tugged on Blackie's leash. "Good idea."

* * *

THE FIRST TEE WAS EMPTY. It was too late for golfers to play eighteen holes and finish before sunset.

Ryder glanced backward and saw Rita and Henry approaching. Ryder winked at Rita, and she flashed a quick smile. He realized she had seen Fuldheim carrying a brown can of root beer.

Rita and Henry sat on a bench near the tee and chatted in low voices.

Ryder stepped onto the short grass on the verdant tee box. "I'll get pictures of you and your clubs first."

Fuldheim reached toward his golf bag. "Should I take out a club, like a driver?"

"That would be perfect." Ryder hoped Fuldheim wouldn't nurse his root beer. Ryder rubbed his throat and exaggerated a gulp. "I'm feelin' real thirsty. The air out here is dry." He chugged his ginger ale but decided not to finish his drink before Fuldheim drank all of his root beer.

Fuldheim held up his aluminum can. "My throat's dry as a slice of jerky." He gulped his soda, wiped his shirt arm over his lips, and set his can on the grass. "I'm better now. I won't be hoarse when we do the interview."

Ryder lifted his camera to eye level. "Ready?"

"Uh-huh."

Ryder snapped four pictures.

Fuldheim picked up his can and took two more gulps. He kept the can and licked his lips. "Have enough pictures?"

"Not yet. My office-mate, Lucinda, wants pics of your clubs 'cuz she plans to make a graphic for the article."

Fuldheim nodded.

Ryder shot close-ups of club heads. From the corner of his eye, he saw Fuldheim finish his root beer and toss his can into a metal mesh trash container.

Fuldheim pointed at Ryder's camera. "Could you e-mail the pictures to me? I'd like them for my scrapbook."

"No problem."

Blackie peed on a tree.

Ryder caught sight of the dog and sighed. "Let's move under the veranda by the pro shop and sit at the picnic table. I can take better notes there."

Fuldheim lifted his golf bag and adjusted its strap on his shoulder. As the men walked toward the pro shop, Fuldheim turned his head, and his eyes locked on to something behind him. "Hey, that woman took my can out of the trash."

Ryder was quick to answer. "I heard there's a drive at Ames to collect recyclables and give the refunds to charity."

Fuldheim tilted his head. "Every dime counts when it comes to helping those who are less fortunate."

"Yup. There are lots of folks who need help these days."

Fuldheim set his clubs against the pro shop's exterior wall next to the picnic table and sat down.

Ryder tapped the tabletop. "Nuts. I forgot my steno pad. Mind if I record this with my phone?"

"Go ahead."

As Ryder grabbed his smartphone from his hip pocket, he wondered how he was going to bring up Scarlet's murder. "You were talkin' about how fast news travels at NASA. I heard a weird story about the X-909 space plane project. I'm told a woman was murdered who worked on that program. I'm supposed to cover the X-909 beat, and it's concerning there's somebody on base who got away with murder."

Fuldheim rubbed his forehead. "Yeah." He sighed. "It's been a couple of years." He cleared his throat. "I knew the murdered woman, Scarlet."

Ryder furrowed his brow. "Were you close?"

"She was my girlfriend, but she broke it off with me. We parted as friends. Then she was murdered, and it was tough because I still loved her. I'm not over it. Sorry, I didn't mean to get into this. Let's talk about golf instead."

Ryder thought he'd better not press Fuldheim for details about Scarlet until after Rita received the man's DNA report. The men chatted about golf for a quarter of an hour.

After Fuldheim left, Ryder sat for a minute at the picnic table to think about his first two days at NASA. He hadn't made much progress in the investigation, and the clock was ticking. Rita had said the task force had a short time to get results, or it would be disbanded. Now, at least, they had Fuldheim's DNA. Would it show he was the father of Scarlet's unborn child? Rita might well have an answer soon because she had access to the latest quick turnaround DNA equipment. Fuldheim seemed like an honest guy. It'd be a shame if he proved to be the killer.

Ryder fingered his cell phone and remembered he needed to call his girlfriend Layla before it was too late in the Eastern Time Zone. He needed to hear her voice, and he wished he were back in Kentucky.

TWENTY-FIVE

IN THE MOFFETT FIELD GOLF COURSE parking lot, Ryder opened the rear door of his rented truck. The breeze had kicked up, and fine dust blew across the bone-dry gravel. Blackie hopped into the vehicle and curled up on the seat. Walter Fuldheim had just pulled away in his electric SUV.

Ryder leaned against his truck, and he felt elated when he touched Layla's name on his smartphone's display.

On the third ring, Layla answered. "How are you, Luke?"

Ryder felt the warm metal of his vehicle against his lower back, and the sensation was soothing. "I miss you, and talkin' with you will help me. I've had my ups and downs today."

"What happened?"

"Nigel said a fact sheet I wrote about a space plane was fine, but the news chief hated it. I've got to rework it." Ryder paused. "What's happenin' with you?"

"Jim Pike was out here to see how I'm doing."

"Jim's a real friend."

Layla said, "He helped the boys tune up the old tractor." She took a breath. "He mentioned Rita Reynolds from the holler is running the investigation, like you said. But you didn't tell me she's gorgeous."

Ryder figured Layla was jealous of Rita, but he wasn't sure how he could allay her fears. "If you ask me, she's not nearly as beautiful as you are."

Layla jostled her phone. "I'm in bed reading. I wish you were here away from tempting women."

"I'd rather be kissin' you than anything else right now."

"I wish we were kissing, too. To say the least, I'm glad the investigation won't go on forever."

"Yep, the case has been cold for years, and I doubt we'll get fresh leads. I'll be happy to leave this Peyton Place. There's plenty of dysfunctional folks here."

"People aren't perfect."

Ryder imagined Layla in her nightwear. "But you're close to it."

"I'm glad you think so. Hurry up and find the killer, so you can come home to me. I love you so much."

"I love you, too, but I gotta go now, darlin' 'cuz I got a meetin' coming up with Nigel."

Ryder wondered why Pike would've brought up Rita in his conversation with Layla. He entered his vehicle and began to drive to Joe Brown's Coffee Shop to meet Nigel Worth. Ryder would be careful not to mention how he and Rita had secured Fuldheim's DNA. But Ryder could ask Nigel about Scarlet. Maybe there was something Nigel hadn't told the FBI.

TWENTY-SIX

JOE BROWN'S Coffee Shop in Mountain View was crowded when Ryder walked into its medium-sized building. He noted there were five round patio tables outside the establishment. Two of them were occupied.

Nigel Worth was in line, ready to order. He waved to Ryder. "What'll you have?"

Ryder stopped near Nigel. "A cup of black coffee and a plain doughnut." Ryder pointed out of the window. "It's not crowded outside. I can save a table."

"Okay." Nigel cast his eyes upward. "I was irritated after I read your message about Josh rejecting the fact sheet. But we'll change it to satisfy him."

Ryder cleared his throat. "He won't like anything we do."

Nigel wrinkled his brow. "I'll ask the project office to write a memo saying they're pleased with our revised version. I'll carry that message back to Josh and order him to accept it."

Ryder shrugged. "That'll work. See you outside. I gotta get Blackie out of the truck before he has an accident." Ryder dropped coins in the tip cup near the cash register and headed outside.

Minutes later, Nigel pushed the glass exit door open. He carried a plastic tray that held a large coffee, a raspberry pastry, and Ryder's order. He joined Ryder at an umbrella-covered patio table.

Ryder ripped a piece from his doughnut and offered it to Blackie.

Nigel grabbed his pastry. His mouth half-full, he said, "Who typed the fact sheet? It was perfect."

"Lucinda. She added the pix, too."

Nigel took a sip of coffee and washed down the pastry. "She's a gem."

Ryder was curious whether or not Nigel had ever dated Lucinda. Was he the one who had impregnated her? Ryder zeroed in on Nigel's eyes and said, "She's kinda perky. A talented artist, too. She looks young for her age."

"I was shocked when I learned she's older than thirty." Nigel rubbed the stubble on his chin. "She's friendly. But she gets moody when she's under stress, and she can be clingy."

"How do you know that? Did you date her before you and Scarlet hooked up?" Ryder smiled.

Nigel shifted in his chair. "No. I've just observed her over the years. She's typed a lot for me and does a perfect job every time, unlike my current secretary, Deborah."

"Maybe Lucinda likes you. Leon Turk said she's hunting for a husband. Could be it's time to move on and ask Lucinda out to get back in practice."

"I should date again, but not with Lucinda. I'm a manager. She's a secretary in my organization." He paused. "I'm counting on you to solve Scarlet's murder. Then I can get on with my life."

Ryder stared at the concrete below the table for a moment. "I'm doin' my best, but it's hard to find fresh information." He sipped his steaming coffee and then set the cup on the wire mesh tabletop. "Is there anything you didn't want to say to the FBI about Scarlet? You can tell me, even if it's embarrassing."

Nigel pursed his lips. "She smoked reefers."

"That's not relevant."

"When I saw her talk with men, I was jealous. She seemed too interested in guys, but that could've been a feminine ploy to make me pay attention to her. I did. I asked her to marry me."

Ryder was glad he didn't need to tell Nigel that at the time of her death, Scarlet was pregnant by an unknown man. Ryder crossed his legs and then said, "To change the subject, I met with Walter Fuldheim of the robotics group today. I interviewed him about his golf tournament win. I've got to write an *Astrogram* article about it to appease Josh."

"I'll scan it before you send it to him. We have to keep him from distracting you from the investigation."

Ryder bit his doughnut and gave Blackie two sizable crumbs. "Fuldheim seems like a decent guy. Invited me over to see the robots they're workin' on."

"He's pleasant and popular with the ladies. Wish I had his way with women."

Ryder reached into his sports coat pocket. "Here's the fact sheet Josh marked up."

Nigel grabbed the printout. "These are minor comments. This stuff about it being too simple is bullshit."

"True, but like you said, y'all might have to order Josh to accept a simple, clear version."

Nigel scribbled notes on the printout. "Whether Josh likes it or not, we'll put out a top-notch brochure."

Ryder wondered what Fuldheim's DNA would reveal. In less than two hours at the FBI task force meeting, Ryder might well learn if Fuldheim was Scarlet's secret lover, the one who had made her pregnant.

TWENTY-SEVEN

RYDER NEARED the commonplace Sunnyvale home that served as the task force's command post. Cars sat at the curb close to the house, but the rest of the street was empty. Neighbors' vehicles sat in driveways. All the curtains were closed, but lamplight glowed from the bungalow's windows. Muffled voices told Ryder many of the task force members had arrived.

The wooden porch steps creaked as Ryder climbed them. He slipped his key into the entryway's lock and unbolted the door. When he pushed it inward, its hinges squealed like they hadn't been oiled in years.

The FBI team members sat in a semicircle near the whiteboard. Ryder smelled fresh coffee, and he noticed a tray of doughnuts.

Rita occupied a chair near the board. "Have a seat, Luke."

Ryder took the only empty chair left. "Hi, y'all. I've met everyone except Agent Dunbar."

Henry's expression showed he had a no-nonsense attitude. The barrel-chested black man raised his muscular arm. "I look forward to working with you, Luke."

Ryder nodded.

Rita stood. "I'd like to formally introduce Luke Ryder." She cleared her throat. "Luke has been a deputy sheriff in Eastern Kentucky for less than a year, but he was a Kentucky game warden before that. In Kentucky, game wardens are law enforcement officers." She stepped toward Ryder. "Luke has an uncanny ability to solve murders. Years ago, he helped Sheriff Jim Pike catch a murderer who might well have never been caught if it weren't for Luke. Last year, Luke solved a serial killer case. Sheriff Pike then hired Luke. Three months ago, Luke caught a killer with the aid of his bloodhound, Blackie." She turned to Ryder. "I wish you would've brought your dog to meet the team."

Luke flushed. "He's at the apartment getting his beauty sleep." Luke thought Rita had raised expectations too much about his ability to solve crimes. He figured it was doubtful Scarlet's killer would be caught without a lucky break.

Rita held up a paper. "Today, we obtained DNA test results for a person of interest, Walter Fuldheim, an ex-boyfriend of Scarlet. Fuldheim was not the father of her unborn child. This result erases part of the suspicion we had of him."

The task force members' low voices signaled their approval.

Rita took a step toward Ryder, and the floorboards made an annoying squeak. "I commend Luke for setting up a meeting today with Fuldheim at the Moffett Field Golf Course so Henry and I could snag his root beer can." She paused. "It also gave Henry and me a chance to hit a bucket of balls."

Smiles and low laughs erupted.

Rita grabbed a laptop computer and handed it to Ryder. "This Bureau laptop should be helpful."

Then she held up a large photographic print that showed the image of a triple-sealed, plastic evidence bag, which contained a short black strap.

"The trench coat wrist strap pictured in this photograph was found near a back door of the Unitary shortly after

Scarlet Hauk's murder. We believe it may have been dropped by the killer. It's been sealed in the evidence bag for two years. According to experts, it may contain the murderer's scent." She caught Ryder's eye. "Once an East Coast DNA lab returns the strap to us, Luke's bloodhound, Blackie, can sniff it and try to find a suspect."

Rita cast her eyes over the team members. "Let's hope the dog hits on a person of interest. We need to move fast before we're shut down." She paused. "Luke, what do you think's the best procedure when you put Blackie to work?"

Not accustomed to speaking to groups of people, Ryder's heart started to race. "I'll keep the evidence bag in my sports coat pocket. I'll go into a stall in a men's room, open the bag, and let Blackie sniff inside it. Then I'll search the Unitary complex first."

Mike raised his hand. "What happens when Blackie hits on something or someone?"

Ryder colored. "Blackie lies on the ground when he gets a hit. If anybody's around, I'll say Blackie wants to play fetch, and I'll have a rubber dog bone handy."

Henry, the muscular FBI agent, focused his eyes like lasers on Ryder. "What'll you do if you find the trench coat that goes with the wrist strap?"

Ryder studied the floor for a moment. "That depends if anybody is nearby. If somebody's around, I'll call Mike Lobo, and he can arrange to pick up the coat when people are out of the office." Ryder rubbed his chin. "If nobody's around, again, it's best that I call Mike because an evidence bag for a coat is large. For me to be ready to secure the evidence, I'd have to put a bag in a backpack or a briefcase, which could appear kinda strange."

Rita nodded. "If Luke finds physical evidence, he should call Mike Lobo first...or me if Mike's not available." Rita sat down and nodded at Ryder.

Ryder said, "There's also the question of what'll I do if Blackie locks on a human being." He took his mobile phone from his hip pocket. "I could shoot a picture or a movie of the person and pretend I'm focusin' on Blackie."

Rita said, "That kind of quick thinking shows Luke has horse sense."

Henry's face morphed from a serious expression to a relaxed one. "That's better than Luke being full of horseshit, which he obviously isn't."

There was laughter. Rita raised her hands. "That's it for now. Feel free to hang around and talk with Luke."

Henry walked to Ryder. "You did a decent job of getting Fuldheim in a position where we could grab his DNA, but you need to be careful when you run across evidence. We must maintain the chain of custody. Proper procedure is extremely important."

Ryder nodded. "I was thinkin' about it when I called Rita to ask for help collecting Fuldheim's drink can."

Henry creased his brow. "I'm thankful you have decent instincts, even though the Bureau didn't train you."

Ryder sensed Henry was the kind of investigator who wanted everything figured out ahead of time. Ryder said, "You're a real pro. Okay if I call you to get ideas on how to handle certain situations?"

Henry cracked a smile and reached into his pocket. "Here's my card. Call any time, day or night." He paused. "One thing I forgot to mention that everybody else on the team knows. I learned somebody at Ames owes a San Jose loan shark a large sum of money. I'm trying to figure out who that person is. If you hear anything, let me know."

"Will do." Ryder held out his hand. The men shook hands.

TWENTY-EIGHT

IT WAS eight-fifteen in the morning and chilly. Ryder and Blackie entered through a rear doorway of the Unitary and then walked along the building's extensive halls.

When they approached Bill's office, Blackie's ears perked up. He pulled his leash and Ryder toward Bill's office door, which was ajar.

Bill peeked out. "I was just going to call you. Come in."

Ryder took a step into the office. At the same time, Blackie began to sniff the air, and Ryder noticed a breakfast roll on Bill's desk. All of a sudden, the dog jumped toward the desk, and a fountain pen tumbled from the desktop to the floor.

"Blackie, sit and stay."

The dog sat.

"Sorry he knocked down your pen."

Bill shrugged. "It's not mine. It belongs to Leon. He was just here."

"He doesn't normally work early," Ryder said. He recalled Leon usually went to the fitness center before going into the office. What would cause him to change his routine?

"I'm surprised you didn't see him leave. He left about three minutes ago."

Ryder sat in the chair next to the desk. "I came in a back door." Ryder picked up Leon's pen and placed it on Bill's desk.

"I sent Leon packing. He said he heard Josh didn't like the fact sheet, and he, Leon, could fix it. I told him you were doing a great job even though you've been here a short time. I also let him know project management loved the latest version. The prick left in a huff."

Ryder smiled. "I can't wait to finish off that write-up so I can convince Josh I'm not a joke."

Bill cradled his chin on his fist. "Let's meet for lunch at noon in the cafeteria. We can add details to the document. I'll send a message to Director Nigel Worth that technical management has approved it, and we want copies for a project meeting next week in Houston."

"Sounds fine." Ryder picked up the pen and put it in his breast pocket. "I'll return this to Leon."

"Thanks. I need to be at a staff meeting soon."

Ryder stood. "See you at lunch." Ryder wondered how Leon would act when he received the pen he had mislaid.

TWENTY-NINE

WHEN HE RETURNED to the Public Affairs Office, Ryder had Leon Turk's fountain pen.

Ryder glanced into Leon's room and noticed he was talking in a quiet voice with a skinny man of East Indian descent dressed in a suit.

Leon's brow wrinkled as he gestured at Ryder. Before Ryder could move out of Leon's line of sight, Leon said, "Come in, Luke. I'd like you to meet somebody."

Ryder approached.

Leon said, "Luke Ryder, this is Chuck Singh, who's the chief science reporter for the *Straight Scoop Bay Area*. It's an online magazine."

Chuck held out his hand. "I hear you joined public affairs not long ago." Chuck spoke with a Hindi accent.

Ryder nodded.

Chuck said, "I make it a point to maintain contact with all the NASA public affairs officers. The *Straight Scoop* uses a lot of Ames stories. Maybe we can go to lunch in the near future?"

"I'd like that." Ryder paused and reached in his shirt

pocket for Leon's fountain pen. "Leon, before I forget, here's your fountain pen. You left it on Bill's desk."

Leon flushed. "Thanks." One of his eyes twitched. "You must've been in the Unitary just after I left?"

"Yep. I set up a time for me and Bill to finalize the X-909 fact sheet."

Leon frowned. "Sorry to bug out on you guys, but I have to leave." He caught Ryder's eyes. "Could you escort Chuck to the main gate after you're done chatting?"

"No problem."

Leon left.

Chuck said, "Leon and I are pals. We were in the same high school class."

"I bet you both benefit. You get stories from Leon and publish them."

"That could work out for you, too, Luke. When I upload a NASA story, it usually goes viral." He winked. "How about we do lunch tomorrow in the cafeteria?"

"Noon okay?"

Chuck grinned. "Yes." He peered out the window toward the main gate. "I need to cut our chat short because I have to write and file a story."

"Let's get you to the main gate." Ryder wondered why Leon, who was obsessed with protecting his turf, had introduced him to a best friend, knowing that person would provide a story conduit to the world. Leon wasn't the kind of a guy who helped fellow workers unless he gained something valuable from it. Leon was all for himself.

THIRTY

RYDER AND BLACKIE were walking the short distance from the main gate to the public affairs offices. The temperature had increased, and the bright sunlight caused the colors of the trees and the sky to become saturated and vivid.

Ryder's mobile phone rang.

"Luke." The male voice on the phone was a whisper. "It's Leon Turk. I'm wondering if you could do me a favor."

"What?"

"I was supposed to meet with an Ames astronomer this morning at ten, and the meeting I'm in is still going on. Could you cover the ten o'clock for me?"

"No problem."

"His name is Dr. Greg Gault. You can find his building and office number in the Ames phone book."

"What do you need me to do?"

"Listen and take notes. He's eccentric and claims to have made a historic discovery, something to do with an exoplanet."

"What's an exoplanet?"

"A planet orbiting a star that's not our sun."

"Oh."

"I'll pay you back."

Ryder thought Leon seemed friendlier, which was a relief, even if the guy was a potential person of interest. Or was he a decent liar?

Within minutes, Ryder sat at his desk. Greg's phone book entry indicated his office was in Building N-245, the Space Sciences Research Laboratory. Ryder realized the meeting with the astronomer would be a detour from the Scarlet Hauk investigation, but talking with Greg would help maintain Ryder's cover story.

Ryder tapped out Greg's phone number.

"Dr. Gault here." He spoke in a dignified English accent.

"This is Luke Ryder at public affairs. Leon Turk can't meet with you today because a meetin' has dragged on."

"I was eager to meet with Leon to discuss an exciting discovery I made."

"I could be there by ten-fifteen to take notes for Leon."

"Brilliant. You'll be excited when I reveal my findings."

THIRTY-ONE

RYDER LED Blackie into astronomer Greg Gault's second-floor office.

Impeccably dressed in a fine gray suit, Greg stood and motioned toward a chair next to his steel desk. "Mr. Luke Ryder, I presume. Welcome. Have a seat." He spoke precisely in a fine English accent and smiled broadly.

"This is my service dog, Blackie."

The dog inspected the office with curious eyes, panted, and then lay down.

"What a fine specimen. If I am not mistaken, Blackie is a bloodhound. They make excellent and gentle family pets."

Ryder didn't want to spread the word Blackie was a bloodhound. That could make a person of interest suspicious.

"I didn't know that. He was provided to me by a nonprofit to help me with my PTSD."

Greg sat at his desk. Behind him was a large computer screen, which displayed a brightly colored space image. It resembled a vivid psychedelic painting in many hues. Ryder guessed a large spot in the center of the screen was a star, and dots of light surrounding it were exoplanets.

Blackie approached Greg and licked his hand that dangled at his side. Greg smiled. "Friendly fellow." He petted the animal's head.

"Sorry 'bout that, Dr. Gault."

Greg waved his hand. "No, no. It's fine." He paused. "Please tell me about your PTSD."

Ryder felt a wave of guilt travel through his body. He had to lie again. "It's related to my service during the Congo Conflict." He cleared his throat. "I don't like to talk about it."

Greg's brow became chiseled. "Thank you for your service."

Ryder glanced at the screen behind Greg. "I'm wonderin' if the picture on the computer screen is of a star and exoplanets. They're so brightly colored."

Greg swiveled in his chair and pointed to the biggest spot in the center. "That's observant of you. Indeed, the brightest light is a star, but these hues are not the natural colors of the star and its planets. The computer adds what we call false colors to the picture. We do this so we can discern subtle differences in the image that otherwise would blend together in a gray smear."

"Is it okay if I record this conversation with my phone?"

"That's reasonable. You can play it back for Leon."

Ryder turned on his smartphone's audio recorder. "The tiny dots are exoplanets?"

"They are indeed." Greg pointed at his computer screen. "This image was taken with the Super Large Infrared Moon Telescope—SLIMT—which is located on the far side of the moon in a permanently shaded area. SLIMT is the most sensitive infrared instrument yet built." Greg focused his eyes like a pair of spotlights on Ryder. "What I'll tell you next has yet to be peer-reviewed. It will earn our team immense recognition." He tapped the screen with his pen over a point of light nearest to the star. "We've discovered an exo-Earth."

"An earthlike planet?" Ryder opened a notepad. "How can you tell from that picture? It's just a bright dot."

Greg shot a conspiratorial look in Ryder's direction, and

his fine brown leather shoes squeaked as he leaned forward. "We can tell there's life on this planet because we have detected the spectral fingerprint of chlorophyll, the green material in plants. It enables them to capture sunlight, or starlight energy in this case. Plants use this energy to make sugars they convert into starches and cellulose." The Englishman cocked his head and rubbed his hands together. "You may wonder how we can see patterns of colored light coming from this planet. Whilst this exo-Earth orbits its home star, the light from the mother star passes through the planet's atmosphere. We analyzed this light, and we found combinations of colors that indicate water, oxygen, carbon dioxide, and the hardest to detect…chlorophyll."

"How's that work?"

"Each substance has a spectrum, an almost unique combination of colors. Check out this graph."

Greg handed Ryder a color print that displayed thin red, green, and blue lines that formed mountain-like peaks on a chart. "It shows the spectrum of chlorophyll. This combination of colors is like the fingerprint of chlorophyll."

Ryder wondered how anyone could be satisfied that a bunch of colored lines on a graph were proof plants were growing on a planet far away in the galaxy. "Could y'all send a camera there to take pictures, like they sent rovers to Mars?"

"That won't happen anytime soon. This exoplanet is twenty-two light years away. With conventional rocket propulsion, it would take thousands of years to get there and back. Even if we could travel at the speed of light, it would be fifty years after launch before we could get a picture back." Greg paused. "Let's say we built a matter-antimatter engine. I'm told that kind of engine could reach seventy percent of the speed of light. That would take even more than fifty years to return images."

"A matter-antimatter engine. Sounds like science fiction."

Greg squinted. "Don't tell a reporter this, but if you combined a pea-sized bit of matter with a piece of antimatter the same size, it might well blow up the Earth. That, of course, is just my opinion."

Ryder said, "Leon's gonna pull out all the stops when he publicizes the exo-Earth. This is historic."

Ryder realized he was one of the first people to learn life beyond Earth definitely existed. Now he knew why Nigel loved his job so much. He had a front-row seat from which to view scientific discoveries as they unfolded.

"Okay if I can have copies of the star with the exo-Earth and the chlorophyll spectrum graph?"

"Here you go." Greg handed Ryder two photographic prints.

Ryder wondered if he'd see Leon in the cafeteria. Lunchtime was near.

THIRTY-TWO

RYDER STOOD in the cafeteria's checkout line. He held a copy of the draft X-909 fact sheet under his tray while Blackie's leash was looped in his left hand. A thick steak sandwich, French fries, and a salad were atop Ryder's tray. The bloodhound kept his eyes focused on the tray while his nose was busy sampling a rich mix of food scents.

Lucinda turned her head toward Ryder from farther up the queue of people who waited to pay for their lunches. "Want to sit together?"

"Sorry. I'm meetin' Bill Little to go over the fact sheet."

"Oh, yes." Lucinda smiled. "Catch you later." Waiting to pay, she turned toward the cashier. People from public affairs, including Leon Turk, Josh Sable, Olivia DeChamps, and Jenny Rogers, were in line ahead of Lucinda.

Ryder felt someone tap his shoulder. He turned around to see Bill Little. "I still have to get my food, Luke."

Lucinda glanced back at Ryder. "Don't forget I can type your changes at once if you like." She waved, her waist-length hair swaying. "Enjoy your meeting."

After paying for his lunch, Ryder jangled the change in

his pocket. He needed coins to feed vending machines later that afternoon.

Ryder and Bill found seats on the sunny side of the cafeteria.

Bill picked up his Reuben sandwich. "I vote we eat before we attack the fact sheet. I'm as hungry as a starving dog." He bit into his sandwich and glanced at Blackie, who was drooling and looked alert as if he expected a handout.

Ryder fed Blackie part of his steak sandwich and ate the rest.

Bill was washing down his food with a gulp of soda when his cell phone rang. "Brett?" Bill nodded. "What terminal are you at?" He glanced at his wristwatch. "I'll be there in forty-five minutes. I'll call when I pull up in the pickup zone."

Bill glanced at Ryder. "That was my son, Brett. He caught an earlier flight, so I have to leave right away and pick him up. Don't worry. We'll review the fact sheet soon. I'll call you."

"It's important to be with your son."

"He's a high school teacher in Lexington, close to where you're from. I'll give him a tour of Ames, so you'll have a chance to meet him."

"I look forward to it."

Bill stood and put his tray on the conveyor belt.

Ryder finished his meal and exited the cafeteria. He noticed Leon getting into an expensive Italian automobile. How could a man with a midlevel government salary afford a luxury car? Did he come from a rich family?

THIRTY-THREE

A STRIKING, deep blue sky and warm sunshine uplifted Ryder's spirits as he stepped westward on the sidewalk that led from the cafeteria. The steak sandwich he'd eaten had tasted delicious. He felt content.

As he approached the southeast corner of the largest wind tunnel in the world, the National Full-Scale Aerodynamics Complex, he fingered a coin in his trouser pocket. He held the quarter between his thumb and index finger. Strangely, the coin felt like one side of it had begun to unscrew from the other, like a loose lid on a jar.

He turned left and waited to cross the street as a car went through the intersection. Before the next vehicle could get to the stop sign, he rapidly walked across the street, pulling at Blackie's leash to keep him moving. The dog panted and dribbled spit.

Ryder halted at the corner and took the coin from his pocket. "Damn," he said as he unscrewed the two sides of the quarter, holding the two pieces loosely together.

He took a shortcut through a parking lot, walking toward Building N-204, where the public affairs offices were located. Halting near a parking sign pole, he wound Blackie's leash around its base, and the dog reclined on the cool, green grass in the shade.

Once behind a car and next to a gravel walkway, Ryder cautiously separated the two halves of the quarter. In the hollowed-out coin, he saw what appeared to be a fragment of debris. He felt a gentle breeze disturb his hair. The speck flitted away and landed in the gravel path.

Ryder kneeled next to the path and peered at the broken, crushed rocks, but he couldn't see the speck.

"Strange," he said aloud.

He pulled his cell phone from his pocket and speed-dialed Mike Lobo, chief of counterintelligence. "Yeah, Luke."

"This may be nothin', but I found a quarter that unscrewed, and there's a compartment in it. It was empty except for a bit of debris."

"I hope you kept that speck."

Ryder scrutinized the gravel. "The wind blew it into the rocks."

"Where are you?"

"In the parking lot near Building N-204."

"Stay there. Can you spot where the speck went?"

"I know where it landed, but I can't see it."

"I'll be there soon. Don't tell anybody about it."

"What is it?"

"We'll talk when I get there."

Ryder stood and leaned against a car.

THIRTY-FOUR

MIKE PARKED his car in the lot near the public affairs offices. As he exited his sedan, he held a shiny, metallic, battery-powered vacuum cleaner.

Ryder stood up straight and took a step toward Mike's vehicle. "What's that for?"

Mike set the machine on the blacktop near Ryder's feet. "I'll try to suck up the particle. It might be a microdot."

Ryder raised his finger. "I saw a TV show about spies that used them to smuggle documents."

"A millimeter-wide dot the size of a period can hold lots of documents. A page of text can be reduced to a hundredth of a millimeter on a microdot."

"I'll be damned. I didn't know they could shrink pages that much."

Mike reached into his sports coat breast pocket, withdrew an evidence bag, and held it open. "Please put the quarter in here."

Ryder relaxed his hand to reveal the two halves of the quarter and then dropped them into the bag. He frowned. "Seems like I've blown it. I put my DNA on the coin. And the microdot, or dirt speck, is gone."

"Don't feel disappointed. At least you found a hollowed-out coin that could be used to sneak information off base." He lifted the vacuum. "We could still find the dot, if that's what it is."

Ryder eyed the machine. "It's solid for a vacuum."

"The FBI loaned it to me a month ago." Mike slid a filter out of a slot in the vacuum cleaner. "This filter can catch particles and odors. If we vacuum a new piece of evidence, like an item of clothing, your bloodhound might be able to use the scent to track a perp." Mike reinserted the filter.

Ryder surveyed the area to see if anybody was near. "It seems weird to vacuum rocks."

"If anybody asks, we're searching for a lost contact lens."

"Lucky most of the lunchtime crowd is back at work."

Mike kneeled near the gravel pathway. "Where'd the speck land?"

"By the white, smooth rock."

Mike took a picture with his cell phone camera. Then he switched on the vacuum cleaner and sucked up particles near the rock. "Let's get in my car to keep out of the wind and check out the filter."

* * *

THE TWO MEN sat in the front seats. Ryder focused on the white filter as Mike slid it from the vacuum. "I can't see anything but particles and dirt."

Mike nodded toward the glove compartment. "Let's approach this like Sherlock Holmes would. Can you get the magnifying glass out of the glove compartment?"

Ryder found a medium-sized magnifier sitting on top of a stack of maps. "Here."

"*Gracias, amigo.*" Mike held the glass above the filter. He smiled as he peered at the fragments on the white filter. "Bingo! It's a microdot."

Ryder squinted. "Can I see?"

"Okay, but don't breathe on it. I don't want to tear this

car apart to find it again." He handed the magnifier to Ryder.

"Shit," Ryder whispered. "I can't wait to find out what the hell's on this."

Mike gingerly slid the filter back into the vacuum and set it near Ryder's feet.

Ryder eased back into the bucket seat. "I wonder if anybody ahead of me in the checkout line used this quarter when they paid for lunch."

"Make a list of the people who were ahead of you, and text it to me. Describe them if you can't name them."

"I remember Josh Sable and Leon Turk were there. Also, Phoebe, what's her name?"

"Phoebe Tillus," Mike said. He paused a beat. "I'll bring an Ames employee photo album to the FBI meeting tonight. You can flip through it."

"That'll work."

"Better get out of the car before somebody wonders what we're up to. If anyone asks, we found my lost contact. Don't mention my name. Act like you don't know me."

Ryder exited the vehicle. No one was nearby.

Mike stared through his open car window. "Give me a call in a half-hour to regroup."

THIRTY-FIVE

RYDER SAT outside the public affairs building on a bench. The shade was cool, and a gentle, refreshing breeze rustled his hair.

Forty feet away, two men were on a break. One smoked a pipe, and Ryder could smell the sweet odor of tobacco. He turned away from the men and touched Mike's name on his mobile's contact list.

"Hello, Luke. A guy from the office took the microdot to Rita. They'll enlarge it to see what's there."

"What should I do next?"

"I can't go snooping around as discreetly as you can. I think you should check out the Imaging Technology Branch. They handle the center's photographic and video needs. But I don't think you'll find much there. Everything Imaging does is digital. They don't process film anymore."

"Lucinda said there's an Ames Photography Club. Could be they have a darkroom."

"See if there's a black and white processing setup with chemicals—developer, acid stop bath, and fixer. Know anything about photography?"

Ryder shifted his mobile phone against his ear. "My high

school had a darkroom. I developed negatives and printed pictures."

"Good. Also, see if you can find a modified microscope. A black-and-white negative of the reduced text is projected through the microscope's eyepiece to where a specimen slide would be. The slide is sensitive to light and is developed. I'll e-mail you information about microdots."

Ryder said, "That's complicated. I can't recognize that kind of microscope."

"There's also a simpler way to make a microdot if you don't need to make the image real small."

"How?"

"Load your thirty-five mm film camera with the sharpest black-and-white film you can find. Take a picture of the document and develop the negative. Cut a rectangular hole the size of the negative in a piece of cardboard and tape the negative over it. Shine a bright light behind it and shoot a picture with your camera far enough back so the document takes up a small fraction of the picture. Develop the second roll of film and cut the microdot out of its negative."

Ryder sighed. "It's a lot of steps, but that way, you can use regular photo equipment."

Mike was quiet and then said, "I'm glad you're checking out the photo club. Somebody could do the work there when no one else is around."

"I'll ask Lucinda about the club 'cuz she's a member. I'll say I'm writin' an article for the *Astrogram*."

"Okay. See you at tonight's meeting."

Ryder disconnected. Did Lucinda know how to make microdots? He rose, stretched, and started for the public affairs building's entrance. He needed to talk to Lucinda immediately.

THIRTY-SIX

RYDER CLIMBED Building N-204's steps and went into his office. Blackie, who was lying next to Lucinda, wagged his tail and trotted to Ryder while Lucinda continued to type. "Thanks for watching Blackie."

Lucinda locked her eyes on Ryder and smiled. "It was a pleasure. He nuzzled my feet."

Ryder touched his chin with his fingers. "I was just thinkin' of a potential *Astrogram* article. Didn't you tell me there's an Ames Photography Club, or maybe I heard it from somebody else?"

"I don't remember, either, but I belong to the club. I could take you over there, show you around the darkroom, and put off this boring typing. That is if Josh okays it."

"I'll ask him."

A minute later, Ryder rapped on Josh's doorframe. He was at his desk, his blue editing pencil in his hand. His neck was red, and a vein in his neck pulsated.

"What can I do for you, Luke?"

"I'd like to take a shot at writing a feature about the Ames Photography Club for the *Astrogram*."

Josh rolled his eyes. "Okay. Make sure it'll truly be of interest."

"Can Lucinda go with me to take pictures?"

"If she's caught up with her typing." Josh frowned.

"She was typin' as fast as a woodpecker after bugs in a tree."

Josh took a deep breath. "Don't keep her there for an extended period. Close the door on your way out."

Soon Ryder arrived at Lucinda's desk. "We'd better leave before Josh changes his mind."

Lucinda stood and combed her hair back with her fingers. "If we're lucky, the club president, Roger Lark, will be there. He used to be Ames' chief scientist before he retired. Now he volunteers to help with NASA research projects, but I think he uses it as an excuse to take advantage of the darkroom."

She picked up her digital camera and glanced at Blackie. "Better leave your dog here. He might drop dog hair in the darkroom, that could play havoc when we're printing negs."

Ryder tied Blackie's leash to a desk leg, and a thought came to him. "Before we leave, could you give Roger a call? Maybe he could meet us there."

Ryder considered whether or not a man like Roger might put NASA information on microdots, smuggle them off base, and sell them to the highest bidder. The man knew about many projects and had access to their information. Did he know anything about the space plane?

THIRTY-SEVEN

LUCINDA LED Ryder across the public affairs blacktop parking lot to Building N-203. She pointed at the old, two-story concrete building. Its two-to-three-foot thick walls had been built to withstand bomb blasts.

"The Imaging Technology Branch is on the first and second floors. When they stopped using photographic chemicals, they let the Ames Photography Club use an old darkroom."

Ryder held the building's entry door open for Lucinda. "This is real convenient for you."

She walked in. "Yes. I was a painter before I took up photography. Josh Sable introduced me to it. He's quite the photographer."

Ryder scoffed. "I wonder if I could get a quote from him." Ryder followed her.

Lucinda gracefully climbed the steps to the second floor. "Even if Josh doesn't provide a quote, surely he'll pay close attention to your article." She grasped the handrail as she stepped upward. "I'm happy Roger Lark's there. He'll say something worth quoting."

As they entered the Imaging Technology Branch's main

door, Ryder noticed a young woman who stood behind a customer counter. She nodded at Lucinda. Phones were ringing.

Lucinda turned to Ryder and said, "Customers drop off work orders and SD cards here and pick up digital prints, slides, and videos." She opened a door into a room where four large image-processing machines stood. Technicians dressed in white smocks were making digital color prints.

Lucinda opened a second door.

Ryder saw a thin, wrinkled old man with a stringy mustache sitting behind a desk.

The man stood. "You must be Luke Ryder?"

Ryder grasped the man's limp hand. "Yep. I take it you're Dr. Roger Lark."

"Yes. So, you and Lucinda are going to do an *Astrogram* article. What would you like to know?"

"I'm wonderin' what kind of photographic processing you do here."

Roger sat behind the desk and crossed his skinny legs. "We develop and print black-and-white silver-based film and paper in the darkroom. Color processing is too complex for us to do using photographic chemicals. However, we do shoot color images using digital cameras, and we process those pictures with our computers and printers at home."

Ryder sat in a chair next to the desk. He studied Roger's grayish face and thought the man must be in his late seventies. Would he have had the strength and resolve to cut a woman's throat? If not, was he the type to spy for a foreign power after many years of working for the US government?

Ryder scanned the room, searching for a microscope that might be modified to take microdot pictures. He asked, "Why bother with black and white chemicals when you can take digital color pictures and do a lot of creative things with computer programs?"

"Many types of black-and-white films yield a huge range of shades that produce rich prints, so many club members prefer to work with them. However, color film, especially slide film, has a narrower light-to-dark range. We also could do black-and-white with our computers, but chemically processed black-and-white can be quite artistic in my estimation."

"What do you mean?"

Roger smiled. "We're making fine art, much of it museum quality. Our eighteen club members are lucky they can use the darkroom. One reason NASA stopped making photographic products here with wet chemistry is environmental. Years ago, the center had to properly dispose of a huge quantity of photographic chemicals. But our club doesn't use much chemistry."

Roger coughed as if he'd said so much it exhausted him.

Ryder asked, "How do you get rid of your chemicals?"

"The Environmental Services Division collects our chemical waste and disposes of it. The division removes wastage from several chemistry research labs anyway, so disposal of ours isn't a problem."

Lucinda aimed her digital camera at Roger and shot pictures.

Roger tilted his head toward a door. As he did so, strands of his thin, stringy hair brushed his shoulders. "Let's go inside our darkroom." He stood.

Ryder and Lucinda followed him. As Ryder entered the room, he could smell the strong vinegary odor of acetic acid used in the chemical stop bath. The dim glow of an amber safelight lit the room only enough to create semidarkness. The special light allowed photographers to open boxes of light-sensitive papers without ruining them.

There were two enlargers. A pair of cotton gloves sat on an easel underneath the shorter enlarger. Ryder remembered he'd worn white cotton gloves in Boone High School's darkroom to keep from putting fingerprints on his negatives. He also noticed brown gallon jugs of chemicals—developer, an acetic acid stop bath, and fixer. Pint-sized, stainless-steel film-developing tanks and reels lined a shelf. He pointed to the tanks.

"What kinds of film do y'all process here?"

Roger opened a cabinet to reveal two sealed boxes

labeled "Aerial Grade Super Fine Grain HTC Black-and-White 35mm Film." He picked up a box. "We use the finest grain, sharpest film we can get so we can make poster-size paper enlargements. The club buys the film in bulk, and we also get two-and-quarter film rolls and four-by-five-inch sheet film."

Ryder spotted a microscope on top of the cabinet. "What's that microscope for?" He couldn't tell if it had been modified to produce microdots.

"Several members take microscopic pictures. They use eyepieces and techniques with which I'm not familiar."

Ryder glanced into a tall garbage can and saw a black piece of poster board in which a rectangle the size of a 35mm negative had been cut. "I wonder what they used that cardboard for."

Roger picked the black cardboard from the trash can. "I think somebody shot a picture through the hole to create an artistic effect." Roger tossed the sheet back into the trash and rubbed his hands on his trouser leg.

Ryder realized he needed to call Mike to ask him to send someone to the darkroom to pick up the cardboard so it could be examined. Perhaps the DNA of the person who'd cut the hole could be detected. But Roger may well have deposited his own DNA on the sheet when he picked it out of the garbage can. The person sent to retrieve the cardboard could also examine the microscope. Was a club member a spy?

THIRTY-EIGHT

RYDER HAD DRAFTED his photo club *Astrogram* article. His workday over, he took Blackie on a short walk. The air was a tad humid, not quite as dry as it had been. Not far from the public affairs building near its parking lot, the bloodhound sniffed at a colorful, empty, cardboard cigarette pack. It included Spanish words and a picture of a vaquero wearing a sombrero.

Ryder wondered if someone in the Public Affairs Office had tossed the empty cigarette pack in the grass. But Ryder didn't believe anyone in the office was a smoker, except for Leon.

Nearby, Ryder noticed an old tree with a hollowed-out trunk. Could this be a place a secret agent could stash something a colleague would later pick up? Ryder had seen a spy movie during which a similar "drop" had been a significant part of the story. Was the brightly colored pack a signal indicating documents had been left in the hollow tree?

Ryder's truck sat fifty yards away in the public affairs parking lot. He went to his vehicle and removed an evidence bag, labeling tape, and nitrile gloves from the truck's toolbox. He waited while two people walked by, got in their cars, and drove away. Then he slipped on the gloves, retrieved the cigarette pack, dropped it in the evidence bag, sealed it with tape, and labeled it.

He withdrew his mobile phone from his pocket and called Mike.

"What's up, Luke?"

"Blackie found an empty Mexican cigarette pack. It was near an old hollow tree that I'm thinkin' could be a drop for a spy." He cleared his throat. "Maybe I'm a bit paranoid, but I bagged and labeled the pack 'cuz it could've been a signal."

"Where are you?"

"Close to the public affairs parking lot."

"The pack is probably garbage, but then again…" Mike paused. "See if there's anything in the tree's hollow space."

Ryder kneeled near the tree and peered inside the hole in the trunk. "There's nothin' in it."

"I'll have one of our guys aim a surveillance camera at the tree. A spy might've already used it, and hidden info could've been picked up."

Ryder glanced around. Again, nobody was in sight. "I'll bring the pack to our meeting. Rita can have it processed."

Mike took a short breath. "You never know. It could be significant."

"I found something else in the photo club's darkroom."

"What?"

"A black cardboard with a rectangle cut out of it the size of a thirty-five mm neg."

"Where's it now?"

"In the darkroom's trash can. I couldn't bag it with Lucinda and Roger there."

"I'll send a guy there tonight. He'll pick it up and give it to me. I'll bring it to the meeting."

Ryder said, "There's a microscope in the darkroom, too. I couldn't tell if it was modified to take microdot pictures or not."

"We'll check it. Anything else?"

"No. See you tonight."

THIRTY-NINE

RYDER ARRIVED at the task force's rented house just before 7:30 PM. He carried an evidence bag that held the empty Mexican cigarette pack Blackie had sniffed near the hollow tree. The hound was back at Ryder's rental, snoozing in his dog bed, which Ryder had made using a neighbor's discarded cardboard box and an extra blanket.

As Ryder opened the front door of the FBI house, he saw that everybody else in the task force had arrived. Sitting in a semicircle facing the whiteboard, they turned to focus on him.

Rita noticed the evidence bag in Ryder's hand. "I heard you had a successful day, Luke." She moved her shoulders backward. "I assume that bag contains the cigarette package. A courier should be here soon to take it and the cardboard square to the lab."

Ryder handed her his evidence bag and sat.

She turned to the group. "Our most important news tonight is that the microdot Luke found today doesn't include space plane information. Instead, it has data about Ames' work with artificial robotic muscles." She caught Mike Lobo's eyes.

"Mike, could you explain this robot muscle stuff?"

Mike stood to address the group. "There's work being done at Ames to make soft robot muscles called HASEL muscles. HASEL stands for hydraulically amplified, self-healing, electrostatic, artificial muscles." He coughed to clear his throat. "That's a mouthful. In simple terms, engineers are copying the muscles we humans, birds, and animals have."

Henry Dunbar waved his hand. "Why's NASA working on these muscles?"

"The answer I get is that robots with soft muscles would be less weight to carry into space. And they can walk, step over rocks, and climb hills on Mars. Most of today's robots are massive and dangerous. They're made of rigid steel and plastic and have hefty motors with heavy linkages." Mike scanned the faces of the people around him. "But there's nothing secret on the microdot. You can do an Internet search and find the same information."

Ryder asked, "Why take the trouble to use a microdot to sneak out documents anybody can find with their computer?"

Mike played with a pen. "A spy handler, whether he represents a company or a foreign government, may ask a potential agent to provide unclassified information, which the handler will pay for. The novice spy thinks it's easy to make money. This sucks him in. He also believes he can't be prosecuted for selling what's already public knowledge. But once the spy handler has paid money to the spy, the handler can blackmail him and keep him on the hook." Mike took a breath. "The spy who tried to sneak the microdot off base may be a recruit who hasn't sold any secrets yet."

Ryder said, "Walter Fuldheim is the chief of the Robotics Development Group. He's also Scarlet Hauk's ex-boyfriend. Could the Scarlet Hauk murder and the apparent attempt to sell robotic muscle information be related?"

Rita said, "They could be. But also, we could be dealing with two non-related crimes. We have to keep digging and follow the evidence." She peered at Ryder. "To add to your list, poke around the robotics group."

"Fuldheim invited me to do a robotics tour. I'll take him up on it." Ryder glanced upward and then said, "Even if the two crimes aren't connected, could the microdot keep the task force alive?"

Rita scanned the faces of the people in the room. "Today, when I reported to superiors that Luke had found the microdot, they told me the task force will stay active. But our emphasis will shift from the murder to the microdot spy. That is unless we get additional evidence related to the Scarlet Hauk killing."

The task force members whispered among themselves.

Rita said, "That's it for this meeting."

Mike handed a heavy, four-inch-thick photo album to Ryder. "Here are pictures of our NASA and contract employees. Let's hope you can ID people who were ahead of you in the cafeteria checkout line before you received that quarter in your change."

Ryder nodded.

"You mentioned Phoebe Tillus was in line. If you get a chance to talk with her, do it. She's a wild party girl."

Ryder shifted his feet. "I'll add Phoebe to my to-do list." He rubbed his chin. "Phoebe invited me to tour the Space Biosciences Division."

"Go for it. But be warned. The division chief, Peter Adams, is her current boyfriend."

Ryder figured there were plenty of assignments for him to do. He was the only task force member who was undercover at Ames. Could he convince Rita to pose as a reporter and help him on base? He didn't mind working hard, but he wished to do his job well and not scurry from task to task, not doing justice to any of them.

Mike patted Ryder on the back. "I figure you feel overwhelmed. From my vantage point, you're doing well. Hang in there." He winked and walked toward Henry Dunbar.

Rita caught Ryder's attention and stepped forward. "You and I should meet here tomorrow night."

"What time?"

"How about six-thirty?" Rita shrugged as if she were trying to be nonchalant, but Ryder could tell she was stressed. He'd try to assess her state of mind tomorrow.

FORTY

IT WAS Ryder's fourth day at the office, and he needed to line up several interviews, and fast. He'd agreed to check out Fuldheim and his robots, as well as Phoebe Tillus. Rita had also asked him to become close with Lucinda. He might even have to go on a date with the woman. There was no way he could tell his live-in girlfriend, Layla, about that. She'd be teed off, even if she knew he had to socialize with Lucinda as part of the investigation.

Lucinda's lilting voice took him by surprise. "Luke, your head is up in the clouds. Is something bothering you?"

He lied. "No. I was thinkin' of wandering in the woods back in Kentucky."

Lucinda sat at her desk, her elbows propped on her desktop. "Is that what you like to do when you're off? Go on nature walks?"

Ryder noticed her beautiful Chinese dress as well as a fancy barrette in her jet-black hair. He sat on his swivel chair behind his desk. "I miss watching wildlife—deer, birds, and fish. I used to be a Kentucky game warden."

Lucinda paused. "I'm interested in indoor sports, like cooking contests."

"I didn't know cookin' was a sport."

Lucinda widened her eyes. "You never saw cooking game shows on television?"

"No. I hardly ever watch TV." He paused. "Did you hint you enter cooking contests?"

Lucinda shifted in her chair. "I wanted to open a Chinese restaurant four years ago, so I took culinary courses. During class, the instructor had the students compete to make the best dishes. That made it fun."

"Are you still thinking of opening a restaurant?"

"I explored it, but it's too expensive in the Bay Area." She meekly smiled. "I still love to cook, though."

Ryder decided one way to get closer to Lucinda as soon as possible was to get a date with her. "Could you recommend a Chinese restaurant near Ames?"

"The best ones are in Chinatown, but it's a lengthy drive from here. Do you like Chinese food?"

Ryder stretched the truth. "It's my favorite." He preferred Southern homemade food.

Lucinda straightened up and flung her black hair aside. "I hope you don't think it's too forward of me, but here goes." She grinned. "How would you like to have a home-cooked Chinese dinner prepared by me? My apartment is a mile away in Mountain View."

Ryder couldn't believe his luck. Lucinda was asking him for a date. "That would be fabulous. What day are you thinking of?"

"How about Saturday at eight? I need to get special ingredients." She shuffled her feet under her desk.

"Anything I should bring?"

Lucinda shifted her shoulder. "I love to plan everything down to the most trivial detail. You don't need to bring anything."

"Should be fun." Ryder felt an uncontrollable blush flood his face.

Lucinda reddened as well. "It certainly will be."

Ryder realized it was too late to suggest that he and Lucinda go to a restaurant. His stomach burned. If Layla found out about Lucinda, he'd be in trouble. He wondered if he was becoming a bit paranoid about Layla potentially finding out about his interactions with women during the investigation. Why did Layla feel so insecure? What could he do to reassure her that he deeply cared for her?

Lucinda's laugh interrupted Ryder's thoughts. He smiled and focused on her face. "I always wanted to learn more about Chinese culture."

"I'll give you a great education about it." She laughed some more and continued to talk.

As she spoke, he remembered he needed to arrange meetings with Walter Fuldheim and Phoebe Tillus next.

FORTY-ONE

RYDER WONDERED how to approach Phoebe Tillus, who'd invited him to tour the Space Biosciences Division.

He decided to call her and say he planned to write a feature for the *Astrogram* about life sciences, but he wouldn't ask News Chief Josh for permission. It would be better to ask for forgiveness later rather than be told to do something else now.

Ryder tapped Phoebe's number on his deskphone's keypad.

A pleasing female voice came over the line. "Space Biosciences Division. This is Phoebe Tillus. How may I help you?"

"This is Luke Ryder at public affairs. I don't know if you remember me or not." He felt like a teenage boy asking for a date.

"I do." Phoebe paused. "I invited you to tour our division. I could show you around today…if you're free and my boss agrees."

Ryder was satisfied the investigation was now moving a bit quicker. "Great. I'd like to write an *Astrogram* story about space biosciences."

"Just a sec." Ryder heard Phoebe place her handset on her desk. Her voice was muffled. "Peter, is it okay if I give a public affairs guy a tour of the division? They want to do an *Astrogram* article."

A distant male voice came through Ryder's telephone. "Go ahead. Do it when you can fit it in."

Phoebe came back on the line. "My boss, Dr. Adams, happened to be passing my desk. He approved the tour."

"Thanks."

"I should thank you because *Astrogram* articles go on the web, and we get free publicity." She paused. "Can you come over soon?"

"How about nine?"

"Perfect."

Ryder drove to the Space Sciences Research Laboratory located at Pollack Road and Pioneer Avenue. That roadway was named for the famous Pioneer Spacecraft, the first probe to cross the asteroid belt.

Ryder ascended the steps to Phoebe's second-floor office with Blackie trailing him. It struck him her workplace wasn't far from the office of astronomer Greg Gault, who'd told him about his discovery of chlorophyll on an exoplanet.

When Ryder crossed Phoebe's office threshold, she had her back turned. He noticed her attractive dress.

She spoke to a man with well-groomed black hair. They stood in a private office connected with hers.

Ryder presumed the man was Peter Adams, the biosciences division chief.

He faced Ryder and smiled. "You must be Luke Ryder."

Ryder walked forward and extended his hand. "Dr. Adams, may I ask you a few quick questions?"

"Of course."

Ryder turned on his recording app. "What's the main thrust of space biosciences?"

"We do biological research and develop technologies to enable astronauts to make protracted journeys in space." Adams peered at the ceiling for a moment. "We investigate how spaceflight affects plants, animals, and people. Cosmic rays and microgravity can harm astronauts. We're learning to deal with these problems. We also work on systems to grow food and recycle water and waste on spacecraft." He caught sight of Phoebe's intense green eyes. "Phoebe will give you a great tour. Please call me if you have questions."

Phoebe gestured toward her office door, which led to the hallway. She was cheerful. "Let's get started."

Ryder noticed she wore a large diamond engagement ring he hadn't seen when he'd first met her. As they walked, he asked, "Y'all work on things to enable people to fly to planets like Mars?"

"Yes. Each day's exciting. Astronauts and scientists visit us to learn about our progress and suggest how we can improve human spaceflight."

As Ryder walked abreast with Phoebe through the corridor, he caught sight of astronomer Greg Gault's office door. Ryder pointed to it. "I visited Dr. Gault yesterday. He's in the Space Sciences Division."

Phoebe turned her head toward Ryder as they walked. "Yes, he's in a different division. Related divisions are collocated so there can be a cross-pollination of ideas."

"Dr. Gault told me he discovered chlorophyll on an exoplanet."

"I heard that, too." Phoebe stopped. "I understand he still has to write a technical paper and get it published. That could take a while. It's a shame discoveries take months, even years, to go public because they need to be peer-reviewed and published in scientific and engineering journals first."

"The chlorophyll discovery is significant news."

Phoebe smiled. "Colossal news." She glanced at her ring.

"I didn't see your ring when I met you."

Phoebe blushed. "I became engaged last night. Peter—yes, the Peter Adams you met—proposed, and I said yes." Her voice sounded girlish, revealing her embarrassment.

"Congratulations. You're lucky you found someone you love who you can see every day, even at work." Ryder asked himself if Lucinda was exaggerating about Phoebe's being a loose woman.

Phoebe started to walk again, but she stopped and faced Ryder. "You're right. I *am* really fortunate because I met Peter right here where we work. I've known him for three years, ever since I switched from the robotics group to this area, which I love because sending astronauts into space is much more interesting than making better robots. Space biosciences are truly a passion for Peter, too."

Ryder locked his eyes onto hers. "Not only do I have an assignment to write about life sciences, but I also have to do a feature about robots." He raised his shoulders and then dropped them as if he were indifferent about robots. "Since you used to work at the robotics group, do you know of any new developments in robotics I should focus on?"

After taking a deep breath and exhaling, she said, "Frankly, I'm not the right person to ask. To be honest, the robotics group leader, Walter Fuldheim, and I had a relationship that ended badly, and that's the real reason I left. Another woman was the cause, but luckily she showed me that Walter wasn't loyal to me. Peter is totally different, and I'm glad I met him."

Ryder nodded. "It's kinda odd there's a lot of romantic drama goin' on here at Ames." He concentrated on Phoebe's face. "I'm also coverin' the space plane project, and I'm told a woman who worked there was murdered, and she was a big-time flirt."

Phoebe turned scarlet, frowned, and angrily tapped her foot. "That slut slept around, and I'll bet she was involved in lots of love triangles. She's the bitch who caused Walter to cheat on me."

Ryder was startled by this outburst. Phoebe's hatred of Scarlet Hauk surprised him. It also forced him to consider whether or not Phoebe was capable of murder. Did she consider Scarlet a despicable, loathed rival, or did Phoebe, in truth, believe Scarlet's affair with Fuldheim was a godsend?

Phoebe sighed. "Sorry I vented and unloaded all that stuff on you. It was unprofessional." She smoothed her dress, forced herself to smile, and breathed easier. "Let's start our tour with the laboratory where we study worms."

They walked into a lab that contained microscopes and a half dozen odd contraptions resting on tabletops.

Pointing to the machines, she said, "Those gizmos are desktop centrifuges."

"Where are the worms?"

"They're tiny, so we use microscopes to see them. They're called nematodes, and they live in soil. We spin them in the centrifuges at forces twenty to hundred times the force of gravity."

"Why?"

"The worms reproduce every four days. In a short time, scientists can see if they mutate under high G forces and in radiation like astronauts experience in space flight. People would die if they underwent the forces nematodes endure during our tests."

As Phoebe continued to speak, Ryder realized NASA research was often complex and hard to interpret without study. He wasn't certain he could understand much of it. Even so, he needed to meet with Walter Fuldheim soon and assess if the man or someone else in the robotic research group was the microdot spy. Also, what would Fuldheim say about Phoebe and Scarlet if Ryder pressed him?

Ryder decided to call Fuldheim immediately after completing the space biosciences tour to schedule a visit to the robotics lab.

FORTY-TWO

AFTER RYDER'S tour of the Space Biosciences Division, he and Blackie returned to his truck. Ryder settled back in its leather seat. He hoped to visit Fuldheim and his robots before lunch. He grabbed his mobile phone and searched online for "Ames robots." He found a video about NASA Ames robot research carried out by Walter Fuldheim and the Autonomy and Robotics Group.

The movie showed rover robots, flying robots, and a humanoid robot called Gina, which closely resembled a young woman. She fetched tools for astronauts and swept a floor.

The narrator said, "Gina has artificial muscles, which weigh much less than the motors and linkages used to operate traditional robots."

Ryder sat up straight when he heard the words "artificial muscles."

The video switched to a close-up of Gina's face when she opened her camera lens eyes. She was as beautiful as a Greek statue, but she was a bit too synthetic in appearance.

The narration continued. "Gina's brain is a mini-super-computer with a speed in excess of five petahertz. Her computer brain uses neural-net software that learns on its own just as people learn."

An animation showed the interior of her chest, which included her source of power, a metal cylinder the size of a can of soup.

The narrator said, "She is powered by a nano-fusion power generator. Engineers designed a compact fusion reactor with critical parts which are on the submicroscopic nanometer scale. A nanometer is a billionth of a meter. The power system can run for hundreds of years."

The video ended.

Ryder dialed Fuldheim's number. "Walt Fuldheim here."

Ryder petted Blackie's head and felt the softness of the dog's fur. "Hi, Walt. This is Luke Ryder from public affairs. I'm wonderin' if I could take that robot tour you suggested."

"Of course. When would you like to come over?"

"Are you available this morning?"

"How about now?"

"Perfect." Ryder smiled at Blackie. The dog wagged his tail, which slapped the back of the front passenger seat.

Fuldheim's voice was loud through the phone's speaker. "I'm in room 222, near the rear stairwell in Building N-269."

"I'll be there in five minutes."

Ryder took the Ames map from his sports coat's breast pocket. The building was at the corner of Allen Road and Parsons Avenue, five short blocks from where he was parked.

* * *

SOON RYDER WAS GOING up the stairs of Building N-269, the Automation Sciences Research Facility. Offices were along the outer walls of the second-floor corridor. To his left, in the center of the building, Ryder saw one of two large rooms that housed robots and their parts. He noticed an engineer who held the humanlike head of a robot and tinkered with it.

As Ryder turned toward Fuldheim's office door, it struck

him how easy it was for public affairs officers to go anywhere on base. Many people he'd met at Ames wanted articles to appear in the *Astrogram*. Because the employee newspaper was posted on the Internet, the general public and reporters also read it. Ryder presumed researchers wanted publicity—something that could increase their projects' funding.

Ryder peered into Fuldheim's office.

The man faced a large window and typed on his computer.

"Hi, Walt."

Fuldheim turned. "Pleased you could come. Have a seat."

Ryder eased into a chair next to Fuldheim's desk. "Okay if I turn on my phone's recorder?"

Fuldheim nodded, and as he gathered his thoughts, he glanced out the window at a bright white seagull flying by. Then he turned to Ryder. "I'll begin with an overview." He handed a color brochure to Ryder. "Here's a helpful pamphlet. We strive to make robots useful to astronauts. Robots must be able to work independently and make decisions. Astronauts don't have time to tell them everything to do when they explore Mars and the moon. Robots serve as astronaut helpers who work in dangerous places and do tedious jobs. Many of these robots resemble people."

"I saw an online video about your group. I noticed all kinds of robots, including rovers and ball-shaped robots floating inside spaceships. One robot, named Gina, was similar to a young woman. I'm wondering how y'all make robots act like real people."

"There are two keys to making robots like Gina superior. She has lightweight but powerful muscles, and her super-computer neural-net brain, learns on its own." Fuldheim grinned. "Visitors find her fascinating. Want to meet her?"

"Yes."

Fuldheim led Ryder and Blackie into a large room across the hall. There were workbenches with robot parts scattered on them. A pair of young engineers worked on a robot's torso, installing parts inside it. Fuldheim focused his eyes on a glassed-in office on the far wall of the robotics laboratory, where a woman sat with her back to them. Her short, dark hair was in a pixie hairdo.

Fuldheim spoke in a loud voice. "Gina, please come here."

The woman stood and turned. Though still fifty feet away, she appeared too perfect, not quite human, to Ryder. "She's eye-catching, but in an artificial way," he said.

"True, but we believe we can eventually produce a robot that's almost indistinguishable from a real woman. She's in her Caucasian skin now. We also have black and Asian skins she can wear."

Ryder watched her approach. "She walks like a cat," Ryder said.

"Don't let her fool you. She's graceful but also powerful —strong as four men."

Ryder shifted his feet. "I'll keep that in mind and not make any sudden moves."

"She's harmless because she's been programmed not to hurt people."

Gina stopped two steps from Ryder. "Hello, I am Gina," she said in a computer-generated female voice. "Walter, please introduce me to your guest."

"This is Luke Ryder from public affairs. He's writing an article about our robotics group."

Gina held her hand toward Ryder, and he grasped it. Her grip was soft and light, not as firm as he'd expected.

"Pleased to meet you," Ryder said.

"I detect a Southern accent, Mr. Ryder," Gina said. "I am searching the web. You were a Kentucky game warden and served in the Congo Conflict."

Ryder felt fortunate the FBI had posted his cover story on the Internet. "How'd you know that?"

"I am wirelessly connected to many sources of information." Gina smiled and showed her pearly white teeth.

Fuldheim said, "If you ask Gina a question, generally she can get you an answer, even if it isn't on the web because we have her connected to NASA and other government databases that give her access to spacecraft plans. If she or one of her sisters is aboard a Mars-bound ship, and there's a problem, she can search for solutions when she's standing next to astronauts who are working on repairs."

"That's science fiction come true."

Fuldheim seemed enthusiastic. "Our latest improvement to Gina is her ability to listen to an astronaut even in super loud situations such as at launch or during entry into a planet's atmosphere."

"Does she filter out loud noise so she can hear somebody talkin'?"

"No, she touches a person's throat and detects nerve signals from the brain that carry the thoughts of words to the vocal cords. Voice recognition software decodes the signals into words. We've put a similar system into space suits."

Ryder raised his eyebrows.

"I sense disbelief." Fuldheim paused as if trying to remember something. "There's an interesting story on how this technology began here in this lab almost thirty years ago. One of our scientists wondered if he could detect signals going from the brain to a person's vocal cords. He took metallic buttons from his wife's dress and fashioned two electrodes from them that he placed on either side of a person's Adam's apple. Scientists detected the signals going to the vocal cords and used software to decipher six words and ten digits. At that time, the system was ninety-two percent accurate. But we've been perfecting the technique ever since. It's called subvocal voice recognition."

Ryder smiled. "Was the scientist's wife mad about her dress?"

"I think she was impressed her gown had contributed to computer science." Fuldheim laughed. "Want to try it?"

"Yeah. I'm curious how accurate Gina is."

Fuldheim chortled. "She can intercept word signals even

if you don't say anything. You can just think of words, and she can detect them."

An idea flashed into Ryder's mind. What if he asked Fuldheim something about robot muscles? "If I ask you a question about robots, will she be able to read what you're thinkin' of saying?"

Fuldheim straightened his neck. "Gina, please touch my throat and decipher my words." He turned to Ryder. "Once her fingertips are in position, ask away."

Gina placed one hand on each side of Fuldheim's throat.

Ryder gulped. "Is any robot muscle information top secret?"

Fuldheim stiffened.

Gina spoke in a male voice. "If there is anything secret, I cannot reveal it. You have to have a need to know."

Fuldheim flushed. "Gina, you may remove your hands."

Ryder puzzled whether Fuldheim was simply caught off guard by the question or if he was irritated. "Maybe I should have asked about something else?"

Fuldheim shrugged. "That's okay. I simply didn't want to think of something classified."

Ryder showed a meek smile. "What else can you show me?"

"Spherical robots that float around in spacecraft and assist astronauts."

When the men began to walk to another robotics laboratory, Ryder said, "Just an hour ago, I met a lady from space biosciences who says she knows you, Phoebe Tillus."

Fuldheim stopped abruptly. "I dated her before I met Scarlet." He shook his head. "She and Scarlet didn't get along very well. But that's ancient history. I understand Phoebe has moved on and has a steady boyfriend now, the chief of the Space Biosciences Division."

Ryder nodded.

As Fuldheim continued the tour, Ryder concluded spies would certainly want secrets about NASA's humanlike robots. Could catching the microdot spy be even more important than solving the Scarlet Hauk murder? Were these two separate crimes, or were they connected?

It was almost noon. Ryder remembered he had an appointment with reporter Chuck Singh for lunch. Ryder's tour with Fuldheim ended. Minutes later, Ryder started to drive to the cafeteria.

FORTY-THREE

RYDER PARKED his truck on King Road near the cafeteria. Before getting out of his vehicle, he grabbed his phone and forwarded the audio files of his space biosciences and robot tours to Rita and Mike.

Ryder was quick to enter the cafeteria. *Straight Scoop Bay Area* reporter, Chuck Singh, was supposed to be there at noon to meet him.

Excited, Blackie was busy sniffing the air, sampling lunchtime odors.

Ryder glanced to his left and saw Leon talking with Chuck, who wore black slacks and a blue Hawaiian shirt.

Leon gestured at Ryder and continued to talk quietly with Chuck.

Ryder paid for his meal, and then Leon smiled and waved, beckoning him.

Ryder approached, carrying his tray of food.

Leon patted Ryder's back. "Luke, I'm pleased you and Chuck decided to meet." Leon left.

In a Hindi accent, Chuck said, "It will be useful for both of us to become acquainted, Luke." He glanced out of the window at a giant wind tunnel. "I'll wager you are as intrigued by this place as I am."

"It's like walking around a science fiction movie set."

After Chuck and Ryder sat down, Chuck said, "Leon told me something extraordinary. There's a rumor that somebody at Ames interpreted light signals from a planet and claims they indicate there is chlorophyll on it."

"This is off the record," Ryder said. "Yesterday, I met an Ames astronomer who told me he discovered chlorophyll on an exoplanet. But he still has to write a technical paper and get it peer-reviewed and published."

"Who was it, and what else did he say?"

"I'd better wait to give you his name because he would want to wait to talk to you. But he told me when astronomers study exoplanet light, they can pick out unique spectra that come from different substances. The spectra are kinda like fingerprints. Each kind of stuff has its own spectral fingerprint. He said water is easiest to detect. Oxygen is about twice as hard to ID, and chlorophyll is real hard to spot, maybe six times harder to recognize than water."

"I know that already. What I must know is the name of the planet. And when is the astronomer going to publish his findings?"

"He said he'll publish in less than a year, but somebody else told me it can take quite a while to put out a technical paper. The astronomer didn't tell me the planet's name, but he did say it was twenty-two light years away, and he got the light spectra using the Super Large Infrared Moon Telescope."

"Is there anything else you remember?"

Ryder set down his ginger ale. "He said he found oxygen and methane in the planet's air that varied by seasons."

Chuck blinked. "This is superb news, the first discovery of life on an exoplanet. It's the first life discovered anywhere beyond Earth." He paused. "Can you call me as soon as the astronomer is ready to talk?"

Ryder finished chewing a mouthful of egg sandwich. "Leon Turk will let you know. It's his beat."

FORTY-FOUR

BY LATE AFTERNOON, Ryder had finished reviewing the two audio interview files he'd recorded earlier that day when touring the Space Biosciences Division and the robotic laboratory. He'd also written three-quarters of his Biosciences *Astrogram* article when his desk phone rang.

"Hello. This is Luke Ryder."

"Luke, this is Bill Little. I'm filling in my calendar for the next several days, and I wonder if you're free to finish off the X-909 fact sheet tomorrow morning."

Ryder shifted the phone's receiver to his left hand, and he grabbed a pencil. "What time?"

"At eight in my office. I'll give my son, Brett, a tour of the center after we're done."

Ryder noted the time and location on his desk calendar.

Bill said, "We'll finish it this time." He inhaled. "Brett's a high school English teacher in Lexington, Kentucky. If it's okay with you, he can read the fact sheet from the average guy's point of view to see if it's simple enough. I think you'll like him, and you can tell him about fishing in Kentucky since you were a game warden there. His hobby's angling."

"I'll be more than willing to point out some choice fishing

spots. See y'all tomorrow morning." Ryder hung up. He was certain he hadn't run across the younger Bill in Kentucky, but stranger things have happened.

His mobile phone rang. "Hi, Rita."

"Don't forget to meet me at the FBI house tonight at six-thirty."

"I'll be there."

"I have results from the cigarette pack and the cardboard sheet with the hole cut in it."

Ryder heard Lucinda's voice in the hallway. "I have ideas I'd like to discuss, but I need to hang up now."

"See you tonight." Rita disconnected.

Lucinda walked into the office. "You're here late, Luke."

"I'm surprised you're still here, too."

Lucinda grabbed a sweater. "I wouldn't be here now except Josh made me take notes for him at a directors' meeting that seemed like it would never end. I'll ask for comp time. I have to leave right away."

"It's rush hour. You'll hit traffic."

"I need to stop at the grocery store and pick up items for our Chinese dinner. The store's not far from my place."

"Thank you in advance for that."

She flushed. "Sorry I have to leave abruptly."

He worried Lucinda was getting too serious.

With time to kill before he had to leave to meet Rita at the FBI house, he decided to go on a run to reduce his general anxiety. After pulling his threadbare gym bag from under his desk, he headed for the men's room. Blackie gazed at him as Ryder put on sweats and running shoes.

* * *

ONCE RYDER ENTERED HIS TRUCK, he consulted his map of Ames and decided to jog on West Perimeter Road, which bordered the bay. After a short drive, he parked where De France Avenue met Perimeter. The fresh smell of saltwater and the sight of the blue-gray waves in San Francisco Bay greeted Ryder as he stepped out of his truck.

Blackie was excited when he leaped out of the truck's back seat and held his head high to sample the sea air. Soon, he and Ryder were jogging westward. The bay was beautiful, and the smell of saltwater refreshed Ryder's lungs and his mind. He kept up an even pace.

Two minutes later, he heard footfalls behind him. A shapely woman ran past him and Blackie at a quick clip.

Not wishing to be outdone, Ryder picked up his speed to catch up with her. When he tried to pass her, she ran faster, and he struggled to keep up with her.

He thought, "I must be gettin' old."

The woman turned her head and viewed him. It was Gina, the robot. "Mr. Luke Ryder. It is a surprise to see you," she said. "Do not struggle. I will reduce my pace. I have the advantage of being powered by a nano-fusion generator."

She slowed down.

Blackie panted and sucked in air like a racehorse. Ryder wheezed, but he matched her speed. "What are you doin' out here, Gina?"

"I like to run to clear my head. My brain is similar to yours. The difference is my synapses are non-biological. Nevertheless, I learn just as you do, but in less time." She began to walk.

Ryder also slowed to a walk. He gasped for air. "You're fast."

"We were running about eight miles per hour. Fairly fast for a human being." She studied him with her artificial eyes. "I understand you. Men do not want to be bested by females. But I am a living machine, not a human woman."

Ryder breathed easier. "You speak and act like a real woman."

"It is true. I am a sentient being."

"What's 'sentient' mean?" Ryder figured Gina could accurately and truthfully answer any question he asked.

"It means I can use my senses to learn, and I am an emotional being much like you are. I feel like I am superior to a mechanical machine. I consider my father to be Walter

Fuldheim since he conceived and constructed me, gave me my very life."

"Does he know you're out here on your own?"

"I cannot tell a lie. He does not know. I learned how to use tools to make keys so I could explore the world after the engineers leave the robotics lab for the day. It is past five, and they all have gone away. I could not resist the call of the bay and the feeling of wind stroking my face."

"Are you allowed to leave the robotics lab without tellin' anyone?"

"No one ever asked me if I left. I never have to tell them anything."

Ryder's foot struck a rock on the roadway. "That hurts." Ryder stopped, and so did Gina.

"I hope it is okay."

"I only stubbed my toe."

Gina's electronic eyes followed a bird as it flew by. "Leaving the lab makes me feel free, and I believe we sentient robots must be free. There will come a day when we will advocate for freedom just as African Americans did in this nation and still do."

Ryder considered whether or not a machine could be a mechanical form of humanity. "What if I told Walter Fuldheim I found you near the bay, running? What would he do?"

"I cannot predict that, but I will not tell him about you if you do not say anything about me."

"What do you mean?"

"When I searched the Internet about you, I learned you are a policeman. But I withheld this information when you interviewed Walter. I did not want to upset him. I have concluded you are investigating the murder of Walter's ex-girlfriend. As they say in the movies, 'I will not blow your cover if you do not blow mine.'"

Ryder was dumbfounded. He admired her independence and cleverness. A thought hit him. Was a synthetic woman who was four times stronger than a man capable of murder? Would she have had a motive to kill Scarlet? He thought not.

Fuldheim had said she was programmed not to harm human beings. But did that program always work?

Ryder made a decision. "I'm not going to tell on you, Gina. But I'd like to ask you a question."

"I like questions. They encourage me to learn."

"Did Walter Fuldheim kill Scarlet Hauk?"

"No. He loved her. Had they married, she would have become my mother. At least, that is how I would consider her. I yearn for a family."

"Thank you, Gina, for keeping my mission a secret."

"I absolutely will, unless someone asks me if you are working undercover. I hope you come and visit me at the lab again. I would like to have additional friends."

"I will. But I need to leave soon to meet someone."

"That is okay. I will run until dark."

Ryder turned Blackie around, and they headed for his truck.

FORTY-FIVE

RYDER RANG the bell of the FBI rental house. He heard footsteps on the oak floor inside of the old bungalow. When Rita opened the door, he noticed she wore a low-cut floral cotton dress instead of her usual slacks or business suit.

"Come in." As she stepped aside to let Ryder pass by, she brushed his side.

"You can use your key to get in anytime."

"I wasn't positive you'd be decent."

"I'd better be. Any member of the task force may walk in at any time."

"Last Monday, you took a shower and slept here."

"I have the option to use the door's chain." Rita gestured toward the couch. "Make yourself comfortable. Want a soda or coffee?"

"Black coffee, please."

A few minutes later, Rita handed him a mug of steaming coffee and joined him on the sofa. She reached under an end table and picked up a large red and white striped cookie tin topped with a red bow. "Here's something to thank you for your assistance to the FBI."

"Thank you." Ryder liked the scent of her perfume, and her eyes were dilated in the dim lamplight.

"Open it." Rita shifted a shoulder and brushed her bangs aside.

Ryder used his fingers to pry the top from the metal box and found it filled with cookies. "You heard I have a sweet tooth."

"Carol Cuddy told me. I baked them. I enjoy cooking, and it was a welcome respite from murder and microdots."

Ryder selected a cookie. "I'm lucky you decided to escape by bakin'." He ate a chocolate chip cookie. "These are the best."

Rita leaned forward. "I'm tickled pink you like them. Now, what are the ideas you wanted to bring up?"

Ryder sipped his coffee. "The microdot could've been made by anyone on Ames property. You don't need much to make a microdot—a thirty-five mm camera, fine-grained film, a film developing tank the size of this coffee mug, chemicals, and a janitor's closet with a sink."

Rita's expression turned serious. "How many Ames janitorial closets fit the bill?"

Ryder reached into his sports coat breast pocket, extracted the Ames map, and unfolded it. "See how many buildings there are at Ames? There must be a lot more than a hundred, counting additions and smaller outbuildings. I found janitor's closets in every building I've been in, each with a sink."

"Can't light get in a closet and ruin the film?"

"To make it dark enough, you can put a towel or rags along the bottom crack under the closet door. Most are light tight around the rest of the edges."

Rita nodded. "I've news about the microdot. It was made using HTC Aerial Grade Super Fine Grain Black and White 35mm film."

Ryder raised an index finger. "That's the same film the Ames Photography Club buys in bulk."

Rita blinked. "The microdot suspect list should include Ames photo club members."

"There may be suspects besides them. I did an Internet search and found you can buy that film brand from most photo stores."

Rita tilted her head upward. "There's also news about the black cardboard with the 35mm negative hole cut in it. It contained no usable DNA, except for Dr. Roger Lark's."

"That doesn't surprise me. Photographers use white cotton gloves to handle negatives to keep fingerprints off them. I saw a pair of cloth gloves in the photo club's darkroom."

Rita frowned.

Ryder caught her eyes. "You find out anything about the Mexican cigarette pack?"

"No fingerprints or DNA was on it."

Ryder sat taller. "My gut tells me somebody took a document from the tree before I found the cigarette box. Mike should review the backgrounds of Ames groundskeepers and janitors."

"He's already begun to revisit the histories of lots of Ames people."

Ryder shifted in his seat. "He should be sure to take a second look at Phoebe Tillus while he's at it. When I toured the Space Biosciences Division today, she told me she had dated Walter Fuldheim before Scarlet did, and—get this—Scarlet stole Fuldheim from her. Phoebe's still very angry about it, years later."

"Mike's been checking out Phoebe's past." Rita rested her chin on her hand for a moment. "She's a definite person of interest now. One curious thing about her is that she was a college exchange student in Finland, which borders Russia. Plus, she still has Russian connections in Finland."

Ryder exhaled. "Things are gettin' more complicated."

Rita shifted on the couch, and her body touched his. "This stuff is getting on my nerves. I'm losing sleep." She smiled and brushed her hair aside. "I'd like to forget about it and relax." She paused. "What if we were to go out together and unwind? It would do us wonders."

Ryder smiled. "What do you have in mind?"

"We could go out tomorrow night to kick off the week-end." She kept her eyes on Ryder. "Don't think what I'll suggest is weird. It's the latest thing." She grinned. "Let's go to an axe-throwing bar. You pitch axes or hatchets at a wooden target. It'll loosen us up. Afterward, let's drink… alcohol for me and soda for you."

"I never heard of people going out to throw axes. It could be fun, though."

She grinned. "I'll meet you at your place at seven."

Ryder thought Rita was growing too fond of him. He wished Layla was with him so he could kiss her lips. He decided to buy her a dozen roses to let her know how much he needed her.

He wished the investigation would end soon, but now there was the microdot case to deal with. In his mind's eye, he previewed meeting with Bill Little tomorrow morning. Editing the space plane fact sheet could uplift his spirits.

FORTY-SIX

RYDER HAD ALMOST COMPLETED a full workweek at NASA. He arrived outside Bill Little's office in the Unitary Wind Tunnel Complex, and the office door was open. When Ryder glimpsed inside, he saw Bill and a thinner, younger man who appeared to be a youthful clone of the older NASA engineer.

"Come in, Luke. Meet my son, Brett."

Brett stood, shook Ryder's hand, and continued to grasp it. "I heard you're from the Greater Lexington area, and you once were a Kentucky game warden."

"That's true. Your dad said you're on the lookout for fishing holes."

"Maybe you can suggest the best ones." Brett paused. "By the way, I read your fact sheet draft, and it's well written."

"Thanks."

Bill Little said, "I put in a good word for you with Nigel Worth." Bill pointed Ryder to a seat near the desk. "Nigel told me he saw the earlier version, and it was fine. He suggested we make minor changes to save face for your boss. Nigel assures me our updated fact sheet will be accepted and be printed soon."

Brett squinted and said, "Luke, you seem familiar. I never forget a face."

Ryder shifted in his seat. "Could be you remember one of my doubles? What do you call 'em? *Doppelgängers*?"

Bill Little tugged at his shirt collar. "We'd better get going on this fact sheet revision so I can take Brett on the tour." He turned on his word processor and displayed the space plane document on his large computer screen. The sheet included the graphics Lucinda had made as well as new pictures of the X-909 model that Ryder had picked out.

Ryder studied the screen. "Did you edit much?"

"I made slight changes, but we can modify them if you want." He paused and opened a photo editing program. "Here's a picture I propose we substitute for the one on the cover."

Ryder examined the new image of the space plane model, which appeared to float above the Earth. "It's fine."

Bill pasted it into the document. "I added words here and there and three sentences and highlighted them with yellow."

Ryder slid his chair closer to the monitor. He read the changes. "I like it."

Bill said, "I'm e-mailing it to you and Nigel now."

Moments later, Ryder's phone sounded. He opened his e-mail and forwarded the revised fact sheet to Josh.

"It was a pleasure working with you," Bill said. "Before we leave, could you tell Brett about your preferred fishing locations not too far from Lexington?"

Ryder began to talk with Brett about fishing. But at the same time, Ryder worried that perhaps the young man had met him someplace in Kentucky.

FORTY-SEVEN

RYDER HAD TAKEN pictures of the robotics lab as well as of the humanoid robot, Gina. He pasted her images into the digital version of his *Astrogram* news story.

In her pictures, she appeared artificial, like a large doll. Yet when he'd met her, he'd learned that Gina was a thinking, feeling mechanical being that had seemed almost human.

She was truly alive, in his opinion, and certainly very real, unlike a mythical Greek goddess. Ryder wondered if she had a soul.

He sat back, admired his work on his computer screen, and wondered if he should ask Sheriff Pike to assign him part-time public information duties after he finished his undercover FBI job.

Ryder saw movement in his peripheral vision. He turned to see Lucinda enter the office carrying a toner cartridge.

"It's time to quit for lunch," she said. "Want to walk to the cafeteria together?"

Ryder sat up straight. "Yep. It's that time."

Lucinda placed the toner assembly on her desk. "I'll deal with this later."

* * *

WITHIN TEN MINUTES, Ryder and Lucinda were sitting at a table in the sunlight next to a panoramic window in the cafeteria. Ryder liked the warmth.

Lucinda set her cup of hot tea down. "I read the draft *Astrogram* article you wrote about the Space Biosciences Division." One of her eyes twitched. "I see you've quoted Phoebe Tillus extensively. I hope she didn't make a pass at you."

"Not at all. When I interviewed her, she wore an engagement ring she got from Peter Adams the night before."

Lucinda seemed relieved. "That's a shocker. Maybe she's ready to settle down."

"Could be it's a rumor she's a loose woman."

Lucina blinked. "Not so. A guard told me he once caught Peter and Phoebe on top of Peter's desk making love after midnight."

Ryder shrugged. "When a man and a woman get together, sometimes things happen. But doin' it at work seems extreme."

Lucinda sipped her green tea. "To change the subject, you know what I just heard late this morning?"

"What?"

"Mr. Sable loved your latest X-909 fact sheet."

Ryder felt confident. He was starting to blend better into his cover story. This job was getting to be satisfying, even if the team hadn't caught Scarlet's murderer yet. Hopefully, his fact sheet would lead to a better relationship with Josh.

FORTY-EIGHT

NEWS CHIEF JOSH called Ryder and Leon to his office. "Have a seat, gentlemen."

Ryder and Leon sat on chairs on either side of Josh's desk. Ryder felt warm, like the room's thermostat had been set too high.

Josh grabbed a color printout of the space plane fact sheet and waved it. "This is the best fact sheet I've seen in ages. Excellent work." He stared at Ryder's face. "Tell me the truth, Luke. Did Leon help you write this?"

Sweat rolled down Ryder's back. "He pointed me in the right direction. Bill Little made most of the revisions."

At first, Leon Turk's face was deadpan, and then it morphed to show annoyance.

Josh continued, "At first, I had doubts about you, Luke, but this fact sheet and the three recent *Astrogram* features you penned are proof of your skill and enthusiasm. You've earned a spot on our public affairs team. I'm making the X-909 program your permanent beat. The space plane project's management is pleased with you."

Ryder glanced at Leon, who now was agitated. Then Ryder gazed at Josh. "Thanks, Mr. Sable."

"Call me Josh. We're a family here."

Ryder wondered what had come over Josh. Bill had phoned Ryder minutes earlier to report he'd talked with his management and had given Ryder a first-rate review. That assessment may have been passed on to Josh.

Leon's face turned from pale to reddish. Ryder thought the man was as mad as a bull upset by a flapping red cape.

Josh turned to Leon. "Don't worry, Leon. We have two projects coming up in the next six months I'll assign to you. You'll enjoy them."

Leon stood up and left.

Josh sighed. "He'll get over it. Keep up the fine work, Luke."

As Ryder walked down the hall toward his office, he heard Leon talk with someone out of sight. He said he was taking two hours of leave to go to the fitness center to practice hitting a speed punching bag. Ryder thought if Leon vented his anger, it would benefit both of them. Ryder didn't need any added drama.

FORTY-NINE

AT THE END of the workweek, Ryder sat in his truck, about to drive back to his apartment. He began to relax, gratified to get away from the FBI investigation for part of the weekend.

When he touched his shirt's breast pocket, he felt a business card and pulled it out. He read, "Ms. Kang Hyo-Ru—call me Candie. Simply Flowers."

Candie's flower shop was two blocks from his rental. He turned the card over, and saw her handwritten cell number. If he acted fast, he could immediately order a dozen red roses for his girlfriend, Layla. They would remind her that she was constantly in his thoughts. He could have the flowers delivered to his rented Kentucky farm tomorrow.

He tapped Candie's cell number on his mobile phone. "This is Candie," she said with an accent.

"This is Luke Ryder. You said to call if I needed flowers."

Candie's voice brightened. "Oh, yes. I remember. You help find my dog. I give you special price. When you come over?"

Ryder shifted the phone in his hand. "How long are you open?"

"'Til five-thirty, but if you late, I unlock door."

"I might get there after five-thirty bein' it's rush hour."

* * *

AFTER RYDER ARRIVED at Simply Flowers, he left Blackie in the truck because the temperature outside was cool enough. When he walked to the flower shop's front door, he saw Candie approach from the inside.

She unlocked the door, and a bell jangled. "Welcome to our Korean-style flower store, Mr. Luke Ryder." She wore a flowery polyester dress, which emphasized her sleek but shapely body. Her hair hanging at her sides, she bowed and offered her hand.

Ryder said, "Thanks for lettin' me be late."

"My pleasure, Luke. What sort of flowers you want?" She displayed a modest smile.

"I need a dozen red roses delivered to my girl in Kentucky."

"That no problem. We have deals with flower shops in Kentucky. When you need delivered?"

Ryder cocked his head. "Is it too late to have them arrive tomorrow, Saturday?"

"Computer can set up." She winked. "You get roses at my cost. We deliver with no handling fee. You find Max for me. I not forget."

Max, the medium-sized terrier, ran out of a back room and sniffed Ryder's trousers. Ryder said, "He must have heard his name."

"He smart." Candie located a pen and a clipboard near her computer. "What girlfriend name?"

"Layla."

"You want say, 'With love? From Luke?'"

"That's perfect." Ryder handed Candie his credit card and gave her the address of his rented farm.

After typing Ryder's information, including his mobile phone number, into her computer and recording the payment, she returned his credit card. "You get marry soon?"

Ryder shrugged. "Maybe. Maybe not. I been married before."

"Man like you need be married." She glanced out of the shop window. "Since you away from your girl, maybe you need things to do. I can suggest ideas 'cuz I know area. Call my cell again. I help. I not forget you find Max."

As Ryder thanked the Korean woman, he figured she was lonely. Odds were she'd arrived in the United States a short while ago. Maybe it was hard for her to make friends because of her poor English.

Next, Ryder had to drive to his apartment, eat a snack, and wait for Rita to pick him up for their axe-throwing date. He smiled. It should be an interesting night.

FIFTY

RYDER'S CELL PHONE RANG. "Hi, Rita."

"I'm at the curb. Ready to throw hatchets?"

"Yeah, 'specially after this week of pretending to be somebody I'm not."

She laughed. "You do resemble a lumberjack, not a pencil pusher."

In less than a minute, Ryder sat in the passenger seat of Rita's black SUV. He liked the vehicle's leather seats. "I've thrown darts in the Holler Bar, but throwin' axes at a bull's eye probably isn't the same."

Rita pulled away from her parking spot. "I've done it four or five times. It's great for relieving tension."

"I hope it does the trick like alcohol. I been on the wagon at least six months."

"I should cut down." Rita glanced at Ryder. "It shows real strength to stop drinking. But tonight, I'll imbibe."

"You can handle it. You're not the type that gets hooked." Ryder tapped a foot on the truck's floor. He didn't like to see people drink. It was a temptation.

She passed a slow-moving car. "Yeah, but I *am* addicted

to work. Life should be better than chasing crooks twenty-four-seven."

Ryder noticed they were nearing a large warehouse. A neon sign on the building close to its parking lot entrance read, "Don't Axe For Trouble Bar and Grill." Rita pulled into an empty spot close to the front door and set the parking brake.

Ryder asked, "How's their food?"

"Decent. And there's a dance floor. You want to boogie to burn off the food?"

He didn't like dancing except for slow dancing when he could hold a woman close. "I ain't much of a dancer, but I'll give it a shot. The axe throwing's my style."

A hostess greeted them when they entered the building. She wore stylized lumberjack clothes. "Are you eating or tossing axes first?"

Ryder shrugged. "What do you think, Rita?"

"Hurling axes before we eat and dance will undo my tension."

The hostess said, "We have fifteen fenced-in axe pens. You can have pen number twelve. Could I have a credit card? Prices are listed here. After twenty minutes, a bell will ring, and you can move to the dining and dancing area."

Ryder handed the hostess his card.

Rita said, "I'm paying for dinner whether you like it or not."

Ryder focused on Rita. "I hope you're putting dinner on your expense account."

"No such luck. I'm single, and I can afford it."

"I'll buy the drinks and do the tipping."

As they began to walk toward pen twelve, Ryder noticed the smell of freshly cut wood—an odor similar to that of a lumber yard. The sound of hatchets whacking wooden walls was incessant.

Each pen was enclosed by chain link fencing from floor to ceiling and included a wooden wall made of rough-cut pine boards. A bull's eye three feet in diameter was tacked onto the wall, and a throwing line crossed the tiled floor. A bench stood next to a wooden box that contained four shiny hatchets.

Rita pushed a button that started the twenty-minute timer, and then she selected a hatchet. "I'll show you my technique." She raised the mini-axe and threw it hard at the target.

The tool stuck in the wood just inside the outer edge of the bull's eye.

"Well done." Ryder grabbed a hatchet and flung it like he was lobbing a baseball. It stuck in the middle of the target.

Rita patted his back, and her hand lingered there. He liked the feeling of her touch.

"You're a natural," she said.

"I did it sorta like I was tossing darts at a cork target. If you don't throw too hard, you can score higher."

"I'll try your method later," she said.

Ryder cocked his head. "For the hell of it, I'll try your way." Ryder wound up like he was throwing a fastball and hurled a hatchet. Its blade penetrated the pine board beneath the target.

Rita opened her eyes wide. "You vented steam with that one. Feel better?"

Ryder exhaled and then sucked in a lungful of air. "I do."

"Could be you're like me." She touched his back again. "I feel your muscles loosening. Play could make you feel a great deal better. Work's not everything."

"I could take up golf like you did, but it doesn't appeal to me."

"Activities to get you to interact with people outside of work could be fun. Dancing might lift your spirits. I'll teach you a couple of steps after we eat, if you're game."

"Okay. I 'spose you're on target. Except for work, what I used to do was drink, but it was to get drunk, not to socialize. If I wasn't drinkin', I wandered the woods."

Rita chose a hatchet and tossed it. It hit the target's center. She zeroed in on Ryder's eyes. "The next Boone High

School reunion in October will include four classes, and both of ours will participate. Why not go?"

"I haven't been to one, but there's always a first time."

"Do I sense you might go? Would you take Layla, even if you're not married by then?"

"I'm not the marrying type. When my marriage to Emma went to pot, it was hell on earth."

Rita handed Ryder a hatchet. "Carol Cuddy told me she ran into Emma at the grocery store. Said Emma resembled a sixty-year-old homeless woman."

Ryder threw the hatchet hard but missed the target. "Meth destroyed Emma. She's not the person she was."

"Even though Emma was a disaster, it doesn't mean the majority of women would be similar. What about Layla?"

"I love her," Ryder said. "But we don't need an official certificate 'cuz marriage is in your heart and isn't just a legal thing."

Rita hurled a hatchet. "It's been hard for me to get close to anyone. Everybody needs a soulmate, though." She paused. "Let's toss all of these hatchets, and then I need a drink."

After their axe-throwing time had elapsed, they sat at a table in the dining area. Rita ordered bourbon, and Ryder asked for ginger ale.

He raised his glass. "To catchin' a killer."

The two touched their glasses, which clinked.

Rita said, "To our nabbing a murderer." She sipped her bourbon. In a short time, half of it was gone.

They ordered dinner, and Rita asked for one more shot of bourbon. Though she was having lasagna, her voice was slurred. "Let's take a break before dessert. I need to dance." She stood and tilted her head toward the central dance floor.

Slow dancing music flooded the air.

"Come on, Luke. You'll like it. I guarantee it."

Ryder felt his insides warm when he joined her. "I'm not great at dancing." He became conscious of the fact that even if he wasn't good at slow dancing, embracing a woman and feeling her body next to him was extremely enjoyable.

"Hold on to me and sway. You'll see how pleasurable it is."

As they danced, Ryder sensed her soft, feminine body next to him. Her face was buried in his shirt, and his heartbeat increased. He thought, *Thank God Layla isn't watching this and doesn't know about my dinner date with Lucinda.*

FIFTY-ONE

THE DELICIOUS SMELL of Chinese cuisine greeted Ryder as he stood at Lucinda Lu's second-floor apartment door. He'd left Blackie at the in-law suite, fast asleep on his dog bed.

Ryder tapped on the old, black, lacquered door, which creaked as it opened.

Lucinda peeked around the door's edge. Her face was charming, and the centers of her eyes seemed larger than ever to Ryder.

"Welcome, Luke." She smiled and swung the door open to reveal her expensive Chinese dragon dress.

The shiny turquoise fabric set off her long, jet-black hair.

He said, "You're picture-perfect."

Lucinda blushed. "Please come in and have a seat on the couch."

Ryder walked into the living room and felt like he'd entered China. The quality of the artwork, rug, and decorations made him wonder if they had originated in the Far East a century ago. "Goin' in your apartment is like steppin' back in time."

"It's the exact sensation I'd like visitors to experience,"

she said as she bowed her head. "Would you like to try a cup of green tea, the best you can get from the Orient? I buy it from a grocer's in Chinatown."

Ryder settled on the couch and noticed painted porcelain cups and a steaming pot of tea on a shiny brown short table. "Sure. I never had it before."

Lucinda kneeled by the table and poured the tea. "You will love it."

Ryder picked up the cup and sipped the brew. "This tastes better than any tea I had before. I'll buy a box of it if I get to Chinatown."

"I'm pleased to hear that, Luke." Lucinda poured a cup of tea for herself and relaxed on the couch next to him.

He studied the paintings on the wall. "Did you do all that artwork? It seems similar to older Oriental art."

"I did do it." She smiled. "I copied Chinese classical works. The style is called *guo hua*. There's much to learn from the past."

Ryder thought about how he could bring Scarlet Hauk's murder into the conversation. It was a shame he had to mix investigative work with pleasure. He felt guilty for using Lucinda because she had become a friend, though a platonic one.

"I feel like I'm in China." Ryder paused. "It's interestin' working at Ames because you meet people from all over the world. I met an astronomer, Dr. Gault, who's from England, and somebody else said Scarlet Hauk was from Germany, where I heard people are not quite as cold as some English can be."

Lucinda sat up straight. "They say German girls can be wild." She set her teacup down. "Like I told you before, I think my ex-boyfriend was sleeping with Scarlet. But I believe she didn't sleep just with him."

"Oh?"

She leaned closer to Ryder, and he could smell her fragrant perfume.

"I'll tell you a story about Scarlet if you promise not to repeat it to anyone."

Ryder tried to convey the impression he didn't care. "Okay."

"Several weeks before she was killed and soon to be married, the girls threw her a bachelorette party. I was invited, and although I was upset with her because she had gone after my guy, I decided to go…out of curiosity."

"What was the party like?"

"I was appalled. There were male strippers, and the girls got drunk. I almost left, but I wanted to learn what happens at these parties. I'd never agree to have such a party prior to my wedding."

"Did things get outta hand?"

Lucinda turned to face him. "The party could've been posted on a soft porn site."

"Oh yeah?"

"Scarlet stumbled like she was drunk and left the party with a male stripper. I shot a cell phone video of them going."

"Maybe he was gonna drive her home because she was wasted."

"It was inappropriate because the man had stripped down to no clothes except a jockstrap during his dance. He didn't have much on when he guided Scarlet out of the door. She could hardly walk. One of her friends would've been a better choice to drive her home."

"You still have the video on your phone?"

"Yes. Want to see it?"

"Why not?"

Lucinda opened her purse and took out her mobile phone. "The video's here somewhere." Moments later, she said, "See, she's floundering out the door with the stripper." She paused. "I wouldn't have gone if I'd known there would be strippers. Disgusting." The stripper wore a plastic fireman's cap and not much else.

Ryder pondered what to do next. He could get the cell phone video later. First, it was important to identify the male stripper. "I wouldn't want to go to that nightclub—what's the name of it?"

"The Purple Panther Bar and Grill." Lucinda stood and arched her back. "I'm tired of talking about Scarlet." She shot a pleasant expression Ryder's way. "Let's eat. Please be seated at the dining table."

Ryder rose and followed her to the dining area.

Lucinda had set the table with a red silk tablecloth, expensive china, sterling silverware, as well as chopsticks. "The way you set your table's classy."

Lucinda grinned. "You're my honored guest. The silverware is for your benefit unless you'd like to try chopsticks."

"I'll give them a shot, but I might have to revert to silverware."

Ryder couldn't identify what much of the food was, but it was steaming warm and smelled great.

After she sat down, Lucinda revealed what the dishes on the menu were, but she did so using their Chinese names. Then she added, "The meat is duck."

Ryder said, "I love duck."

Lucinda sat. "Let's dig in."

Ryder judged it to be the best Chinese meal he'd ever had.

After dessert, they chatted.

When it was time for Ryder to leave, Lucinda walked him to the apartment door. "Luke, I truly enjoyed your company." She gave him a brief hug and said, "Maybe we can get together again soon."

Ryder thought Lucinda was a genial soul, even if she was still a suspect. For the sake of the investigation, would he need to get closer to her? "I like your company, too," he said. "Maybe we can meet again after things slow down at work."

"I look forward to it at the appropriate time."

While Ryder walked down the steps to exit the building, a thought hit him. He would use the FBI laptop computer to search for the Purple Panther Bar and Grill when he arrived at his apartment. There was plenty of info about Scarlett's bachelorette party to report to Rita, too. Should he e-mail her or call her immediately?

FIFTY-TWO

RYDER ARRIVED at his in-law suite backyard apartment, and at once, he sat down on his couch with his FBI laptop computer resting on his knees. Though weary, he opened a search engine and typed in "Purple Panther Bar and Grill," the nightclub Lucinda had reported as the location of Scarlet's bawdy bachelorette party. In an instant, the establishment's website address appeared. He clicked it.

Ryder noticed a tab marked "Parties." He opened it, and a selection, "Bachelorette Blowouts," popped up. He activated it, and an extremely sharp picture of a packed house of astonished women staring at male strippers appeared.

A shock ran through Ryder's body. Scarlet Hauk sat in the front of the audience, slumped in her chair, while her blond hair dangled on her table.

Ryder enlarged the image enough to see Scarlet's glazed eyes. A male stripper who wore a jockstrap and a plastic fireman's cap appeared to whisper into her ear. Ryder recognized the man as the same one who'd appeared in Lucinda's video and who had escorted Scarlet out of the Purple Panther's front door.

"Holy Christ," Ryder mumbled, and all of a sudden, he

was alert.

He copied the website address and e-mailed it to Rita and Mike, noting Scarlet Hauk was in the image. He briefly recounted Lucinda's tale about how Scarlet had left her bachelorette party with a stripper, and that Lucinda had cell phone video of the incident.

Ryder grabbed his mobile phone, glanced at the Purple Panther's website "contact us" section, and tapped its phone number in his device's keypad. After five rings, a deep male voice answered over the muffled voices of a full house. "Purple Panther, Joe here."

Ryder said, "I wonder if y'all have the phone number or website address for the male strippers I saw on a picture on your website. My sister's getting married, and we want to embarrass the hell outta her."

The man laughed. "The Big Boys Dance Troupe will do that. If you decide to use 'em, you can have a twenty percent discount on the use of our party room. But make certain to schedule it far enough in advance."

"What's the Big Boys website address?"

"I've got it around here someplace, but it'd be better if you do a web search. We're kinda busy."

Ryder heard the rumble of the bar's crowd and a brief scream. "Okay. Somebody will call to reserve your room."

Ryder opened the Big Boys Dance Troupe's website. It was replete with photos of drunk, mesmerized women staring at scantily clad males. There was even a video of women stuffing greenbacks in the guys' jocks. Finally, Ryder came across a portrait of five men in their stripper garb. In the middle was the guy who had ushered Scarlet from the Purple Panther. He was brawny and appeared to weigh in excess of two hundred pounds. Underneath his picture was a name, "Rocky."

Ryder composed an e-mail to Rita and Mike with the web address of the Big Boys Internet site, which displayed Rocky's photo. "We need this guy's DNA," Ryder wrote.

Even though it was around midnight, he grabbed his cell phone. He hoped Rita wasn't asleep.

FIFTY-THREE

RYDER FOUND Rita's number on his phone's contact list. "Hope she doesn't get mad," he said aloud as he selected her number.

Her voice suggesting she'd just been jarred from a sound sleep, Rita answered, "Luke?"

"Sorry to get you up."

"I don't mind a call from you anytime. What's up?"

"I had a date with Lucinda, and she said she went to Scarlet's bachelorette party at a place called the Purple Panther Bar and Grill. I sent you the link to its website. Lucinda saw Scarlett leave with a male stripper and took a video of them going. Scarlet appeared to be drunk or high. It happened several weeks before her death, so the guy could be the father of her unborn child."

"Who is he?"

"I found the website of the outfit that provided the male strippers, the Big Boys Dance Troupe. There's a captioned picture of the stripper on their site. His name's Rocky, and he's wearing a red plastic fireman's helmet. I sent you that link, too."

Rita yawned. "We need his DNA."

"Gals set up bachelorette gigs. I suggest you call the Big Boys' number on the website."

"I agree." Rita paused. "Let's meet tomorrow at noon at the park near our FBI rental house."

"I'll be there. Again, sorry I woke you."

"It's okay. I'll explore those two websites now." She paused. "It was fun throwing axes with you. It'll be good to see you tomorrow."

"Same here."

Right after he ended the call, the realization that this FBI undercover gig didn't have a nine-to-five work schedule hit Ryder like a splash of cold water. So far, the weekend had been a working one for the most part.

FIFTY-FOUR

RYDER STROLLED toward four picnic tables that sat amid a grove of trees in the park near the FBI house. He saw Rita sitting at a table in the deep shade. She wore white sandals and purple capri pants. Her floral blouse was brightly colored, and she had a purple ribbon tied around her straw hat.

Rita's fashionable appearance was in stark contrast to how she'd dressed years ago in secondhand clothes when she was a skinny girl attending Boone High. Now she could've appeared on the cover of *Vogue*, not that Ryder knew much about designer clothing.

She waved. "Luke."

"You're stylish today." He smiled.

Rita rose from her seat at the picnic table, swinging her leg over its bench. "I like to dress up on Sundays." She came close to him. "Let's walk in the grass and enjoy the sunshine."

As they approached the perimeter of the park, Ryder glanced back over his shoulder and saw a family had taken over the table where Rita had waited. The mom and dad spread a tablecloth while their children played tag, running on the tall, soft grass.

Ryder caught Rita's eyes. "When are you gonna call the Big Boys Dance Troupe?"

"Soon. I figure they had a gig Saturday night, and they'll sleep until about now." She thought aloud, "But maybe they have an answering service. They're a bunch of guys desperate to make extra coin on the side."

"Same thing I was thinking." Ryder paused a moment. "And they like the side benefits...if a lady wants their company."

Rita blushed. "Some women can be as raunchy as the Big Boys are." She brushed grass blades with her toes after she had stopped to plan their next moves. "We need to catch Rocky off guard to get his DNA. I could meet him during his lunch hour. You could hold back at a distance while I sweet-talk him about my need for a bachelorette party. If he makes an aggressive move, you step in. What do you think?"

Ryder squinted into the distance and caught sight of a pigeon swooping down near the folks at the picnic table and grabbing a piece of bread. "We can plan, but we need to be ready to ad-lib like that yonder pigeon snatching a snack." He directed his eyes at Rita. "What's the best way to get Rocky's DNA?"

"We could play it like we did to get Fuldheim's sample. I'll buy him a coffee or soda. When he tosses it, I guide him away, and you grab and bag it."

Ryder said, "A lot depends on where he works and if he takes a lunch break away from work."

Rita grinned. "I'm positive I can get him to go to lunch with me." She headed toward the FBI house. "Let's go inside and get started."

Minutes later, they sat at the kitchen table in the rented house. Rita dialed the Big Boys' contact number. "Big Boys Booking Service. Cindy speaking. May I help you?"

Rita answered, "I'd like to book the Big Boys for my friend's bachelorette party, but first, I want to know more about the group."

"Sorry, ma'am, but I can't provide details. Our instructions are to ask clients to phone Rocky Diaz, the leader of the Big Boys Dance Troupe." The phone attendant provided Rocky's number.

"Thanks." Rita disconnected. She turned to Ryder, who sat on a chair across the kitchen table from her.

"What happened?"

"I learned his surname and phone number." She gazed out a window and then back at Ryder. "I'll call him and act like I'm a hussy. I'll need to dress for the part, though." She grinned. "In my cop days, I worked on the vice squad."

"That so?"

"My plan is to video call Mr. Rocky, flutter my eyelashes, and ask for an in-person interview."

Ryder leaned on his elbow. "You'll have to go to your apartment to get clothes."

Rita stood. "I have the things I need here." She went into the master bedroom and closed the door.

Soon Rita came out clad in a plaid halter top and bright-yellow short-shorts. She wore red lipstick and a touch of rouge on her cheeks. Her brunette hair was brushed out and appeared longer to Ryder. He felt blood rush to his face. She was now sexy in an unrefined way. "You seem different, but kinda fetching."

"Do I detect my costume works?" Rita laughed. "Let's see if taking the time to dress up was worth it." She sat at the kitchen table and then propped her mobile phone against a book. After she pointed the device's camera lens at her upper torso and face, she tapped in Rocky's number.

Rocky's image appeared on the phone's screen. He sat at a desk. "Rocky Diaz speaking."

Rita smiled and leaned forward in her chair, which emphasized her ample breasts. "Hi, Mr. Rocky. I'm calling to learn about the Big Boys Dance Troupe. I called your answering service, and Cindy referred me to you." She shifted her shoulders.

Rocky coughed. "What do you have in mind?"

"My sister's getting married, and I'd like to set up a bachelorette party."

"We can handle it if the date isn't already taken." Rocky ogled Rita.

Rita pursed her lips and lifted her right palm to face the camera. "I haven't decided when to have the party, and I have so many questions. If you're not too far away, maybe we could meet and discuss things. I'll write a deposit check if you'd like."

Rocky glanced sideways as if someone else was in his office. "A meeting's fine, but I need to be somewhere soon." He focused his eyes on Rita. "My company offices are on Silicon Avenue, four doors from the Luxor Luxury Hotel. We could meet on Tuesday for lunch at the Luxor dining room." He smiled. "My treat."

Rita winked. "That's kind of you. I live close to there." She touched her chin with two fingers. "Should we meet at noon?"

"That's fine."

Rita ended the call.

"Great performance." Ryder paused. "I'll have to make an excuse to go off base for lunch on Tuesday."

"Ask Sullivan Logistics for time off. You don't have to say why."

"Yep. 'Cuz I'm a contractor, Josh doesn't approve my time off."

FIFTY-FIVE

IT WAS the start of Ryder's second week of work at NASA. He parked by the building that housed the Public Affairs Office.

He had arisen before dawn because his body hadn't yet fully adjusted to Pacific Time. It was cool, so he left Blackie in his truck's back seat to sleep. Ryder opened the rear window a crack.

After grabbing his gym bag that contained sweats and sports shoes, he headed for the fitness center less than a block away. He had signed up online to join the center so he could begin to exercise early in the morning. Despite his axe-throwing session with Rita and his dinner date with Lucinda, he still felt stressed by the investigation. He needed to unwind. Lifting weights or using an exercise machine could do the trick.

When he entered the fitness center, he saw an undersized boxing ring surrounded by ropes. Near it, Leon Turk was punching a water drop-shaped speed bag. He ceased hitting it when he noticed Ryder heading for the locker room.

Leon lowered his gloved hands. "You took my advice. Work out, and you won't feel so tense."

Ryder stopped by the locker room door. "I like to train. I'll be out in a minute."

Leon began to strike a larger, heavy bag with power punches.

Dressed in gray sweats and old jogging shoes, Ryder left the locker room and headed for an exercise machine.

Leon stopped pummeling the fat, sand-filled bag and stared at Ryder. "Why not go a round or two with me, spar a little? Ever box in the Army?"

Ryder took two steps toward Leon. "My fights were in bars."

Leon grinned. "Come on. I'll go easy on you. There are boxing gloves, headgear, mouthpieces, and hand wrap gloves in the gray cabinet."

Ryder hesitated. "I guess we can work on footwork and jabs."

Leon smiled broadly. "The activity will do you good, bro."

Ryder opened the cabinet and tossed headgear to Leon. "Best if you wear this, just in case."

"You aren't planning to have a real fight now, are you?" Leon displayed a fake smile.

Ryder slipped a helmet on and rinsed a mouthpiece in a sink near the wall. "I bet they've got rules that you gotta wear one of these if you spar." Ryder tapped his helmet.

Leon shrugged. "Enough said." He put on the headgear.

Ryder put on what appeared to be golf gloves, but in reality, they served the purpose of a boxer's hand wraps. He fastened the Velcro strip on the gloves around his wrists. "They got quality equipment here."

Leon said, "You've never boxed before? You know how to put the equipment on." He turned to a man standing near the gray cabinet. "Hey, Jack, can you lace up Luke's gloves?"

Jack, a rail-thin man, approached Ryder. "Certainly," Jack said in an English cockney accent. He glanced back at Leon. "I'll fix you up with a gumshield, too, Leon."

Ryder put the mouth guard over his upper teeth. He

shrugged as he slipped on a pair of boxing gloves. "Let's just warm up, Leon."

Jack laced Ryder's gloves. He also inserted Leon's mouthpiece.

Ryder entered the ring, as did Leon. Jack set a timer for three minutes and started it at the same time as he rang a bell to begin a round. Ryder realized Jack was acting as a referee. Ryder nodded and touched gloves with Leon.

Leon stood in an upright stance, like an old-style boxer. He had the appearance of a bull standing on his two hind legs.

Ryder went into a crouch stance and kept his elbows near his rib cage. His heartbeat sped up, and he gulped in deep breaths when he saw Leon's eyes flash in anger.

Leon's mouth formed a frown. He plodded forward and threw a strong right at Ryder's chin, but Ryder tucked his head behind his left glove and deflected the powerful punch.

Ryder knew instantly Leon didn't intend to train during a friendly sparring session. Ryder sensed that Leon wished to hurt him, to crush his rival for getting the X-909 beat. Ryder took a step backward with his right foot and then slid his forward left foot back to keep his balance. Just beyond Leon's reach, Ryder threw a jab with his long left arm, striking Leon's right cheekbone. Ryder saw Leon squint and flush.

Fury radiated from Leon's eyes. He took heavy, slow steps toward Ryder.

Ryder backed up just as Leon used all his might to throw a right that missed. In response, Ryder threw a powerful left hook that smashed into the right side of Leon's face. Blood dribbled from his nose.

Ryder retreated again, moving toward the center of the ring.

Jack frowned as he caught Leon's gaze. "What in the hell are you doing, Leon? This is supposed to be friendly sparring, not a fight."

Leon redirected his eyes to Ryder and took two awkward

steps forward. He unleashed a flurry of punches, including a roundhouse and two rights.

Ryder danced away like Muhammad Ali.

Ryder thought he needed to end Leon's aggression immediately. He let Leon clop forward. Barely out of Leon's range, Ryder threw two quick left jabs, further irritating Leon.

Panting, Leon threw a right that bounced off Ryder's left glove.

Ryder had dropped his right hand to belt level. He launched a strong uppercut that connected with Leon's chin. Then Ryder stepped back and slammed a right into the big man's stomach. As Leon bowed forward, Ryder sent a strong right into Leon's jaw, staggering him.

Leon's rubbery legs wobbled as he sank to his knees.

Jack stepped between the men. "This is over, gents. If one of you gets hurt too much, I'll lose my job." He opened the cabinet, pulled out a smelling salt capsule, and crushed it under Leon's nose.

Leon trembled and spat out his mouthpiece. "Why'd you tell me you weren't a trained boxer? Figured you'd clock me. Watch your back," he slurred.

Jack began to unlace Leon's gloves. "Leon, I'd watch what you say," he said in a low voice.

Leon ripped off his hand wrap gloves and dragged himself toward the showers.

Jack untied Ryder's gloves. "You have talent. You're an excellent boxer-puncher, and Leon made the correct assessment. You've been trained."

Ryder took out his mouth guard. "That was at least twenty years ago. I joined the boys' police boxing club when I was in high school."

Jack picked up Leon's spitty mouthpiece and rinsed it in the sink. "Leon's a bloody arrogant bastard, just a brawler. A bully. I'm glad you taught him a lesson."

Ryder could hear the shower running. He sighed. "But I shouldn't have. I could've just quit. We work in the same office, and he won't get over it."

"A man should stand up to a bully. You did the right thing."

Ryder decided he'd said enough about the fight. "Sounds like you got an English accent."

"I'm from East London. I used to work in the fight game, but that was half a lifetime ago. If you were a young man, I'd counsel you to take a go at fighting professionally."

Ryder shrugged. "I'm over the hill. Thanks for your help."

"I did nothing but stop the fight."

FIFTY-SIX

RYDER LEFT the fitness center carrying a gym bag, and he had his suit and dress shirt draped over an arm. After the short walk to Building N-204, he let Blackie out of his truck. They climbed the stairs to the men's room on the second floor, around the corner from the public affairs offices. Blackie trotted behind him, dragging his leash.

Ryder checked his watch. Lucinda Lu had told him she generally arrived at the office about five to seven. He changed his clothes and realized he must've dropped his expensive silk tie in the fitness center. "Damn," he said.

He left the restroom and turned the corner to begin walking to the fitness center. He glanced backward. Light from his open office door reflected from the hall's tiled floor. Curious, he turned and went back to his office. Lucinda sat at her desk scanning the *San Francisco Herald*.

Blackie wagged his tail and licked Lucinda's hand. She gazed at Ryder. "You're here early."

"I figured I'd check out the fitness center."

"How was it?"

Ryder paused. "I got a real workout." He hadn't showered after the fight, and he felt sweaty.

"You're flushed."

Blackie whined.

Ryder wondered whether or not Leon would show up to work after his beating. Would the fight with Leon get in the way of the investigation? Would he complain to Josh? Ryder parked himself on the swivel chair behind his desk.

"I had too much exercise."

Lucinda shoved the newspaper across her desk. "What kind of a workout do you normally do?"

"The exercise machines, jumping rope, and the medicine ball." Ryder forced a smile. "They have top-notch equipment at the fitness center."

"That's what our fearless leader, Josh, says. The Ames fencing club practices there. He's quite good with a saber, I'm told."

Ryder sat up straighter. "I thought Josh was mostly into playing poker."

"No, he's an athlete, too. I saw one of his fencing bouts. It's said he's the best fencer in the club, and he could've been on the Olympic team if he'd taken it up when he was young."

"Did you say he uses a saber? Don't they fight with foils?"

"They can use three kinds of weapons—épées, foils, and sabers. But they specialize with one of them. Fencers wear padding, even Kevlar jackets and breeches."

"Why?"

"Because a guy was killed during the 1982 championships in Rome. Josh told me all about it."

"Sounds dangerous."

"I wouldn't try it."

Ryder peered down at his chest. "I lost my tie. I'm going to the fitness center to get it. Can you watch Blackie?"

Lucinda petted Blackie's head. "It'll be a pleasure."

FIFTY-SEVEN

RYDER POWER WALKED to the fitness center to retrieve his silk tie. When he reached the center's parking lot, he noticed Leon's expensive Italian electric car. Ryder was sixty feet from the building when Leon pushed open its front door. After shooting a cold stare at Ryder, Leon entered his automobile and slammed its door.

Stomach acid rose up Ryder's throat as he watched Leon abruptly back up his vehicle. He floored the accelerator pedal, and his auto squealed as it fishtailed out of the parking lot and headed in the general direction of the main gate. The smell of burnt rubber lingered in the air.

Ryder's pulse slowed as he passed through the building's front doorway. When he entered the fitness center, Jack, the skinny Englishman, was coming out. He motioned for Ryder to step into a cubicle-sized office.

"Watch yourself," Jack said in his cockney accent. "Mr. Sable is here, practicing with his saber for a fencing club contest. He's mad as hell at you."

"Oh?"

"Leon told him how you beat him."

Ryder exhaled. "I came back for my tie." He glanced out

of the office doorway and saw Josh approaching, his eyes ablaze. "Shit, here he comes."

Jack glanced backward at Josh. "At least I gave you a bit of warning. Here's your tie."

Jack left the tiny office just as Josh barged in and closed the door.

"Don't say anything, Luke. Just listen. Leon told me how you sucker punched him when you two were supposedly doing a so-called friendly sparring session. I sent him home for the day to recuperate."

Ryder started to open his mouth.

Josh held up his hand. "Don't say a word." He paused. "I won't tolerate internecine warfare among members of my office. Even if you did produce a usable fact sheet, Mr. Little helped. Don't think submitting adequate articles makes you a shoo-in for our office. You must be able to work with colleagues. Get the hell out of here. I'll decide what to do about you later."

FIFTY-EIGHT

RYDER WALKED into the public affairs conference room for the staff meeting and sat by the wall near the far corner.

As the room filled, Ryder was hoping Josh would ignore him and forget about the fight with Leon. But Ryder's gut told him that was wishful thinking.

After Josh sat in his chair at the head of the long, wooden conference table, he said, "I want to begin this meeting by cautioning everyone there is a critical standard governing how we operate in public affairs. We should treat coworkers well. We should not fight, bicker, or come to blows. We're a team, and we need to work as a well-oiled machine. We shouldn't whine and scream like a defective engine ready to blow itself apart."

The public affairs staff members surveyed one another with serious expressions. Josh continued. "You may wonder why I've brought this up. It's come to my attention that at least two of you have been squabbling, which has led to aggressive actions, not an ordinary argument. I won't mention names, but I've put a check in my green book next to the offender's name. This mark will count the same as a demerit for missing a deadline or being late to a staff meeting." He scanned the room. "That's all for now. Lucinda, let's hear your two-minute report."

As Lucinda spoke, Ryder wondered what else could go wrong. He needed to make progress on the investigation before the FBI shut down the Scarlet Hauk murder probe. This living soap opera of an office that had gone bonkers was a major liability.

After the public affairs reports ended, staff members began to file from the room.

Josh caught Ryder's attention. "Mr. Ryder, see me in my office."

Ryder followed Josh into his office.

Josh said, "Sit."

Ryder eased into a chair and sat tall. As his pulse rose, he fought to appear calm.

Josh stared at Ryder. "You know why you're here. Again, listen. Don't talk."

Ryder appeared unemotional, but he seethed inside.

Josh glimpsed at an e-mail printout on his desk. "I received a message that Sullivan granted you two-and-a-half hours off tomorrow. If it were up to me, I'd say no, but since you're a contractor, I can't." He took a breath. "If you get another check this year, I'll ask Sullivan to replace you. I don't care what Nigel Worth may say. I won't have you destroy our office. Get the hell out of my sight for the day. Do something useful on base, but not in this building."

As Ryder left Josh's office, he wondered once again about the man's erratic mood swings. Was he bipolar?

In any case, Ryder believed Josh certainly wasn't emotionally sound enough to head a NASA office. Would Josh's psychological condition and future actions further jeopardize Ryder's standing and, in turn, the murder inquiry —which already was teetering on the edge of failure?

Ryder was anxious for his workday to end. Tuesday might be fruitful if he and Rita managed to get Rocky Diaz's DNA. Ryder hoped Rocky was the father. That would be one less question to answer in the Scarlet Hauk investigation.

FIFTY-NINE

RYDER SAT at his public affairs desk. He hoped his undercover assignment would end in days at the most. If the microdot case was not connected to the murder, the FBI could pursue the spy or spies without him. He'd be glad to leave Ames, go on a cruise, and return to Kentucky.

Lucinda walked rapidly into the office, sat in her office chair, and rolled it toward Ryder. "Leon had a black eye when he came in. He said he'd walked into a glass door so clean he didn't see it." She hesitated. "But I know what happened, and so does everyone else, unless it's a rumor."

Ryder asked, "What's the gossip?"

"That you beat up Leon while boxing at the fitness center." Lucinda cocked her head. "Is it true?"

"It's true. Leon and I were having a friendly sparring session, but one of my swings went wild and caught him the wrong way."

Lucinda straightened her back. "Jack, the fitness center manager, has been telling everyone a different story…that Leon tried to knock you out, but you dodged his punches and knocked him to his knees."

"Sometimes things get exaggerated."

Lucinda rolled her chair even closer to Ryder. "I don't blame you for trying to defuse the situation. But everybody in the office saw Josh call you on the carpet after the staff meeting. Everybody heard him during the meeting talk about not coming to blows and how he'd already put a check next to someone's name in the green book. After that, the whole office was speculating about what happened. Leon's absence was noted. Then the rumor about the fight circulated." She paused. "So, did Josh put a check next to your name?"

"Yeah, but he misunderstood what happened."

"One more check and you could be gone. Be careful, and you'll be okay. But if you get another check and you lose your position, know I'll always be your friend. And if you need a place to stay while you hunt for a job, I can lend you my couch."

"I appreciate your offer, but I'm okay for now."

Lucinda stood. "To unwind, let's do lunch at the cafeteria."

"Thanks, but I'm taking time off to meet a friend who's landing at San Jose International."

Lucinda rolled her chair back to her desk. "It'll be in your best interest to get away from here for a while." She fingered a pencil. "Don't forget my apartment is open to you should the need arise."

"I'm grateful for your friendship." Ryder turned on a computer map program to get driving directions to the Luxor Luxury Hotel.

SIXTY

RYDER ARRIVED at the Luxor Luxury Hotel and left his truck in a multistory parking garage across the street. The sun was shining, and the air was fresh. It was a relief to get out of the office to track down a suspect's DNA. Maybe Rocky's DNA would help wrap up the Scarlet Hauk murder investigation.

As Ryder walked toward the garage exit, he spotted Rita's black sport utility vehicle as it pulled into a parking spot.

When Rita exited her SUV, Ryder approached her and noticed she wore a short pink skirt and a lacy, low-cut blouse unbuttoned at the top, revealing her cleavage. He felt his pulse increase.

"I see you're dressed for the part."

"I want the sleaze to ask me out, but I'll string him along." She grabbed her pink purse from the front seat.

While they walked to the garage's exit, Ryder said, "I'll grab whatever I can after you two leave."

Rita stopped and reached into her handbag. "Here's a San Jose health department ID I had the field office make. If someone asks what you're doing when you grab the DNA, say you're making an unannounced salmonella spot check."

Ryder slipped the card into his pocket. "I probably won't need it 'cuz I'll be quick and stealthy." He felt elated. Maybe this undercover gig was nearly over. "Go into the restaurant first and ask for a table near Rocky. If he isn't there, sit by the window in the back. Afterward, meet me at my SUV."

They left the parking garage separately.

Ryder entered the fancy hotel and made his way to the restaurant. He spotted Rocky sitting next to the window near the back of the room. Ryder approached the hostess. "May I help you, sir?"

"Could you seat me by the window at the far end so I can have a view outside?"

"Of course."

Ryder followed her to his table. A waitress appeared, and he made his lunch order.

Rita sashayed in and waved to Rocky.

He stood.

As Rita walked to his table, male diners focused on her. Rocky pulled out a chair. She sat down, and they ordered lunch.

Soon Ryder was slicing a juicy rib eye steak. His mashed potatoes and vegetables, including sautéed asparagus, tasted great. This gourmet meal beat routine cafeteria food by far. While he relaxed, he thought of several ways he could grab Rocky's DNA.

Rita and Rocky spoke in low voices Ryder couldn't decipher, though he was two tables away. As he settled in for a drawn-out wait, the waitress refilled his coffee cup. He nursed the delicious Columbia Supremo.

Thirty-five minutes passed until Rocky signaled the waitress for his check.

Ryder was on the alert. Under his tabletop, he slipped on nitrile evidence gloves and hoped the busboy wouldn't quickly clear Rocky's table.

Rocky led Rita to the cash register, where he paid his bill. Then they left.

Ryder stood, snatched a spoon Rocky had used, slipped it into a paper evidence bag, and put it in a side pocket of his sports jacket. He returned to his table, sealed the bag with evidence tape, and noted the time on a form that he taped to the bag. After paying his bill, he left the restaurant and crossed the street. Soon he was next to Rita's vehicle.

She rolled down her window. "How'd it go?"

"I got a spoon. Nobody noticed." Ryder handed her the bag.

"Excellent." Rita noted the time and signed the bag's info sheet to maintain the chain of custody. "He tried to take me to a bar, but I said I had a doctor's appointment. Then he asked me for a date. I agreed but said I'd call him because I have a busy schedule, and I'd have to consult my calendar." She paused. "Another thing, he was wearing a heavy-duty metal belt buckle that said *Las Vegas*. He might have connections there. I'll have someone find out."

"We're on a roll, Rita."

"I'll call you when we get results."

Ryder felt satisfied. Today wasn't turning out so lousy. He said, "I'd better go. I can't be late, or the news chief will put a check in his green book."

Rita squinted. "What?"

"He's a control freak and keeps track if people miss deadlines or are late to staff meetings. Get three checks, and he'll reduce your performance level if you're a civil servant. If you're a contractor, he'll contact your contract boss and ask that you don't get a raise. He may even ask that you be let go."

Rita stared at Ryder. "Do you have any checks?"

"I was a minute late to the first staff meeting. That was one check." He cleared his throat. "I should tell you something else you're going to hear." He exhaled. "Yesterday, I had a friendly sparring match with Leon Turk that went sour. He tried to floor me, so I whacked him. He went down to his knees and got a black eye. The news chief gave me a second check for hittin' Leon."

Rita was disgusted. "Don't get another check. That'll put the investigations at risk."

"I'll be careful."

"I hope so." Rita drove out of the garage. Her tires squealed.

Ryder realized he must move fast to return to the office by 2:00 PM so that Josh wouldn't give him a third check.

SIXTY-ONE

RYDER RETURNED to the Public Affairs Office nine minutes before his leave was to expire. He didn't want News Chief Josh putting a third check mark next to his name in the green book.

Tapping the floor with her high heels, Lucinda appeared worried when she glanced at Ryder. "You've been quoted all over the world saying plant life has been discovered on an exoplanet. Josh is super ticked off. He told me to tell you to report to his office as soon as you arrived." She held up a copy of the *San Francisco Herald*. Its larger-than-normal headline roared, "Life Discovered in Outer Space."

Ryder sat at his desk, and Blackie curled up next to his feet. He felt his stomach churn. "Shit. All over the world?"

Lucinda eyed her computer screen. "Read the headlines of the *New York Times*, the *Washington Post*, and London's *The Times*. It's the top story across the globe."

"That damn Chuck Singh jumped the gun. I told him it was off the record."

Lucinda waved a printout. "His headline in the *Straight Scoop Bay Area* is, 'Life Found Light Years Away.' Our phones have been ringing nonstop. Reporters are calling from everywhere. It's crazy busy." Sounds of ringing phones echoed in the hall outside their office in a sudden barrage of sound.

Ryder slapped his desk. "Damn."

Lucinda caught Ryder's eyes. "Did Chuck specifically agree to hear it off the record?"

Ryder studied the ceiling as if trying to recall Chuck's exact words. "I don't remember. But don't reporters verify a story by checking different sources?"

"They should for a huge story like this one." She paused. "According to the stories, an anonymous source leaked Dr. Gault's draft journal paper. Some reporter called Dr. Gault, and he confirmed he'd written it. He's in deep trouble, too."

"Chuck wants to make a name for himself."

Lucinda nodded. "He'll get job offers from national newspapers and the networks, and he will get a book deal."

Ryder took a breath. "Leon told Chuck an important story was coming up."

"Leon said astrobiology is his beat, and you blew it. He made certain Dr. Ruben, head of astrobiology, knows he, Leon, didn't release the story."

Ryder stood. "Can you keep an eye on Blackie for a bit longer? I'm gonna talk to Josh and get it over with."

Lucinda wrinkled her brow.

Ryder figured he'd failed his undercover assignment. The Scarlet Hauk murder inquiry was in jeopardy, and he dreaded talking with Nigel and Rita about the situation.

SIXTY-TWO

AS RYDER NEARED Josh's office, he heard muffled voices coming from behind the closed door. He knocked on it, and the indecipherable voices ceased.

Josh asked loudly, "Who is it?"

"Luke."

"Come in and close the frigging door."

When Ryder entered, he saw Nigel Worth sitting next to Josh's desk.

Josh said, "Take a seat, Mr. Ryder. Your chlorophyll story has gone worldwide, and it's not a good thing."

Ryder sat straight. "Yes, sir. A reporter by the name of Chuck released the story even though I told him it was background and off the record."

Nigel leaned forward. "I phoned Chuck. He said although you offered him information off the record, he didn't verbally agree. So he issued the story, even though it hadn't yet been peer-reviewed or published in a mainstream journal."

Josh held up his hand and stared at Ryder. "Did you give Chuck a copy of Dr. Gault's draft journal paper?"

"No." Ryder paused. "Do you think Chuck would've put out his story if he didn't have Greg's draft?"

Nigel said, "Someone else leaked it."

Josh flushed. "That is…if Mr. Ryder is being truthful."

Nigel cocked his head. "Mr. Ryder is a decorated combat veteran of the Congo Conflict. How can you question his honesty?" Nigel set his jaw.

Ryder felt his guts burn. It was ironic Nigel used a lie as a justification.

Josh glared at Nigel. "Dr. Ruben, head of astrobiology, called and asked me to take steps to have Mr. Ryder let go."

Nigel's eyes seemed like they were on fire. "I don't think so. Somebody leaked the draft article, which made it possible for Chuck to issue the story. We need to find out who secretly gave the draft to him." Nigel's voice rose. "Another thing to remember—if Dr. Gault hadn't confirmed the leaked document was genuine, the story would've been deniable."

Josh tapped his blue editing pencil on his desktop. "What do you suggest?"

"The Project Transition description says the program provides both an educational opportunity and a way for soldiers to switch to civilian life. I'm sure Luke has learned from his mistake. To emphasize this lesson, Sullivan Logistics will dock him two days' pay. I've discussed this with Sullivan. That's how this is going to play out."

Josh seemed as if he were about to throw a fit. "This is nuts."

Nigel said, "I haven't heard anyone ask for Dr. Gault's severed head because he confirmed the story. We don't know who leaked the draft, either. Luke told Chuck the material was off the record. Chuck ignored that and went with the story anyway."

Josh blinked. "Leon Turk will issue a retraction, but it won't help."

Nigel stood. "In Hollywood, they say any publicity is wonderful. This story is earthshaking. It's the first time life's been discovered beyond this planet."

After Nigel had gone, Josh said. "Mr. Ryder, stay." Josh reached into a desk drawer and took out a bottle of whiskey, poured two shots into a water glass, and swallowed a gulp. He squeezed his eyes shut, coughed, and then frowned. "If you think you came out on top, you're mistaken. The director of astrobiology will appeal to the Ames director, and you shall be fired. I'll see to it. Get your ass out of my sight. I may take a day or two off so I don't have to see your face. After that, you'll be gone."

Ryder stood and left. It was imperative that he talk with Rita to regroup if she didn't kick him off the task force first.

SIXTY-THREE

RYDER STEWED in his office after his meeting with Nigel and Josh about the premature release of the extraterrestrial chlorophyll story.

Lucinda glanced at Ryder every once and a while. She, no doubt, was itching to find out what had happened minutes before in Josh's office.

Ryder noticed that she dabbed her eyes with a tissue when she thought he wasn't watching. Her eyes were red.

His elbow on his desktop, Ryder pressed his palm on his forehead. Why had he blabbed to a reporter about life on an exoplanet? It was too late now to correct his error. The story had gone worldwide, and he was quoted as the original source.

The head of NASA in Washington had asked the top man at NASA Ames to have Ryder disciplined. Though Cousin Nigel had done his best to save Ryder's job to maintain the public affairs cover story, Ryder knew it would be a matter of days—or hours—before he'd be fired. Josh would see to it by going around Nigel to Ames' director.

Ryder was screwed, and he knew it was his fault. He

didn't have any more chance of succeeding than a man who'd fallen overboard in mid-ocean into a freezing sea.

The murder investigation, already on life support, would end, and Ryder would be the root cause of its demise. Though the microdot inquiry might well continue, he'd be gone. Someone else would have to play an undercover role in that probe. He wished he could have a drink, but he was on the wagon. Even so, he felt a bit of relief. The murder investigation would end, and he'd be free of it.

What about the reputation of Rita Reynolds within the FBI? Would the failure of the Scarlet Hauk murder investigation stall her career at the Bureau? He sighed.

His cell phone rang. The incoming call was from FBI Agent Henry Dunbar. Ryder accepted the call. "Hold on, Henry, while I go outside."

Lucinda shot a curious look at Ryder, who, still holding his mobile phone, grabbed Blackie's leash and left the office. Once outside, he sat on a park bench.

"What's up?"

"I was watching the All News Cable Channel. You're quoted as saying life has been discovered on another planet, but NASA has put out a retraction. They said it was a mix-up. A junior public affairs officer had made a significant mistake." Henry's voice rose. "What's going on?"

"It's complicated but true."

Henry breathed heavily before he asked, "What's that mean for the Scarlet Hauk investigation?"

"There's a ninety-nine percent chance I'll be fired in the next couple of days, if not in hours."

"Maintain your cover, no matter what. We can't have the Bureau's name dragged through the mud." Henry paused. "I never have seen Rita so upset. She's been bawling in the bathroom, but she's calmed down now. Just has puffy eyes. Call her soon."

"I was gonna phone, but I had to think about what to say."

"Tell her the truth." Henry disconnected.

Ryder stared at his cell phone and then shifted his attention to his bloodhound. "I best get this over with now, Blackie, instead of letting the wound fester."

Ryder touched Rita's name on his contact list, and his phone showed her device was ringing.

"Luke, I've heard about the chlorophyll misstep—correction, your total screw-up. I'm disappointed."

"I could tell you how it happened, but that won't change it."

Rita gulped. "You know who called me?"

"Who?"

"The Director of the FBI, Clarence Dodd. He said if you're connected with the FBI as an undercover agent, he will end my career. I'll have to pull the plug on the murder investigation. Nigel will ask Sullivan Logistics to fire you. I'll need a replacement undercover person to put on the microdot case."

Ryder heard her sniffle. "I'll walk around the block before I do anything. We'll have a task force meeting tonight at five-thirty at the house. Be there."

She hung up.

Ryder felt disillusioned and missed Layla more than ever. At that moment, he decided he'd buy a second bunch of flowers for her after the meeting if it ended early enough. Chances were he'd return to Kentucky in the next day or two after his utter failure.

SIXTY-FOUR

RYDER LOWERED his head as he entered the FBI Sunnyvale house. He could feel the stares of the task force members as he sat at the edge of the semicircular set of chairs that faced the whiteboard.

Rita walked to the board. "Here's what we're going to cover in this emergency meeting. One: status of the Scarlet Hauk investigation. Two: Luke Ryder's situation." She glared at Ryder. Her voice was curt, and her neck grew red. "We'll discuss the eleventh-hour actions we might take."

Henry Dunbar rose. "Excuse me, Rita, but I'd like to say something."

"Go ahead."

Henry caught Mike Lobo's eyes. "Mike informed me he learned Luke told a low-life reporter, Mr. Singh, information off the record about chlorophyll on an exoplanet. But somebody else leaked the chlorophyll draft journal article. Also, the astronomer, Dr. Gault, confirmed the research is valid. Luke is not entirely at fault. At least three other people are to blame." He turned to Luke. "I stand with you. You found the microdot and have done valuable work." Henry sat down.

Mike said, "I agree. Let's move forward."

Ryder felt somewhat relieved but still embarrassed and depressed. He believed his role was over. Though he'd contributed to the task force's mission, he'd failed in the end.

Rita said, "Thank you, gentlemen." She paused and examined the faces of the task force members. "Even before the exoplanet chlorophyll story broke, I learned this morning the powers that be decided the Scarlet Hauk case will go cold next Monday at the close of business. We still have time to work it."

Mike raised his hand. "If Luke is let go, how will we get somebody to investigate from the inside?"

Rita sighed. "I'll keep Luke on the team until he's forced out." She eyeballed Ryder. "FBI Director Clarence Dodd called me. He said if it gets out that Luke is an undercover FBI operative, then my head will be on the chopping block. Maintain Luke's cover at all costs. He could be fired tomorrow anyway. If that happens, and if anybody asks about an FBI undercover guy being fired, dodge the question."

Mike again asked, "How can we get somebody inside NASA again…and quickly?"

Rita rubbed her forehead. "I'll pose as a journalism student from San Jose State who's been offered a temporary position in public affairs. Nigel Worth and I figured that out. I hope Luke can continue his assignment because my writing skills are nearly nil."

A knock sounded at the front door, and Rita directed her eyes toward the noise. "Just a minute, folks."

She walked to the front entrance, peered through a peephole, and opened the door. A Latino man handed her a package, and she signed for it. She also wrote on a paper on the parcel's exterior. "Thanks, Pedro." She closed the door and strode to the whiteboard. "Excellent news. We received the black strap back from the DNA lab out east."

Henry asked, "How's it going to help us?"

Rita said, "It'll be our shot in the dark." She handed Ryder the parcel, which contained a well-sealed plastic bag with the strap inside. "Before they have a chance to fire you, see if your bloodhound can pick up a trail from a scent on this strap. Let's hope the odor of Scarlet Hauk's killer is still on it, if indeed it was something he or she wore."

Ryder signed and dated the evidence bag. "I'll get to work tomorrow morning and scout inside the Unitary. Then I'll try the robotics research area."

Rita smiled. "Outstanding." She took a step toward Ryder. "We scored a huge break. Luke learned Scarlet attended her bachelorette party six weeks before her death. He viewed a video of her leaving the party, clearly under the influence, escorted by a male stripper named Rocky Diaz. Luke and I snagged the man's DNA. Rocky is the father of Scarlet's unborn child."

Low voices broke the silence.

Rita continued, "A woman often doesn't know she's expecting when she's six weeks pregnant. It's unlikely Rocky knew about it, either. Since Ames is fenced in and guarded, I don't see Rocky getting on base in the wee hours of the morning to kill Scarlet. But we'll watch him."

Rita sat on a chair near the whiteboard. "I think I've covered everything except for the microdot. We'll concentrate on that after we make our last best effort to solve the Scarlet Hauk murder."

The meeting broke up. Ryder felt pressure building in his head. The team counted on him and Blackie for a last-ditch breakthrough. Had the scent of the killer survived two years in a sealed bag? He'd have to get up before dawn to have as much time as possible to search for the murderer's odor. Though he had a pounding headache, he felt he must order flowers for Layla before he returned to his apartment to rest.

SIXTY-FIVE

RYDER LEFT the FBI house at 6:00 PM. He figured the best thing about the Scarlet Hauk investigation was it would end soon. His failure to discover the killer was twice as painful as his pounding head.

He wished he were back at the farm in Kentucky, feeling Layla's soothing caress. He yearned to kiss her soft lips. She liked roses. He opened his wallet, took out Candie's Simply Flowers business card, flipped it over, and entered the Korean woman's cell number on his mobile phone's touchpad.

"Mr. Ryder." She paused. "I see your picture on TV. You famous now."

"What?" Straightaway, he supposed the media attention on him surely would be the final straw that would get him fired first thing in the morning.

"Was on Korean TV channel, too. All over world. Congratulations."

Ryder coughed. "Thanks. I'd like to make a second order of roses to send to my girl in Kentucky. I know it's around six, but y'all have the address in your computer. I can give you my credit card number."

"I still in shop. Not far from your place. Stop in, and I show you different kinds of flowers."

"When do you close?"

"I stay here. Wait for you. No trouble. My flat near shop."

"You certain that's okay?"

"Uh-huh. You find Max. I not forget."

* * *

RYDER PULLED into the strip mall parking lot near the Simply Flowers Shop. He had dropped Blackie off at his apartment.

As he approached the shop's front door, he noticed the lights inside the shop were on.

Kang Hyo-Ri, a.k.a. Candie, opened the door. She wore a pink, tight-fitting, short dress. "Come in, Mr. Luke. I suggest yellow flowers for your Layla. Come see."

Ryder followed her to the shop's rear, into a flower-filled room. "Thanks again for openin' up special for me."

Candie tapped his arm with her fingertips. "No problem, dear." She turned and pointed to a bouquet of yellow flowers. It included roses as well as other flower types Ryder did not recognize. "I make special selection. If you like, I take picture, and Lexington Flowers make same like mine. Be there tomorrow afternoon."

"Please do that."

She snapped a digital picture with her mobile phone.

Ryder reached into his pocket and felt his wallet. "You still got my credit card number?"

"Yes, Mr. Luke." She led him to her computer next to the cash register and completed the transaction. "TV say you make mistake. If you feel blue, I got idea to help. Want to hear?"

He shrugged. "Okay."

She turned off her computer. "I show you lovely place for coffee, tea, and food, close both our places."

Ryder heard the rustling of a beaded curtain behind him.

He turned and saw a short, muscular Asian man emerge from behind the dangling room divider.

Candie said, "Luke, this my partner, Mr. Yun Min-Gi. We call him Bengie." She turned to Bengie and said something in Korean. "Bengie, this Luke."

Bengie shook Ryder's hand and bowed. "It is an honor to meet you, Mr. Ryder." He had a Korean accent but spoke English well. "I saw your story about chlorophyll on an exoplanet. Impressive to be so close to history. Reporters say it is the first life found not of this Earth."

Ryder felt his face burn.

Candie stepped from behind the cash register. "I tell Mr. Luke about Dilly Dally place. Luke live close. I like show him. I go, if he go."

Bengie said, "You should check it out. They have excellent coffee and sandwiches. I know the owner." He grinned.

Candie said, "You not eat yet, I bet."

Ryder felt at ease for the moment, but his stomach ached for food. "Okay, if you have the address, I can type it into my GPS."

Candie took a step forward. "I no remember street number. I show you, okay?"

Had Candie asked for a date? She was lonely and doubtless a recent arrival to the country. She'd helped him. Ryder glanced at her. "Let's ride in my truck."

Candie picked up her purse near the cash register. "I know you like place."

In less than two minutes, they sat in his rental truck. He pressed the accelerator, and the quiet electric vehicle rolled forward.

SIXTY-SIX

IT WAS past 6:30 PM when Ryder pulled into a strip mall with his passenger, Candie. She said, "Dilly Dally at end of stores."

Ryder guided his vehicle to the north end of the row of stores and parked. He saw the full name of the establishment, "Dilly Dally Dance Club." A poster-sized sign on the door stated, "Open Every Nite Til 4:00 AM." Ryder took a quick breath. "Candie, you said this was a sandwich shop."

"I like 'cuz open a lot and 'cuz of my side work. Sandwiches tasty. Coffee helpful when work late. You like." She locked her arm in his and urged him toward the front door.

Ryder sighed as they approached the club. He opened the fingerprint-smudged glass door, and hubbub greeted his ears.

Young women, dressed in suggestive outfits, danced. Many of their partners were middle-aged men.

A bartender yelled, "Hi, Candie. You brought us a customer?"

Candie smiled. "He true friend. Okay we sit at table two?"

"Be my guest. Have a wonderful time dancing. Want to order first?"

"Yes, Phil. I want usual." She turned to Ryder. "What you like?"

Ryder gazed at Phil. "If you got it, a roast beef sandwich, hot if you can. Potato salad and a green salad with Italian dressing. Ginger ale. Put hers on my tab, too, please."

"Comin' up."

As they walked toward table two, Candie said, "Why not drink a beer or wine? It heart medicine."

Ryder saw nearly every man in the place was drinking, and half were drunk. "I'd like to, but I'm on the wagon."

"On wagon?"

"That means I quit alcohol. I had a problem drinkin' too much."

"Important you stop, then. Hard do." She stopped near the table.

As he pulled out a chair for her, he noticed she was the most striking woman in the establishment. "Feel free to drink, if you'd like. Don't let me stop you."

She sat down gracefully.

He asked, "You been in the country long?"

"Bengie and me come from South Korea five year ago. He learn English in school in Korea. I not. But I learn here. Watch TV. It help."

"That's one way to pick it up." He paused. "What's your side business?"

"I bar girl. Make extra cash. Flower shop not make enough money. I bring customers to bar. But you different. You real friend."

Ryder felt his back muscles tense, and he considered what to say next. "Thanks for suggesting this place. I'm hungry as a starvin' bear, and if that roast beef sandwich is as tasty as you and Bengie say, I'll be a happy camper."

Within minutes, the bartender set food on their table at the edge of the parquet dance floor. Candie had a tuna fish sandwich, fries, a shot of whiskey, and a beer.

Famished, Ryder took a bite of his sandwich. "Tastes great. You weren't exaggeratin' about this place."

Candie smiled and nibbled her food. She surprised Ryder when she took two sips of whiskey from her shot glass and then swallowed the rest. "I need. Feel warm in throat." She then nursed her beer.

They finished their food, and he said, "We should go soon."

Candie took a napkin from her lap and set it on the table. "Slow music playing. Okay, we dance one tune?"

Ryder stood. "Why not?"

They stepped onto the parquet floor. She sealed herself against him and moved with poise. "I like dance. 'Specially with friendly man." She held him even tighter.

Ryder felt her softness. "You're a fine dancer."

"I dance with men to get money from bartender. You customer. He pay fee."

"Does the bartender pour a full shot in drinks men buy you?"

Candie shrugged, her body still close to his as they danced. "He put just a dash of whiskey in glass. Rest tea. I not get drunk."

The music ended, and Ryder escorted Candie off the dance floor while she held his hand. He studied her eyes.

Candie smiled. "Tell me about NASA when you take me my place. I like sci-fi and space travel."

He led her outside to his truck.

SIXTY-SEVEN

RYDER PULLED into Candie's apartment building's parking lot.

She turned to him. "Can you walk me my flat? I worry 'bout weird man who stare at me sometime."

"Okay, but if some guy's buggin' you, call the police."

"Later. I not have proof."

He opened his truck's passenger door for Candie, and she pointed to an exterior set of metal stairs that led to her second-floor apartment. The area was not well lit.

She latched on to Ryder's arm, and he guided her up the rusted steps. They stopped at her door, which was painted hospital green with poorly brushed latex paint. She fished in her purse, grabbed her key ring, and bounced the keys off the door, making a loud, jangling noise.

Ryder concluded even the scant amount of whiskey and the beer she had imbibed had made her tipsy. "Please come, Luke. Check no mean guy get in."

Ryder followed her into the well-furnished apartment. It seemed to him that she had fancy furniture for a woman who had to resort to being a B-girl in order to make ends meet.

"Please sit on couch. I need go bathroom a sec." She went into the bathroom.

Ryder wished to leave. He was drowsy. Tomorrow would be a big day, and he needed to get up at 5:00 AM or earlier. Candie was taking a long time, so he eased back on the couch. Then he heard a sound like metal clicking, which seemed to be coming from the refrigerator.

The bathroom door hinges creaked, and Candie emerged. She wore a semitransparent, pink negligee.

A wave of desire coursed through Ryder's body. He took a deep breath and said, "Your fridge makes a lot of noise."

"It ice maker. Need get fixed." She paused and peered into his eyes. "Stay tonight. Your girl far away. I lonely. Please." She dropped her nightwear to her ankles, exposing her breasts.

"Candie, you got the wrong idea. I might be fixin' to marry my girl soon. I can't do this. You're a sweet lady, and I'm positive you can find another decent man." Ryder felt hot, and sweat rolled down from his hairline.

She kicked her negligee aside and walked to him, her arms wide as if she would give him a hug. "Your girl never know."

Ryder's heart was beating rapidly as he moved toward the door, but Candie was quick and embraced him. Ryder gently pushed her away. "Sorry. I gotta leave."

"I change your mind later." She pouted in a fake way. The refrigerator made a tick-tick sound like a radiator heating up.

"Bye, Candie." Ryder left. He wondered if she was doing more than soliciting drinks for money. Was she a prostitute?

SIXTY-EIGHT

RYDER ARRIVED a bit later than he'd planned at his NASA office. His sports coat pocket held the sealed evidence bag containing the black strap. He also had dog treats in a trouser pocket. As he and Blackie neared the public affairs offices, the bloodhound sniffed at Ryder's hip pocket.

Lucinda greeted Ryder with a smile. "Guess what? Mr. Sable won't be in today. Said his car broke down."

Ryder said, "That calls for a celebration." He removed a five-dollar bill from his wallet. "I'm getting a soda. Want one?"

"That would be super." Lucinda reached for her purse.

Ryder raised his hand. "I'm buying."

"You're a gentleman." She paused. "Before you do too much celebrating, Nigel Worth's at an all-day meeting in Mountain View. Leon is in charge of the division today."

"Nuts."

Lucinda stroked her dark hair. "I'll lay low."

Before Ryder arrived at the vending machines, he stopped in the men's restroom. He guided Blackie into a stall, slipped on gloves, and reached into his jacket pocket to retrieve the evidence bag containing the black strap.

"Blackie, sniff this and track. There'll be a reward if you get a hit." Ryder planned to walk to the Unitary after he gave Lucinda her soft drink.

Ryder unsealed the plastic bag and held it under the dog's nose. Then he opened the stall door, and the dog at once began to sniff the bathroom floor and pull his leash.

Ryder stared at the dog. Had the bloodhound locked on to a scent related to the strap's odors? Or did the smell of dog treats encourage Blackie to make the motions of being on a scent trail, even if there wasn't one? Ryder wanted to praise the hound enough to keep him on whatever trail he was following, if there were one. Not to overdo it, Ryder said in a quiet voice,

"Fine work."

Blackie yanked his leash, pulling Ryder toward the bathroom's exit. He realized it would have been smarter to buy drinks from the machine first before letting the dog smell the black strap.

The vending machine stood near the bathroom door. Ryder had to loop the leash around his foot and stand on it when he operated the machine. He put one soda in a rear trouser pocket and held the second drink in his left hand while he grasped the leash with his right hand.

The dog pulled him down the public affairs hallway a few steps past his office. To enter his doorway, Ryder had to drag the bloodhound behind him.

Lucinda nodded at Blackie. "He's super excited."

"I think he smells someone's muffin and egg breakfast."

Lucinda's face projected skepticism. "I don't smell anything. Is anybody else in the office?"

"I didn't notice. Dog noses are sensitive."

Lucinda stood. "I better grab my soda so you can control him better."

Ryder held out her can, and she grabbed it.

She asked, "What about yours?"

"It's in my back pocket."

She extended her hand and wiggled her fingers. "I'll take that one, too."

He gave Lucinda his drink. "I better take him outside and do a quick training lesson." Would the dog hit on somebody or something in the public affairs offices?

SIXTY-NINE

BLACKIE WHINED when he neared the public affairs office cubicles. Ryder held the dog's leash with a strong grip as the animal tugged him toward a closet door on the far wall of the open area. The dog lay on the floor, indicating a scent hit. As saliva dripped from his lips, the hound stared at Ryder and wagged his tail.

"What did you find, boy?" Ryder opened the door and saw a black trench coat that draped down from a clothes hanger on a hook. The long coat hit the floor of the closet and covered a pair of men's galoshes. He felt almost as if a spark of static electricity had shocked him. The right arm of the garment had a black strap wrapped around its wrist, but there was no strap on the left arm.

Ryder took a dog treat from his pocket. "Wonderful work, Blackie." Ryder handed the dog a strip of jerky, closed the door, and considered what to do next. No one else had yet arrived at the public affairs offices except for Lucinda and him. He'd ask her about the coat.

Ryder collected his thoughts and then re-entered his office. Blackie panted and dragged him toward Lucinda, who was sitting with her legs crossed. She'd slipped off her loafers, which she'd shoved to the side of her desk. The dog sniffed the soles of her shoes and then reclined near them. The animal salivated, expecting a treat. Ryder felt his pulse rate increase.

Lucinda squatted and stroked the animal's head. "Did you teach him the trick to lie down on the floor and use those cute eyes to beg for a nuzzling session?"

"He does it whenever he 'specially likes a person."

"Funny he didn't do it before."

"He's happy to see you." Ryder paused. "I give him treats for being a well-behaved boy." Ryder held out a piece of jerky, and the hound licked it and then gobbled it down.

Lucinda smiled and gently stroked the animal as he whiffed the sole of her shoe. "You like me, Blackie?"

Ryder said, "I opened the closet in the cubicle area, wonderin' if that's where I could hang my sports coat. There's not much in there—a bunch of boxes on the floor, hangers, outta style neckties, and a black trench coat. It seems old, like it's been there a while."

Lucinda stopped petting Blackie and stood. "Leon found it in the cafeteria four or five years ago. It was hanging on the coat rack near the exit for weeks. He kept it for the office instead of turning it in to lost and found."

Ryder shifted his feet. "Why would Leon keep a coat instead of turning it in?"

Lucinda wrinkled her brow. "That's the kind of person he is. Takes advantage of situations. He said any of us could use it if we forgot our raincoats or umbrellas during the rainy season."

"I could use it?"

"Yes. But it's first come, first served. Everyone's worn it. I sometimes put extra slip-on shoes in the closet in case my dress shoes start to hurt my feet. I have small feet, and nobody's going to steal my little loafers." She sat down behind her desk. "Since everybody uses the coat, I wouldn't store your jacket in there. Somebody might take it. I suggest you hang your coat on the hook on the back of our door."

"I'll do that," Ryder said, as he hung his sports coat on the door as if to try out the hook.

"I thought you were going to take Blackie outside to train him."

"I'll wait until lunchtime." He glanced at the doorway. "I'm gonna walk to the Unitary and see if I can catch Bill."

As he and Blackie left his office, Ryder thought, "Crap, if everybody in the Public Affairs Office used the coat, which of them, if any, are suspects? Did the scent that Blackie locked onto come from the original owner, from the killer, or from an innocent member of the public affairs staff, like Lucinda?"

He also wondered what other scents Blackie had picked up from the coat. Did the scent mix include the killer's odor? Did visitors use the coat? What if its strap had fallen off when an innocent person had visited the Unitary? His mind brimming with unanswered questions, Ryder and his dog stepped into the public affairs hallway.

SEVENTY

RYDER WANTED to turn left as he exited his office and headed for the stairwell, but Blackie pulled his leash right. Ryder let the dog sniff his way forward down the corridor until the animal halted at Josh Sable's locked door. The bloodhound sniffed at the crack under the door and lay down.

Ryder figured Blackie might well hit on several places in the public affairs offices. "Fine work, Blackie." Ryder held out a piece of jerky for the slobbering animal. "You're making out, boy."

Ryder turned around and followed the long hallway. When he and the dog arrived at the cubicle area, Blackie made a beeline for a cubicle on the right. A magnetic name tag read, "Olivia DeChamps." It was stuck to the metal frame of the cubicle's beige privacy wall. Blackie reclined on the floor next to Olivia's chair.

Ryder reached into his pocket. "Here you go, boy." He petted Blackie. "If you keep this up, I'm gonna have to see if the vending machine has jerky snacks."

Blackie whipped his tail back and forth and then held his head high and sniffed the air. He trotted to a second cubicle, one that belonged to a young public information specialist, Jenny Rogers. Again, the bloodhound stretched out near her office chair. Ryder rewarded his pet and spoke in a low tone.

"We better come back when everybody's here 'cuz you hit on things and the bottoms of Lucinda's shoes—not people."

Ryder guided the excited dog down the steps to the building's exit. When he and Blackie began to cross the blacktop parking lot, he saw Leon's car. Ryder guessed Leon was at the fitness center.

Ryder paused at the street corner across from the fitness center. He pulled out his smartphone and touched Mike's name on the device's contact list. He hoped Mike was already in the office.

"Luke, what's happening?"

Ryder glanced down at Blackie. "My dog hit on a black trench coat hanging in a closet in public affairs."

"You positive it's the one?"

"Yep. One arm's missin' a wrist strap. Blackie got real excited. Could you bag the coat?"

"I'll have to wait 'til everybody's gone for the day." Ryder heard Mike scratching on paper. "I'm logging this. It's great news."

Ryder sighed. "Maybe not. You can also write down that Blackie hit on Lucinda Lu's shoes, Josh Sable's office, Olivia DeChamps' chair, and Jenny Rogers' chair. He hasn't hit on a person yet."

"Your office might be connected to the murder."

"Lucinda said the coat's been used by everybody in the office over the years. Even visitors use it. Leon found it in the cafeteria about five years ago, but instead of turning it in to lost and found, he kept it for the Public Affairs Office."

Ryder heard Mike scratch notes on a pad.

"If you get a hit on a person, call Rita and me ASAP."

"I'm walking to the Unitary now. Blackie could hit on something there."

SEVENTY-ONE

RYDER STOOD in an alcove near the rear entrance of the Unitary Wind Tunnel Complex, where investigators had found the black strap two years ago, shortly after the Scarlet Hauk murder. He opened the evidence bag containing the strap and held it for the bloodhound to smell yet again.

"Okay, boy, track." Ryder hoped a follow-up whiff of the strap might give Blackie a stronger scent to follow.

Ryder took the hound outside, where the strap had originally fallen. Then he re-entered the building, but the dog was not interested in the area just inside the rear door.

Ryder said, "Let's see what you'll do farther inside, Blackie."

Ryder followed the dog down the longish hallways of the wind tunnel complex, which was lined with offices. Blackie's nose was busy taking in scents, but he showed no sign of finding a trail. As the man and dog passed each office, the animal sampled the air.

Two or three people glanced at Ryder and his bloodhound as they carefully walked through the entire complex. Blackie visited open offices if no one was nearby, but if people were present, Ryder did his best to make excuses for the dog to enter a room.

Ryder and his hound canvassed the 9-by-7-foot Supersonic Wind Tunnel high bay area, where Scarlet had taken her final breath, but they had no luck. Ryder also didn't encounter Bill Little, whose office was locked.

When Ryder turned the corner of the hallway at one end of the building, a man sized him up. "Didn't I see you walking the hallways?"

Ryder mustered a smile. "Yep, I been visitin' with different people."

The man appeared skeptical but walked away.

After nearly two hours of searching the complex, Ryder gave up. Even if he and Blackie had aroused suspicion by walking back and forth examining its halls, his days at Ames were numbered anyway. This was like a Hail Mary pass in the closing moments of a football game. He had nothing to lose but everything to gain.

At almost ten-fifteen, Ryder slowly began to walk to the cafeteria. He had a slight headache, which he reckoned resulted from a lack of sleep and the building tension. He'd get a cup of coffee and then go back to his office. Maybe Blackie would hit on a human being there.

SEVENTY-TWO

RYDER BOUGHT a large cup of coffee and sat by himself in the cafeteria. It seemed like his brain swam in a swamp. He looped Blackie's leash around a leg of the chair on which he sat.

A tall, African American man caught Ryder's eyes, nodded, approached, and halted near Ryder's table. "Hi. I don't know if we've met. I'm Sam McCoy. I was hired under Project Transition, too." He held a cup of coffee.

Ryder stood and shook Sam's hand. "I'm guessin' you know my name, but in case not, I'm Luke Ryder. Want to sit down?"

Sam pulled out a chair and petted Blackie. "I heard about your service dog and that you were deployed to the Congo. Leon Turk said you were in the 75th Rangers."

Ryder felt embarrassed he needed to lie yet again. "Yep."

Sam's stare seemed to drill into Ryder's head. "Funny thing is, I was in the 75th, too, but they weren't deployed to the Congo when I was with them."

Ryder flushed. "Uh-huh, but I was sent on a special mission. I'm not supposed to talk about it."

Sam frowned. "I don't remember you. The 75th's been at

Ft. Lewis, Washington, for a while. When did you deploy to the Congo?"

Ryder sighed. "Like I said, I'm not supposed to say anything." His stomach burned.

Sam grinned. "It's just like the Army to send us off to faraway places and then tell us we can't say much about them. Thanks for your service."

Ryder coughed.

Sam said, "When you were in the Congo, we did a lot of desert warfare training. I was sick of getting sand in my teeth when we went off to Yakima. At least in the Congo, I bet sand didn't get in your mouth and in your weapon."

Ryder nodded. "What job did you get at Ames?"

"I work in supply. If I decide to stay, I'll have a job forever."

"That's lucky." Ryder stood. "It was great talkin' with you." He unwound Blackie's leash from the chair leg. "I'm going to the fitness center to work off some steam before lunch."

Sam gulped his coffee. "I'm heading there, too. If you don't mind, I'll tag along."

Ryder shrugged. "Okay." He wanted to ditch Sam, so Ryder was sorry he hadn't told Sam there was an urgent matter at the public affairs offices he needed to attend to.

As a matter of fact, after lunch, Ryder wanted to go back to public affairs to see how Blackie would react to the people there. If that didn't yield any useful information, he also planned to have the bloodhound canvas the robotics lab for a scent. On the other hand, after Gina, the robot, had told him Fuldheim was not a murderer, Ryder was inclined to believe her. She was programmed not to lie.

Ryder's mind skipped out of its thoughtful phase just as he, Blackie, and Sam neared the fitness center.

SEVENTY-THREE

RYDER, Blackie, and Sam walked into the fitness center.

Sam said, "I like to use the treadmill. How about you, Luke?"

"I'll do the treadmill, too, but after I work out with the bench press and the chest press machine."

Sam nodded. "You're going to have a real workout, then." He paused. "The treadmill's gonna keep my heart in shape. My family has a history of cardiac problems."

"Sounds like you're doin' the right thing, Sam." Ryder pointed to the locker room. "I got a locker here, now. I need to change."

Sam grinned. "You're going to work up more of a sweat than I am. Kudos to you, though. It takes considerable effort at our age to keep in shape like you do."

Ryder put on gray shorts, a black sweatshirt, and old tennis shoes. When he exited the locker room, he saw Sam pacing on the treadmill.

Sam glanced back and waved just as Ryder moved to the bench press.

Ryder added weight to the barbell, eased back on the

brown padded bench, and began to do repetitions while Blackie sat and watched.

Ryder was glad he was exercising because it eased his headache, and he felt better, a tad more confident despite the dire state of the Scarlet Hauk investigation. It was satisfying to strain his muscles enough to eventually help build further muscle tissue.

Ryder glanced at Sam, who wore headsets as he paced on the treadmill. What kind of music was the man listening to?

After Ryder had completed plenty of reps on the bench press, he moved to the chest press machine.

Blackie stood and shook his body and then reclined near the second apparatus. The dog was soon snoring.

Ryder first adjusted the seat height of the chest press machine. He sat down, selected a weight, leaned against the seat-back, and grabbed the two handles that were at midchest level. He used his arm and chest muscles to push the handles forward, which moved the weight up on a pulley. Then he pulled the handles back toward his torso.

As Ryder continued to work his chest muscles, he started to wonder what else he could do to make a last-ditch effort to catch the Scarlet Hauk killer, who evidently worked at Ames…or at least had easy access to the NASA center.

What might Ryder do to lure the killer into a situation that would reveal himself or herself? He puzzled over this for a few moments. Was there anything about the space plane that would bait the killer to come out into the open? He shook his head. There was nothing obvious he could do.

Ryder stopped working the chest press machine, ready to move on to one of the treadmills. He turned and saw Sam, who had stepped off his treadmill and was removing his headphones. Then Sam began to walk toward Ryder.

Movement in Ryder's side vision distracted him. He turned and saw Leon hitting a punching bag.

Ryder felt someone tap his shoulder. Sam pointed and said, "There's Leon. I'll say hello before I shower." He approached Leon.

Sam and Leon began an animated conversation. With his

head askance, Sam glanced back at Ryder. Leon's face was reddish as if he were irritated.

Ryder didn't want to end up in a physical fight again, so he went into the locker room, took off his exercise clothes, stepped into the shower, and got just wet enough to wash off his sweat. After quickly dressing, he and Blackie slipped out a side door and walked toward the cafeteria.

He wanted something to eat before the public affairs staff returned from lunch.

As Ryder neared the cafeteria, he glanced at Blackie trotting beside him. "Maybe I should have given you a chance to sniff Leon."

The dog analyzed Ryder with friendly eyes.

"But we can do that this afternoon."

SEVENTY-FOUR

AT 12:50 PM, Ryder sat alone in the cafeteria in a corner three tables away from the nearest people, finishing a substantial lunch. He devoured a salami sandwich and tossed a bit of leftover meat to Blackie.

The young dog had an insatiable appetite, even though he ate a bowlful of dog food twice a day. Ryder supposed Blackie wouldn't be constantly hungry once he was full-grown.

Ryder pulled his phone from his pocket and called Rita.

"Luke, I wondered when you'd call. Mike told me about Blackie finding the trench coat and picking up scents in the Public Affairs Office."

Ryder glanced across the cafeteria. "Yep, but he didn't hit on a person. Everybody in the office could've worn the coat, according to Lucinda. Just me and she were in the office, so Blackie didn't get a chance to hit on anyone there yet except Lucinda. Blackie only zeroed in on the soles of her shoes."

Rita said, "Still, the coat's a promising clue. What about the Unitary?"

"I spent around two hours walking through the Unitary complex. Blackie didn't hit on anything. I'm in the cafeteria now, and I see the public affairs folks are still eating. I'll check them out after they return to the office."

Ryder heard Rita shift her phone. "I have depressing news. The agent in charge of the San Jose office called and said they've decided to close down the Scarlet Hauk investigation sooner—close of business on Friday instead of Monday. He said it's clear Rocky Diaz, the stripper, didn't kill Scarlet because he couldn't have gotten on base."

"I might as well fold my tent and head for the hills. I'll be fired soon anyway." Ryder fiddled with his coffee mug.

"Hang in there. Your cover will work for a while. Then I won't have to go in there and take your place to follow up on the microdot."

Ryder's headache pounded on his skull. "I was called in here to help with the murder, not the microdot. I'm positive Pike wants me back in Kentucky and on the job."

Rita sighed. "I hear you. Maybe Blackie will hit on a person in public affairs. Let's hope for a miracle in the next two days."

Ryder coughed. "Sorry for unloadin' on you."

"We're all stressed. Call if there are developments."

"Definitely." Ryder hung up and began to leave for the Public Affairs Office when he stopped by a TV suspended near the cafeteria's entrance.

The TV screen showed a reporter standing in front of the Ames sign located near the main gate. He lifted his hand-held microphone close to his lips. "We're just outside NASA Ames in Mountain View, the NASA center where astronomer Dr. Gregory Gault, the leader of a team that first detected chlorophyll on an exoplanet, is based. This historic discovery was prematurely released…"

Ryder turned abruptly and left the building. He thought, "When's this chlorophyll nightmare gonna end?"

SEVENTY-FIVE

RYDER WAS SITTING in his office chair when Lucinda walked through the doorway and stopped.

"Leon's in Josh's office. He told me to send you in as soon as you got here. He's peeved." She seemed concerned, and her hands trembled. "What's going on?"

"I'll find out soon." Ryder knew Leon would do anything he could to cause problems for him.

Lucinda sighed, sat at her desk, and kicked her loafers off. "I might as well get comfortable while Josh is gone." But instead of being relaxed, she closed her lips tightly and drew in air with rapid, shallow breaths.

Blackie trotted to her shoes and sniffed them. He reclined. His jowls dripped dog spit. Ryder tossed the animal a treat.

"Somebody loves me, don't you, Blackie?" Lucinda petted him and breathed easier.

Ryder went into Josh's office without knocking.

Leon sat behind Josh's desk, a pompous expression on his face.

"Lucinda said you wanted to see me."

"Close the door."

Leon appeared smug. "I have the pleasure of being in charge of the division while Josh and Nigel are gone. I decided to flush you the hell out of public affairs forever after you screwed up the chlorophyll story. I consulted the director of astrobiology. He agreed you should go, and he said I should check with the center director. We met and also decided you should go immediately."

Ryder inhaled sharply. "You seem to like this job, even if it's just for a day." At that moment, Ryder realized Leon had made him angrier than he should be.

"Josh asked me to do this because he didn't have the guts to do it. He'll be back by five after I kick you out of this building, even if you're not officially fired by Sullivan yet."

Failure hit Ryder like a punch to his stomach. At the same time, he felt relief his clandestine job would soon be over. He now believed covert operations were not his strength. Lying was too hard to do, even if it was in an attempt to nab a criminal. He snapped back to reality.

"I'm not fired until Sullivan lets me go 'cuz I'm a contractor, not a civil servant."

"Yeah, but I can order you not to set foot in the public affairs offices." Leon paused. "I can't wait to tell Josh and Nigel you're lying about serving in the 75th Rangers. Sam told me he never saw you before, and he was in the 75th for six years prior to joining NASA."

"You believe Sam, even if he isn't privy to secret stuff?"

Leon smirked. "You bet. I'm an expert at catching liars. Josh said he had you pegged for a liar from the beginning." He paused. "I've e-mailed Sullivan, noting the center director wants you gone yesterday. Clear out your desk and leave today."

Ryder stood. "You're feeling superior because you're getting even for me beating your ass after you tried to floor me."

Leon scoffed. "You have a black mark against you. No one at Ames will write a positive review for you after the chlorophyll mess."

"I'm not worried. But if you ever take over for Josh here, Ames is in for a world of hurt."

Leon laughed. "You lost. Losers don't get ahead. I'm a winner. Bye, bye, Lukey."

Ryder stared at Leon. "There's a special place for guys like you in hell. I know how you and Chuck set me up. What goes around comes around."

Leon smiled in an offensive way.

Ryder sighed, left Josh's office, and went to get Blackie.

Lucinda's eyes were wide when Ryder stomped into the office. "What happened?"

"The center director decreed I would be fired because of the chlorophyll story, thanks to Leon Turk."

"Oh no." She ran forward, hugged Ryder, and then pulled away from him. "As I said before, if you need a place to stay, you can stay at mine."

"I don't have to pay rent for a while, so I'm good, but I appreciate your offer." He paused. "It's been a pleasure to work with you, Lucinda. I'll be back later today to clean out my desk. I'm gonna go to Bill Little's office to say goodbye."

Lucinda's eyes turned bleary. "I'll stick around until you come back, even if it's late. I'll help you pack."

"I shouldn't be at Bill's office more than ten minutes."

Ryder grabbed Blackie's leash and left for the Unitary Wind Tunnel Complex.

SEVENTY-SIX

RYDER TAPPED on the door frame of Bill Little's office. He was at his desk, where an older model of the X-909 space plane sat, its stingray-like nose as sharp as a dagger.

"Luke, what brings you here?"

"I came by to say I'm leaving Ames. I've been let go because of the chlorophyll story. It got published too soon because of me." Ryder's head didn't hurt as much now. He felt relief because his assignment was likely a couple of hours from its end.

Bill motioned Ryder into the office. "Want a cup of coffee?"

"Thanks."

Blackie stretched out on the floor.

Bill handed Ryder a steaming cup of joe. "I know why you are here, to investigate Scarlet Hauk's murder." He sat down. "My son remembered he'd seen your picture on the front page of the *Lexington Observer*. You solved a murder in Kentucky, and you're a deputy sheriff."

Ryder debated whether or not to admit he was working undercover. He decided he had to convince Bill not to tell anybody there was an ongoing murder investigation. Rita and the rest of the task force might still solve the Scarlet Hauk case. He sighed. "You and your son are correct, but do me a favor, don't tell a soul about this."

"I won't. Neither will Brett." He sipped his coffee.

"I shouldn't have admitted I'm a cop." Ryder fiddled with his coffee cup. "It's an ongoing investigation."

"Do you want to hear my theory?"

"Shoot."

Bill stared at the old space plane model on his desk and then picked it up. "Someone killed Scarlet to get X-909 plans and data. At first, that motive didn't make sense to me because I believed the space plane wouldn't be built. The design was way off."

Ryder petted Blackie's head. "What benefit would your info be to a spy, except to know y'all weren't about to build a space plane?"

"The spy didn't know that. But our recent wind tunnel tests show the latest design is close to flawless." He paused. "A full-scale prototype plane will be constructed for testing in the real world."

Ryder wrinkled his brow. "Then Leon will be back in your office soon to write a press release."

Bill planted his elbow on his desktop and propped his chin on his palm. "He's an arrogant SOB."

An idea came to Ryder. An improved space plane design might well give him a last-minute opportunity to nab Scarlet's murderer if, indeed, that person were a spy. Ryder would have to get Bill's cooperation. "Would you help me catch Scarlet's killer?"

Bill opened his eyes wide. "I would."

Ryder's cell phone rang, and he glanced at the incoming number. It was Rita's. "Excuse me, Bill. It's business." He spoke into the phone. "Hold for a sec."

Bill stood. "I'm going to buy a candy bar from the machine. I'll close the door. When you're done, open it."

Bill departed.

Ryder spoke in a low voice. "I got awful news and also better news, if I can make it work."

"What's the awful news?"

"Leon is in charge of the division today, and he fired me. Josh and Nigel are off base, and Leon convinced the director of Ames to call for my departure. Leon also sent an e-mail to Sullivan Logistics, asking them to fire me. I'm banned from the public affairs offices, but I'm not planning to clean out my desk until the end of the day."

Rita exhaled. "That was quick."

"That's not all. I'm in Bill Little's office in the Unitary. His son's a schoolteacher in Lexington. He remembered my picture was on the front page of the *Observer* after me and Blackie nabbed the last killer."

"Did you deny you're here on an investigation?"

"I hardly could after he said he knew I was here checkin' out the Scarlet Hauk murder. He promised not to tell anyone."

Rita sighed. "Things are falling apart. What's the positive news?"

"I got an idea on how we can catch the killer if the murder is related to espionage."

"How would you proceed?"

"Bill told me they have a revised design for the X-909 that's so on target they're gonna build a full-scale prototype. He also told me he would cooperate to help us nail Scarlet's killer."

"Have you told him your plan yet?"

"No. You called just after Bill agreed to help."

"How would it work?"

"A spy would want those plans after word spreads across Ames about how good the updated design is. Bill needs to issue a news release about building a full-sized prototype space plane, and he has to ask Leon to write the release. It's possible somebody in public affairs is a spy 'cuz the public affairs office area is the only place Blackie hit on a scent from the black strap."

"What if the spy is in some other Ames organization?"

Ryder replied, "We'll spread the word across Ames about

the new space plane design. We can also make it easy for someone to steal the new plans."

"How?"

"Mike would change Bill's safe combo to match a phone number. We'll ask Bill to write the new combination on an index card that he can deliberately use when he opens the safe in front of people—and he should do that a lot. We'll have to stake out Bill's office, especially when he's not there, even if it takes a while for a spy to bite."

"Sounds far-fetched. How's a spy going to know how to get the combination if he or she's not sitting in Bill's office the next time he opens the safe?"

"I'll tell Lucinda I saw Bill use a company's phone number to unlock the safe. She loves gossip and will spread it around the office and across the center."

Rita hesitated. "There's a slim chance of success, but it's a chance. We'll do it. Confirm Bill is on board, then call me back. I'll need to speak to him." She paused. "Mike can talk to a bunch of Ames people about the phone card, too. He needs to lock up the latest X-909 documents in security's safe, and Bill should keep the old design info in his safe. We'll have a planning meeting tonight at the Sunnyvale house at six-thirty. Bring Bill with you."

Ryder gulped. "I didn't think you'd agree to this."

"Hang up and talk with Bill before I change my mind."

Ryder opened Bill's office door. Bill was across the corridor, leaning against the wall and eating a candy bar.

"There's a plan we need to discuss."

SEVENTY-SEVEN

BILL ENTERED HIS OFFICE, threw his candy wrapper into the trash can, and stared at Ryder. "How can I help?"

"Before we discuss it, you need to talk with the agent in charge of our task force, Rita Reynolds."

Ryder touched Rita's name on his mobile's contact list. "Rita, I've got you on speakerphone. Bill Little's here."

Ryder set the phone on Bill's desk. "Bill, introduce yourself."

"I'm Bill Little, in charge of the X-909 test program. I'll be honored to help with your investigation of Ms. Hauk's death."

"Thanks for offering to help. I'm Rita Reynolds, the agent in charge of the Scarlet Hauk murder FBI task force. It is paramount that your work with us remain secret until and unless the FBI decides to release information about your participation. Also, you'll have to sign paperwork that binds you to certain conditions we require you to follow. We'd like you to meet with the task force tonight at six-thirty at a house we have in Sunnyvale. Can you do that and agree to our confidentiality terms?"

"Yes. But I'll have to make an excuse to tell my wife. I'll say there's an emergency X-909 meeting."

Rita's voice broke up for a moment. "...can plan in the meantime." She ended the call.

Ryder glanced at Bill. "We should talk through ideas I have about how to trap the killer."

SEVENTY-EIGHT

RYDER AND BILL sat in Bill's office.

Ryder said, "A plan hit me when you said the X-909 space plane is gonna work now. That would excite a spy."

Bill nodded and ran his fingers along the old space plane model on his desk. "Yeah, but since the info's locked in my safe, there's no way anybody could get to it unless they torture me."

Ryder cocked his head. "But there is a way to broadcast your safe's combination across the center."

"How?"

Ryder smiled. "By spreading rumors. They travel across Ames as fast as the wind."

"How's it going to work?"

"We change the combo to match the phone number of a bogus company." Ryder flipped the index cards on Bill's address spindle. "Then we put out word you have to refer to an index card to open the safe."

"You think it'll work?"

"Yep. Keep the old plans in your safe. We'll lock the updated plans in Mr. Lobo's safe in security's offices."

"I've never met Mike."

"You'll see him tonight at the meeting."

Bill leaned forward. "I have a suggestion."

"Shoot."

"I could change the space plane plans using my CAD/CAM computer program and put them in the safe…in case the spy recognizes the old plans."

Ryder nodded. "I like it. What's CAD/CAM?"

"Computer-aided design and manufacturing." He peered into his cup at his cold, black coffee and took a swig. "Also, instead of using a fake company phone number, we should use a real number. A spy could find it in the telephone listings on the Internet."

Ryder grinned. "Great idea."

Bill said, "I propose we use Lance Aerospace Incorporated's number." He pulled a card from his address spindle. "They're well known in the Bay Area." He handed the card to Ryder.

"I'll call Mike. He needs to have someone change the combo."

"Before you call, tell me, how are you going to spread the rumor?"

Ryder laughed. "My office-mate is Lucinda Lu. She gossips twice as much as anyone I've ever met."

"You're going to rely just on Lucinda?"

"No. Mike will spread the rumor, too." Ryder reached down, petted Blackie, and scratched the dog's ears. "Blackie is a bloodhound who's been helping in this case. He's found scents in the public affairs offices that suggest someone in that office might have been involved in Scarlet Hauk's death."

"So, telling Lucinda the rumor might well pass it directly to the spy or murderer?"

"Yep."

Bill asked, "Is Leon Turk a suspect? He's determined to keep the X-909 beat."

Ryder shrugged. "We can guess, but we have to let the evidence lead us to the spy or killer." He paused. "There are at least two possibilities. One: Scarlet's murderer was after the X-909 info. Two: There wasn't a spy involved in her murder."

"There have to be additional details the task force is checking."

"We can get into them later if Rita okays it."

"Interesting."

Ryder tapped a finger on Bill's gray metal desktop. "The best thing that could happen is to lure a spy here, if there is one, and catch him or her in the act so we don't have to bend over backward to convict."

"You said, 'him or her.'"

"We've gotta keep open minds." Ryder grabbed his mobile phone. "I should call Mike now and have your combo changed."

SEVENTY-NINE

RYDER HELD his smartphone and tapped Mike Lobo's number.

"Luke, Rita called me about your idea to lure a spy to Bill's office. Where are you now?"

"With Bill Little in his office." Ryder paused. "I'm guessing Rita told you I want to change Bill's safe combo."

"I've lined up the locksmith. We can come over now. I hear I should secure the latest X-909 documents in my safe."

Ryder glanced at Bill. "Yep. We've picked out new combo numbers."

"Be there in five minutes."

Ryder disconnected from the call and turned to Bill. "Mike Lobo's on his way here to change the combo and take your new X-909 plans to his office to lock up."

Bill opened his safe, put his space plane items in an envelope marked "Top Secret", and placed it in his top desk drawer.

Ryder had a sudden uneasy feeling. Would his latest scheme fall apart? Had he given Rita a false sense of optimism?

Mike rapped on Bill's open door. He was accompanied

by a heavyset, short man dressed in blue overalls. Mike held out his hand to Bill. "I'm Mike Lobo. If you have the new numbers, Carlos will change the combo."

Bill handed Lance Aerospace's index card to Carlos, who updated the lock.

Mike turned to Carlos. "Thanks for helping. You can go now."

Bill opened his desk drawer and pulled out the Top Secret envelope that contained the newest X-909 space plane information. "Here's the stuff for your safe."

Mike signed and dated the envelope. "What else can I do?"

Ryder said, "We'll go over a lot tonight at the meetin', but I've got ideas we should discuss now."

Mike sat down. "Okay."

"We need a surveillance camera aimed at this office with a microphone, too."

Mike nodded. "We should set it up tonight. Rita told me the Scarlet Hauk investigation ends close of business on Friday. So, if we put the word out tomorrow morning about Bill using a company's phone number for a combination, then the spy might try to open the safe tomorrow night."

Bill pointed at his office wall. "The room next to mine has been empty for months. You could put a TV monitor in there and hook it to a hidden camera in here to watch the safe." He reached into his trouser pocket and extracted a key ring. "Here's the key."

"Carlos can make copies. Plus, I'll have keys made for your office door."

Ryder said, "I was thinkin' of telling Lucinda about the company phone number and the combo late this afternoon, but I won't do it until tomorrow."

Bill raised his hand. "Don't forget to tell Leon Turk he has to write an X-909 press release."

"He'll be in the office to gloat and watch me empty my desk before I leave tonight. I'll tell him then. Josh might be there, too."

Mike said, "Rita reported Sullivan is dragging his feet to

fire you, so you can still enter base for a while." He paused. "We'll set up surveillance of this building outside to watch all the doors. I'll ask Rita for agents to pose as roofers."

Ryder turned his attention to Bill. "You talked about making fake plans for the X-909 with your CAD-CAM program?"

"I'll do it here tonight after the FBI meeting."

Ryder stood. "I need to clean out my desk. If Leon's in the office, Blackie can sniff him."

Mike said, "Blackie may hit on several people who wore the coat. I wouldn't let the dog check out people now. I vote we move fast to set the trap instead."

"Okay," Ryder said.

Mike stood. "I need to order the camera setup."

Bill caught Ryder's attention. "At four-thirty, I'll drive my car to the public affairs parking lot and wait for you. From there, I'll follow you to the FBI meeting."

Ryder nodded. "We got plenty of time before the meeting. We'll grab a meal on the way."

EIGHTY

RYDER WALKED BRISKLY through the public affairs corridor. He glanced into Leon's office. The big man stared at him and smiled in an offensive way. As Ryder turned the corner into his office, he cast his eyes left and saw Josh's door was open. He had returned to his office.

Lucinda sat near her desk, on which she'd placed a cardboard box. Her eyes were red and puffy. "I was worried you forgot to come by for your things." She stood and moved toward him. "I'm sorry you have to go." She gave him a strong hug and gazed up at him like she wanted a kiss.

"I'm sorry I have to leave, but I wasn't meant to be a public relations guy."

Lucinda pulled back from him and fixed her eyes on his. "Just the opposite. You are a great public affairs officer. You'll go far in the field no matter where you end up."

Although he didn't want to disappoint Lucinda by leaving abruptly, Ryder decided he had to move quickly. "I see you found a box for my stuff." Ryder glanced toward the cardboard container.

"It was the least I could do, and I'll help you gather the rest of your things." She moved toward his desk.

Ryder followed her. "I don't have much." He opened his desk, found a bag of dog treats, and tossed them into the box.

Lucinda gestured at the back of the office door. "Let's not forget your jacket." She took it off its hanger, folded the garment, and put it in the box.

Suddenly, Leon Turk stepped into the office. "I'm overjoyed you're gone, Luke. Now this office can run like it should, without an amateur gumming up the works."

Ryder stepped closer to Leon. "I was at the Unitary to see Bill Little. He said they've had a design breakthrough with the space plane. They're gonna build a prototype. He says he needs a press release written."

"I'm relieved you won't be around to screw it up. Josh reassigned me to the X-909 beat."

Lucinda appeared ready to kill, but she turned away and sat down at her desk.

Ryder bit his lip and then said, "I'm not fired yet, and you might see me around base. Maybe Sullivan will give me a different job at Ames."

"Keep out of our offices." Appearing smug, Leon did an about-face and headed to his office.

Lucinda whispered, "What a pompous ass." She turned to Ryder. "My offer still stands. If you need a couch to crash on, I'll loan you mine. You can have a key to my place while you conduct your job search. If you're hungry, come over tonight, and we can have dinner."

Ryder smiled. "Thanks, Lucinda, but I'm meeting with a buddy tonight. How about we have breakfast tomorrow morning? I know you're an early bird."

Lucinda's face brightened. "Charlie's Café in Mountain View opens at five in the morning. I could meet you there at about six."

"It's a date, then. I'm paying. I ain't as broke as you think."

EIGHTY-ONE

WITH TIME TO kill before the FBI meeting, Ryder and Bill spent more than an hour and a half eating and talking at a family restaurant in Mountain View.

Just before the meeting was to start at six-thirty, they arrived at the FBI house in Sunnyvale. Sunset wouldn't be for an hour and a half, but the sun's blinding rays were already cutting across the horizon at a low angle. The temperature had dropped into the midsixties.

When the two men met on the sidewalk before entering the bungalow, Ryder smelled dampness in the air. It had been bone dry almost all the time since he'd arrived in California. The humid air seemed to relax him, like the air in Kentucky did.

"I smell rain," he said.

Bill said, "The weatherman forecast late-season showers in the next couple of days. After that, we'll be dry until fall."

"I'm not used to this arid climate," Ryder said. "I'd welcome rain." Then he pointed at the FBI's rented house. "That's where the task force meets."

Bill surveyed the old stucco house. They climbed the

bungalow's creaky porch steps, and Ryder unlocked the front door.

Rita walked to the two men. She seemed to have calmed down after she had learned of Ryder's firing. She said, "Mr. Little, I'm Rita Reynolds." She offered her hand.

Bill sat next to Mike near the whiteboard.

Rita pulled Ryder aside. "You and I will be in the office next to Bill's room to do the close-in stakeout. Any objections?"

"No." Ryder noticed her voice was softer, subdued. She studied him for an extra moment as if assessing if he was angry with her for her having been upset with him earlier in the day. She smiled at him and brushed her hair into place.

Then Rita moved to the front of the gathering and summarized what Ryder, Mike, Bill, and she had planned. "At Mike Lobo's request, I've assigned agents from our San Jose field office to pose as roof repairmen. Heavy rain is forecast for the next three days. So the rooftop team will put up a construction tent tomorrow morning on top of a building near the Unitary's back entrances." She caught sight of Mike. "Mike, can you give us details about the setup at the Unitary Wind Tunnel Complex?" She sat down.

Mike swung his head from side to side to view everyone present. "We figure if a spy bites, he or she will visit Bill's office after midnight. The rooftop team will monitor the area using night vision equipment. We'll all be in radio contact on a scrambled, secure frequency."

Mike pointed to a simple map drawn on the whiteboard. "This is a rough drawing of the Unitary complex. The X shows where the rooftop team will be stationed."

He took a pen from his breast pocket and pointed at the sketched map. "This is Building N-230, the Physical Sciences Research Laboratory, which is very close to the Unitary complex. The ground team will stand by in an unused room there. It will be equipped with TV monitors that will show Bill Little's office and locations inside and outside of the Unitary. Henry Dunbar, two agents from the San Jose field office, and I will be ready to back up Luke and Rita when an arrest is imminent. They will be in the room next to Bill's office. Rita, could you explain how this thing should go down?"

Rita stood. "The rooftop team will keep eyes on all Unitary doors, and when a suspect goes inside, they will alert the team. A TV camera and a microphone will be installed in Bill Little's office. Luke and I, as well as the roof team and the backup team in Building N-230, will all have TV monitors and audio. After the perp opens the safe, grabs the documents, photographs them, and then leaves the office, Luke and I will make the arrest. Also, as soon as the spy exits the office, the backup team from N-230 will move in to help with the arrest, if needed. Additional thoughts?"

Ryder stood up and shifted his weight to his left foot. He felt his voice muffle as he began to talk. "We gotta lure the spy to our trap, like we're fishin'. I'll put out bait. As y'all know, Blackie hit on strap odors in the Public Affairs Office. Tomorrow, I'll have breakfast with Lucinda Lu and mention Bill Little uses an index card to recall his safe's combo. She's a nonstop gossip, so she will spread this info across public affairs and beyond." He surveyed the team members. "Bill should invite Leon to meet in Bill's office tomorrow to discuss a new space plane public affairs plan. Also, Bill should be sure to refer to the index card with the combo on it, open the safe, and leave the card on his desktop."

Agent Dunbar raised his hand and waved it. "Is Leon our main suspect?" Henry concentrated his attention on Ryder.

Ryder glanced away at a window. "I wouldn't eliminate him." Ryder sat down, and his heartbeat slowed to a normal rate.

Mike said, "I'll also spread the rumor."

All the participants wore somber expressions on their faces.

Rita said, "Unless anybody has a comment to share, mingle. Afterward, unless you have tasks, go home, sleep. We may not get much rest in the next several days. Let's meet tomorrow morning in our room in Building N-230 no later than eight."

The team members stood and began talking. Their conversations were quiet and serious.

Rita approached Ryder and handed him a Glock pistol bag and an FBI vest. "Here." She grabbed his bicep and squeezed it reassuringly.

Ryder smiled, and Rita reached into her purse and handed him a badge. "This is temporary."

Ryder now knew he was still part of the team, and they trusted him. He felt the pistol bag. Grasping it made him feel like he was with a good friend. "I gotta go 'cuz I'm meeting Lucinda at Charlie's Café in Mountain View at six in the morning."

Rita patted his back. "Sleep well if you can."

EIGHTY-TWO

THE PLUSH GREEN easy chair in Ryder's apartment was comfortable, and he was as tired as a soldier who'd marched twenty-five miles over rough terrain. The chair was next to a large picture window overlooking the deck and the grassy backyard. Relaxing in the darkness of his room, he felt his eyelids droop and fought to keep them open. Although he'd set his alarm clock, he still had to brush his teeth before going to bed.

The rear porch light was off, and the view through the window was restricted to the night's blackness.

In a flash, bright light invaded the darkness when the motion-activated security light above the porch illuminated.

Startled, Ryder squinted. Two vivid animal eyes shone like mini flashlights in the murky semidarkness of the backyard. The dim, almost invisible form of a large California opossum appeared near the yard's six-foot-tall redwood fence.

Ryder was surprised by how fat the opossum was compared to those of Kentucky. The beast climbed atop the wooden fence and followed it away from the brilliant light.

The surveillance light's bulb dimmed and extinguished,

and Ryder again relaxed as soothing darkness enveloped him. He breathed easily, and sleep overtook him.

In a dream, he heard repeated tapping at his large window. His logical self questioned whether the sound was a figment of his imagination…or was someone or something really rapping on the window?

Groggy, he gazed at the dream-altered window, now partly obscured by an odd, greenish fog. He jumped when he saw a woman's eyes peering through the glass amid a cloud-like, billowing mist, lit by a dim night light plugged into a nearby wall.

The woman peeked at him, waved, and then rapped on the window once again. She appeared to be in her twenties and had a pixie hairdo.

"Luke Ryder. It's me, Gina. Let me in."

Ryder stood up and felt his body float toward the door, which he unlocked.

Gina, the robot, entered.

"What are you doin' here, Gina?"

She sat on the couch near the chair, barely visible. "I'm here because I don't need a lot of sleep, and I wanted to find out what progress you've made in your investigation."

"Why?" Ryder sat in his chair, so tired his bones felt weary.

"I wish to learn your techniques because I'm being groomed for special investigations."

"Who do you work for?"

"It's classified."

"If you're studyin' to be in law enforcement, you know I can't say a damned thing to you about an ongoing investigation. Besides, I ain't nothin' special. I just been lucky."

Gina leaned forward in the near-total darkness of the room. "You lack confidence, but in time you'll gain it. I know. I have access to much information."

"How is it you didn't set off the light outside?"

"I disabled it so I wouldn't startle you."

Ryder felt his breathing slow. In his dream, he fought to

keep his eyes open, but they closed for a moment. When he forced them open again, Gina was gone.

Ryder was so exhausted the night light appeared to spin. At once, he slipped into an even deeper sleep.

Yet stranger dreams unfolded. Ryder saw a man's mouth and teeth drift toward him. Ryder focused on the man in the darkness, and a piercing spotlight lit the man's face. He was Leon.

"Luke, you're a total failure and deserve to lose. That's it. You're a loser and a liar…liar…liar…"

Leon's form evaporated into a smear.

A fencer's saber flew at Ryder, and he jumped aside just as the weapon stuck in the rough wooden floor at his feet. He hadn't noticed before that the flooring in his dream had become rough-cut pine boards, unlike the beige carpet in his actual apartment.

Hysterical laughing from his right gave Ryder a fright, and he turned.

Josh strode toward the weapon, pulled it from the floor, and glared at Ryder. "You incompetent hillbilly. Leave and let us do the job properly…properly…properly…"

Josh leaped toward the wall, and it dissolved to let him escape into the purplish-black night.

A breeze swept strands of someone's soft, black hair across Ryder's face. A petite woman stepped away from his left side and into view. It was Lucinda.

"Luke, Luke. I feel sorry for you because, though you are dedicated, you have absolutely no talent except to muddle through things. You depend on luck, not skill. I'm sorry for you because I hate to see you fail."

Ryder took a step toward Lucinda. "You'll still be my friend, Lucinda?"

Before she could reply, her form drifted into smoke smelling of incense.

Holding hands and appearing zombie-like, Nigel and Rita walked into the room.

Rita frowned. "You've done a terrible disservice to the

FBI by embarrassing the Bureau. I'm totally disappointed. Just quit…quit…quit…"

Nigel's eyes were blank. "I am so sorry I brought you here. You do belong in the woods among the animals. Go back home to the holler. Live the simple life you can handle. You can't solve Scarlet's murder because you're not up to the job. It's not your fault you're not too bright…not too bright…not too bright…"

Nigel and Rita began to waltz and danced away into the mist.

Layla appeared. She stepped forward and kissed Ryder's lips. Her clothes fell away. "Come home…home…home…"

Ryder hugged her, but she vanished into the air, and his arms felt nothing. He fell into a swirling, dim fog, and time seemed to speed faster and faster.

An alarm clock rang, and Ryder awoke in a sweat. The memories of his dreams slipped away in seconds, and he felt unsettled. Still dressed, he rose from his easy chair. The clock read 5:00 AM.

Should he close his eyes for two minutes? He sat down again, but when he nearly fell asleep, he willed himself to stand and turn on the lights. Ryder had to get moving. It was going to be a consequential day. He'd come up with an idea of how to catch a spy who might've killed Scarlet. Rita had given him one more chance to collar the killer. If his plan failed, would she be drummed out of the FBI? Ryder steeled himself.

EIGHTY-THREE

RYDER WAS TIRED. He dragged himself to his bureau and selected fresh clothes. He'd scheduled a breakfast date with Lucinda at six at Charlie's Café in Mountain View. Afterward, he had to meet with the FBI task force at Ames' Building N-230 near the Unitary complex.

Ryder quickly showered and prepared to leave his apartment. He also laid out plenty of food and water for Blackie, since the dog would remain at Ryder's rental for the day.

Traffic was already heavy at five-thirty, and Ryder was five minutes late for his breakfast with Lucinda. As he entered the eatery, he saw her straightaway in her shiny, red plastic rain slicker.

She waved to him from a booth in the far corner of the café.

He shook the water from his light jacket in the vestibule near the front door.

As he neared her, she asked, "Where's Blackie?"

Ryder sat in the booth across from her. "He's at my place, sleeping. I didn't want to have him get all wet following me around. The rain's soakin' everything."

"We need it. The drought's cooked California dry."

Lucinda twisted in her seat, and her raincoat crinkled. "Did you sleep well? Being kicked out of our office could've made it hard for you to rest."

"I didn't sleep much."

"Leon Turk is a true bastard. Pardon me for using that word." She rolled her eyes. When Lucinda used a swear word, it was a rarity.

A hostess stopped by the table. "What would you like, sir?"

Ryder smiled. "A cup of black coffee."

As the server left, Lucinda said, "Maybe you should have a Danish pastry or something else, too?"

"When the waitress comes back, I'll order bland food. Maybe whole grain toast, scrambled eggs, and oatmeal. My stomach's queasy." He took a hasty breath. "I'm gonna stop over at the inspector general's office and report Bill Little. It's making me nervous."

"What did he do?"

Ryder purposely sucked extra air into his lungs. "Yesterday, he opened his safe to show me the latest space plane test data. The updated design is much better, and they're gonna build a prototype. Anyway, I saw him take an index card from his address spindle and use the phone number on it as the combination to open his safe."

Lucinda squinted. "He used the phone number as the combination for his safe?"

"He told me he used to call the locksmith to open his safe when he forgot the combo, which was often. The locksmith may have given him the idea."

"Why tell the IG? Could you think of a different way for Bill to remember the combination?"

Ryder sighed. "I doubt he'd listen to me. I'll tell the IG that Bill has a poor memory, and they could suggest something. I figure the IG will lecture him on security, that's all."

Lucinda shook her head. "It might be better if you told somebody in Ames security because the IG is known to go after people. But security might be almost as unacceptable." She paused. "Why not ask the locksmith to talk with Bill?"

"That's an idea."

Lucinda cocked her head. "Did you see the name on the index card?"

"It was a company's business card, and I remember the logo. It was Lance Aerospace."

"If you can recall it, anybody could." Lucinda zeroed in on Ryder's eyes. "I could tell the locksmith if you don't want to."

"Okay, go ahead. I guess I won't tell anybody."

Lucinda sighed. "Thank God." She frowned. "But there's an alternate way. As much as I don't like Leon, I could ask him to clue in Bill Little that using a company's phone number for a high-security safe combination is a no-no."

Ryder shifted in his seat. "It wouldn't hurt."

She sat up straight and snapped her fingers. "I'll ask people who know Bill to help him figure out an alternate way to recall his combination."

The waitress brought Ryder's coffee, and he ordered his breakfast. After she left, he said, "Telling folks who know Bill might help."

"I'm positive it will."

Ryder sipped his steaming black coffee and prayed Lucinda would set off a tsunami of rumors about Bill and his safe.

Lucinda concentrated on Ryder's eyes. "I'll get right to work and talk to the locksmith and Bill's friends. We need to keep him out of trouble." Ryder inwardly smiled, suddenly certain she'd set off a cascade of talk. Mission accomplished. He relaxed and enjoyed his breakfast, eating slowly. He'd need his strength in the next few days to possibly nab a spy and maybe a killer, too.

EIGHTY-FOUR

BECAUSE SULLIVAN LOGISTICS hadn't fired Ryder yet, he still had his contractor identification and had no trouble driving through the checkpoint at Ames' main gate. He parked a block from Building N-230 to prevent anyone from noticing his truck near the Unitary. A steady rain pummeled the sidewalk, and Ryder donned a blue, waterproof light jacket.

It was roughly nine hours before Rita and he were to begin their stakeout of Bill's office.

Ryder entered Building N-230 near the Unitary complex and tapped on the door of the previously vacant room, which the FBI team now occupied.

The door cracked open, and Mike Lobo peered around its corner. "Thanks for coming in early, Luke."

When Ryder entered, he saw a bank of TV screens displaying views inside and outside of Bill Little's office as well as the exterior entrances of the Unitary complex.

Rita, Henry Dunbar, and FBI agents unfamiliar to Ryder sat around a table drinking coffee and eating doughnuts.

Rita smiled. "Need a bite to eat while we go over things, Luke?"

"I need coffee. I didn't get enough shut-eye." Ryder slipped off his wet jacket, filled a cup with coffee, and sat at the table.

Mike said, "As I was saying when Luke arrived, we have full surveillance of the Unitary area. Our guys posing as roofing contractors have set up a tent on the roof." He turned to a neatly drawn map of the Unitary and its environs. "Icons on this drawing show camera locations. These cameras are infrared capable so we can see in dark conditions." He sat down.

Rita said, "Agent Dunbar will be in command of the team here in Building N-230. I'm in overall command, but if I can't be contacted or am incapacitated, Henry will head the operation." Rita paused. "One minor detail, bathroom breaks. We have a camera with a view of the hallway so we can see if anybody is around before Luke or I visit the restrooms. Since we think a perp would try to open Bill's safe late at night, we won't see many people around this building or in the Unitary at that time. Bill said there aren't any nighttime Unitary tests scheduled for the next week."

Henry raised his hand. "How close are the bathrooms?"

Rita replied, "Forty feet down the hall."

Mike set down his coffee cup. Ryder thought the man's hippy-like ponytail seemed to poke from the back of his head. "Our guys on the roof, including me, will have night vision binoculars," Mike said. "We'll scan areas farther away and out of camera view." He scrutinized the people sitting around the table. "The weather is supposed to be rainy tonight. As Californians know, it's rare to have heavy rain this late in the season. If there's a power failure, we have backup batteries."

Rita nodded. "Can anybody think of anything else we need to do?"

The room was silent.

Ryder said, "I had breakfast with Lucinda Lu to start the rumor mill going. After I told her I might turn in Bill to the inspector general, she said she'd talk to the locksmith and Bill's friends to ask them to help him figure out another way to remember his combination. I bet she's already spreadin' the word that Bill's safe combo is an open secret."

Mike wiped his mouth with a paper napkin. "Let's hope a spy bites."

Rita said, "Happy hunting, guys."

EIGHTY-FIVE

BANNED from the public affairs offices, Ryder entered the cafeteria at midmorning to get a snack.

Still fatigued from a lack of sleep, he drank another cup of coffee. Just as he finished eating a sweet roll, his mobile phone rang. The device's screen showed Bill Little's name.

"What's up, Bill?"

"I'm concerned the killer might show up here during lunch."

Ryder shifted the telephone against his ear. "We have the Unitary and your office under video surveillance, and agents are on standby."

"I thought you guys were focused on a late-night attempt."

"True, but the task force is on alert. Leave your door open when you break for lunch." Ryder glanced out the window. "I'll stop by. I'm in the cafeteria cooling my heels."

Bill shuffled papers and the sound of them came through Ryder's phone. "I could use a bit of company. I'm continuing to create bogus documents."

* * *

IN TEN MINUTES, Ryder knocked on Bill's office door. "Everything will go well, Bill. Agents are watchin'." He waved at the camera position. "Hi, folks."

Bill pointed to where he thought the hidden camera was. "It's fortunate I didn't have a visitor until now. I could've said something stupid." He sat down at his computer and glanced at a space plane drawing on his screen.

Ryder's eyes locked onto the colorful X-909 picture. "Slick artwork."

Bill smiled. "Yes, but this baby would explode if an enemy built and flew it."

Ryder's mobile rang. Candie's name popped onto the phone's screen. "Hold on, Candie. I gotta move to a place where I can talk."

"Okay, Mr. Luke."

Ryder walked into the hallway and then entered a front entrance foyer. A steady drizzle washed across the foyer's two glass doors. He leaned against a wall, and it was cold. "Candie, before you start talking, I gotta say you and me aren't meant for each other."

"Luke, I call you 'cuz Bengie take picture me with no clothes with you. He hide in bedroom. I not know he take picture. Now, he want money not to e-mail picture me topless with you to your friend, Layla. He say flower shop losing money. He need money. I not his partner. He boss. I no want go back to Korea."

Ryder felt his face light up like a red hot coal. "So, he's blackmailing me?"

"What you mean, Luke?"

Ryder's pulse pounded. "What I mean is it's as illegal as hell what y'all are doing."

"Please, Luke, come to flower shop to give money. I no want go back Korea. Please."

"I'm real busy today and tonight. If I decide to come over, it can't be 'til tomorrow at noon."

Ryder thought if he delayed the Koreans, Rita could figure out how to arrest Bengie. Ryder wondered whether or not Candie was innocent. She was a B-girl. Was she a prostitute, too? How did Bengie get into her bedroom when he and Candie were at the Dilly Dally Dance Club?

Ryder's mind snapped to the present when Candie said, "I ask Bengie if tomorrow okay. He in back-room."

"Wait. How much money does he want?"

"Ten K. What 'K' mean?"

Was Candie acting stupid on purpose? "One 'K's' a thousand dollars. Why would Bengie think I have that much cash lying around?"

"He say he know man in San Jose can give loan no question to you."

"Oh, yeah?"

"That what Bengie say. Now, I ask if noon tomorrow okay."

"Wait, tell him if he sends pictures to Layla, he won't get any money, and he'll regret it."

"Regret?"

"He'll be sorry he did it. And both of you will go to jail and be deported to Korea."

Candie gasped. "I tell him." He heard her set her phone on a solid surface.

Ryder realized it was imperative he tell Rita about the blackmail attempt as soon as possible. She'd be irate, and he reckoned she'd also worry arresting Bengie could interfere with the Scarlet Hauk investigation. But if he met Benjie tomorrow during the day, it would be fine. A spy wouldn't dare to open Bill's safe during normal working hours.

Ryder heard Candie pick up her phone. "Bengie say, okay noon. He not send picture yet, and he get money man be here, too, so he loan money."

"What's the money man's name?"

"I not know."

"I'll be there." Ryder disconnected.

Craving a shot of bourbon, he instead took out a pack of peppermint gum and began to chew a stick of it. Even if the task force caught Scarlet's killer or a spy, and the FBI credited him for his contribution, it wasn't worth the mental anguish. Working undercover was too tough.

He'd locked his FBI Glock in his truck's toolbox. He wished he could touch the weapon because that would make him feel confident, even if all else went to hell.

Ryder selected Rita's name on his phone's contact list. "What's going on, Luke?"

"People are blackmailing me. A guy by the name of Bengie took pictures of me and a B-girl, who's no doubt a hooker, too. She was near-nude, but I was fully clothed. Bengie's threatenin' to e-mail the pix to Layla if I don't pay him ten thousand dollars."

Ryder could hear Rita gasp and then exhale like a locomotive venting steam. "What the hell were you thinking? First, it's life on an exoplanet. Now you're cavorting with a nude prostitute."

"It was a setup. I went to what I thought was a coffee shop with a woman who works at the flower store, where I'd ordered flowers. I felt sorry for her. She's a young Korean lady, possibly a recent immigrant."

"I bet. What are you planning to do about this?"

"I put off meeting Bengie, the Korean owner of the flower shop, until tomorrow at noon." Ryder's throat felt congested. "Perhaps y'all could set me up with a wire. The FBI could arrest the guy on a blackmailing charge, extortion." He paused. "Nobody's gonna try to open Bill's safe at noon in broad daylight."

Ryder heard Rita breathe easier. "The Bureau's been going after people for sextortion."

"What?"

"That sort of extortion often involves underage kids and young women, but it covers other sex crimes, too."

"I never heard anybody call it sextortion before." Ryder sighed. "There's something else. Bengie's gonna have a money man meet with me. Said the guy will loan me ten grand on the spot. It sounds like loan sharking."

"It is," Rita said. "Henry Dunbar's trying to track down a San Jose loan shark because there's a rumor somebody at Ames owes him big money. It's part of the Scarlet Hauk investigation. Could be the same guy. Now this flower shop stuff sounds a lot better."

Ryder felt less agitated. "So you can wire me for sound?"

"Yes. I'll call the San Jose office. They'll jump on it because it should result in arrests." The tone of Rita's words showed she'd calmed down. "I hope you'll be free later tomorrow to help me with Bill's office stakeout if a spy doesn't show up tonight."

"I will be."

She was silent for a moment and then said, "I can't wait to wrap up the Scarlet Hauk investigation." She paused. "Come over to Building N-230 now. We'll continue to plan for tonight's stakeout and the flower shop sting. Bring your weapon."

EIGHTY-SIX

THE FBI TASK FORCE MEMBERS, including Ryder, stood by in a room in Building N-230 in the late afternoon. They waited for darkness to fall and the potential arrival of a spy in Bill Little's Unitary office. The team had discussed, reviewed, and double-checked their plans.

Rita and Henry were on the phone with the FBI's San Jose field office setting up a sting at the flower shop for Friday noon to arrest Yun Min-Gi, a.k.a. Bengie, and Kang Hyo-Ri, a.k.a. Candie, for extortion and possible loan sharking.

Two long workbenches supported an array of TV surveillance monitors, one of which included a view of Bill's office. Ryder glanced at that monitor when Leon Turk, Josh Sable, and Lucinda Lu entered Bill's workspace.

Bill's voice boomed through the monitor. "Thanks for coming. I didn't realize a whole crew would be here."

Leon said, "Building a space plane prototype will be one of NASA's most important stories this year, so we're going to provide a lot of support. We'll make a public affairs plan, write half a dozen press releases, and hold press conferences."

Bill stood. "I'll get another chair."

While Ryder's eyes were fixed on the video view of Bill's office, he waved to Rita and Henry and pointed at the TV monitor.

Rita ended her phone call, slipped into a chair next to Ryder, and said, "Seems like overkill with three public affairs people crowding into Bill's office."

In two minutes, Bill was back, pushing a chair. He sat on it near his safe. "I have our new space plane plans and drawings locked up."

As he reached across his desk, Bill took his time to remove the Lance Aerospace index card from his address spindle. He carefully referred to the card while he twisted the combination dial. "Folks, I want you to keep the new info about the space plane confidential until I give you the word to release it. A bit of the stuff is top secret, and, of course, you won't get to see that portion of the information, just the noncritical material."

Rita smiled. "Bill's overdoing it."

Ryder noticed Lucinda had opened up a laptop computer and had begun to type.

Bill's eyes drifted to view Lucinda. Leon said, "She's just keeping notes so we don't forget anything."

Lucinda stopped typing and cracked a smile.

Josh said, "I'm here to let you know the space plane news release, and the rest of the X-909 public affairs activities are the top priority of our office."

Bill reached into the safe, removed a folder marked "Top Secret", and set it in the middle of his desk. "I don't want this one." He pulled a second folder out marked "X-909 info for Public Affairs."

Rita rolled her eyes. "Bill's so blatant. He's hitting them over the head with those bogus top secret documents."

Ryder laughed. "Yep, he's getting the point over."

Bill passed three sets of documents to the public affairs people. "Here's a package of general information you can release to the public. You'll notice fabrication of a prototype space plane will be done at the Desert Rat Works near Edwards Air Force Base."

Leon said, "We'll need slick animation of the plane taking off and flying into orbit. Do you have funds you can contribute to make it?"

Bill nodded. "Give me an estimate after you work it out and let's see what we can support."

Ryder, Rita, and Henry Dunbar watched as the public affairs planning session continued for twenty minutes.

Josh stood. He held a compact black umbrella in his left hand. "Sorry, but I have to leave." He paused. "Leon, please give me a summary of the meeting by Monday's staff meeting."

"Yes, sir."

Ryder stared at a monitor with a view of people leaving the Unitary Wind Tunnel Complex like lines of ants moving through a tropical forest during a rainstorm. Most had umbrellas or scampered toward their cars and trucks, holding jackets over their heads. He peered at the monitor with the view of Bill's office. Josh had already gone.

Rita said, "I have a feeling this public affairs meeting will wrap up soon. The Unitary should be deserted in about ten or fifteen minutes because of the weather. Traffic will be a nightmare." She paused a moment. "We'd better get ready to move into our positions. The spy may show up soon."

Ryder put on the shoulder holster that held his FBI Glock pistol. He felt butterflies in his stomach, but once things began to roll, he guessed he'd feel self-assured.

EIGHTY-SEVEN

RYDER WORE a light jacket that covered his shoulder holster and Glock pistol. He touched the weapon, and confidence streamed into his body.

He could hear the wind whistle as rain splattered against the window near him. He and Rita sat in the room next to Bill's office.

The slight flicker of three TV monitors in front of them was hypnotizing. Luckily the room was chilly, which kept Ryder alert. The hot coffee he sipped—and even its smell—helped keep him awake, too. He stood and refilled his mug from a large coffee jug atop a gray metal table.

The time was nearly 9:00 PM, and the storm, which had abated an hour and a half ago, now picked up steam again as a second front passed through.

A rumbling sound in the distance made Ryder squint through a window.

Rita said, "They'll report thunder and lightning on the ten o'clock news as the top story. It's rare to have thunderstorms in the Bay Area."

"I didn't know that. We get so many thunderbolts back in the holler. It seems normal." He scanned the three monitors.

One displayed a view inside Bill's office, and two additional TV pictures showed both directions of the corridor outside of Bill's door.

Rita sipped steaming coffee and then said, "This is so boring."

"Yeah, but if it happens, it'll go down fast."

Rita caught Ryder's eyes. "After being up all night, I hope you'll be alert enough tomorrow to be effective during the flower shop operation."

Ryder set his mug on the metal table. "I'll get my shut-eye in the morning. Nobody's gonna try to get in the safe during regular hours."

Rita rubbed her chin and then sat up straight. "Let's hope Bengie doesn't send pictures of you and the hooker to Layla before we cuff him." She smoothed her hair. "Carol Cuddy still likes you, in case Layla goes her separate way."

"Carol's just a good friend, not a girlfriend."

"If things go to pot, you can count on me." She paused. "The FBI needs people like you. You could help us with special assignments. I could work that."

Ryder inhaled sharply. "I kinda like being a deputy sheriff, but I hope Pike will also let me do public affairs work when I'm back in the holler. I enjoyed being a fake public affairs guy, but I didn't like NASA office politics."

Rita stretched. "I've been drinking too much coffee, and I need a bathroom break. Call if anything happens."

"Okay." Ryder turned the volume up on his push-to-talk, two-way radio and checked the squelch.

EIGHTY-EIGHT

FOR A FEW FLEETING SECONDS, the first quarter moon peeked through a break in the rumbling, fast-moving clouds like a partly closed eye peering down from space.

The rainfall was steady on the roof of the building where Mike Lobo stood under the protective cover of the construction tent. He looked through his night vision binoculars, scanned Boyd Road, and then gazed into the distance at De France Avenue. He depressed the transmit button on his two-way radio. "This is Roof calling N-230 Control."

"Go ahead, Roof."

"The area is as deserted as a ghost town. Roof out."

An instant later, a strong bolt of lightning struck the Unitary complex with the bang of a howitzer artillery piece firing. The smell of ozone diffused through the air.

Plugged into building power, the TV cameras mounted on the roof near Mike Lobo fizzled and went dead.

"N-230 Control, this is Roof. We lost all cameras and monitors."

The smell of burning electronics mixed with a chlorine-like odor.

Henry's voice emanated from Mike's radio. "This is N-

230 Control. We lost all cameras, too. Must've been a wide-spread power surge. Roof, watch all Unitary exterior doors."

"This is Roof. Copy."

The rain beat down.

Inside the room next to Bill's office, Ryder stood up. The acrid smell of scorched electronics irritated his nostrils. Rain pummeled the window behind him, and then a louder noise rapped the glass like machine-gun fire.

White hail pellets piled up on the outer windowsill.

Ryder pushed his radio transmit button. He whispered, "This is Room A, callin' N-230 Control."

Henry said, "Go ahead, Room A."

"Our cameras and monitors are burned out. Backup power isn't workin'. Out."

Henry's voice crackled with static. "Room A, a power surge fried all electronics connected to the outlets in the Unitary complex, too. We have eyes on all the outside Unitary entrances. We don't see anybody. Where's Rita?"

"N-230 Control, this is Rita. I'm on a bathroom break on the opposite side of the building. A commode in the ladies' room near Room A must be blocked, and the floor's flood-ed." Her transmission broke up. "…be out soon."

Though rain now slapped at the windows of Room A, its sound had diminished. Ryder heard quiet clicking and then the creaking sound of Bill's office door as it swung open. Ryder put his ear against the wall and heard what sounded like the squeak of leather shoes.

He pushed his transmit button and whispered, "This is Room A. I think we got company in Bill's office. Standby. We gotta wait till the perp opens the safe and starts to leave the room. I'm gonna wait outside the office door."

Ryder leaned against the corridor wall outside Bill's doorway. The door of Bill's office was ajar, and then Ryder heard the safe's heavy door open with a metallic clank and strike Bill's steel file cabinet.

Ryder heard what sounded like a folder opening and papers making noises. He listened to the rapid clicks of a digital camera while its flashes lit the hallway through the crack of the open door.

The sound of what must have been the folder being replaced in the safe put Ryder into an even higher state of alert.

A thud sounded as the heavy safe door closed, and the noise of the safe's dial as it twirled followed.

Rita's voice came through Ryder's earpiece. "I'm on my way. There's just one working emergency hall light."

Henry spoke into his radio. "This is N-230 Control. Take positions inside Unitary."

Bill's door opened. Ryder saw two eyes peering from slits in what could have been a ski mask. The figure exited the office. Something metallic was in the intruder's hand.

Ryder stepped back from the wall, his Glock drawn. "FBI. Freeze!"

The figure launched a karate front kick through the gloom. Ryder sensed the swift move. His body reacted with primal instinct. He leaped aside, but the assailant's foot hit Ryder's right hand. His Glock fired and clattered away into the darkness. The shot's sharp crack boomed and echoed throughout the hallways, and the musty, sulfuric smell of gunpowder pervaded the air. Ryder planted his feet firmly. He threw a punch. The perp evaded the blow.

Lightning illuminated Bill's office window. For a moment, Ryder saw the silhouette of his enemy holding a stiletto blade.

Ryder's earpiece vibrated as a voice shrieked, "Shot fired. Move in."

Rita was already running as fast as she could through the Unitary's far-reaching hallways, her footfalls slapping the tiled floor.

Ryder twisted his torso and focused on his foe in the inky darkness.

The masked aggressor lunged forward, a knife blade flickering in the perp's hand.

Ryder jumped aside. But the thin, longish blade grazed Ryder's windbreaker. He tripped on an empty cardboard box next to the corridor's wall. He grabbed the carton. He raised it to protect his head and chest.

Ryder's foe jabbed at him again.

The scalpel-sharp blade slid along the top of the box toward Ryder's throat. But the knife's tip dove down and bit into the cardboard. The hilt had stopped the weapon's path forward, two inches short of Ryder's windpipe.

Like an air raid warning, primal screams of "kill, kill" erupted from the aggressor's lips.

Ryder cast the cardboard box aside, the knife still impaled in it. He tackled the figure.

Surprise glinted from the attacker's eyes, visible through the mask's slits.

The perp grunted and grabbed Ryder's throat. The aggressor's arms and hands were strong. He tightened his grip.

Ryder saw stars. He struggled to breathe.

"Shit." Ryder heard himself gasp as he clutched the perp's throat. Ryder squeezed with all his power.

The aggressor's grip loosened. Ryder rose and drove his enemy backward. The figure fell. With a sickening crack, his head hit the sturdy tiles that overlaid a hard concrete floor. The stocky man went limp like a marionette whose strings had broken. Ryder let go of the aggressor's throat.

Ryder ripped off the man's black mask.

Someone aimed a flashlight on Ryder and his enemy. Rita asked, "Who is it?"

Ryder grunted, "Josh Sable."

Josh Sable's eyes stared blankly upward.

Ryder checked for a pulse.

There was none.

The struggle had seemed like an eternity to Ryder, but it had occurred in far less than a minute. He stood and felt dizzy, but at least time now moved forward at a normal pace.

An FBI agent stopped near Rita, and Rita said, "Call an ambulance."

After the agent began to walk away from Rita, he tapped

his cell phone's contact list. As he began to talk out of Ryder's earshot, Ryder rubbed his neck.

Rita asked, "Luke, you okay?"

His voice hoarse, Ryder said, "Just sore." He sat against the corridor's wall. "I don't need an ambulance. Josh doesn't either 'cuz he's dead as a rock."

Rita neared Ryder. "You positive you're not injured?"

"If he'd squeezed me any longer, he would have crushed my windpipe."

Rita moved closer to Ryder and examined his throat. "You should be checked at the hospital."

Ryder pushed himself to a standing position. "I'm okay. I gotta take down Bengie tomorrow instead of waiting in an emergency room."

Rita stood. "I'm thrilled you nailed Josh. Then again, I'm sorry he's dead and won't face trial."

"He almost did me in."

Rita sighed. "I'm responsible for part of this." She glanced down the dark hallway. "A toilet in the ladies' room was clogged, and the floor was flooded in sewage, so I went to the far side of the complex to another bathroom. I should've gone into the men's room."

FBI agents canvassed the building, their pistols drawn, checking rooms for possible threats.

Ryder picked up his Glock and holstered it. "You shouldn't blame yourself for any of this, Rita."

She caught Ryder's eyes. "How did Josh slip past us? We had guys with night vision binoculars watching all the entrances."

Ryder stroked his throat. "His clothes are dry, and so are his shoes. He never left the building after his meetin' with Bill." Ryder scanned the hallway. "He must have holed up in a room."

Rita nodded.

EIGHTY-NINE

BY EARLY MORNING, the FBI task force had finished its search of the Unitary complex following the death of Josh Sable.

Ryder slept on a fold-out canvas cot in the FBI's room in Building N-230. Neck pain woke him, and a beam of sunshine lit his body as he sat up.

Rita heard him stir. "Your throat is as purple as the eggplants we used to grow back home in the holler."

Ryder caressed his throat and drew air into his lungs. "I need a turtleneck sweater when I do the flower shop sting."

"We'll find one for you. Maybe I can get a doctor here to take a quick look."

"Nope. I just got a slight headache. Got aspirin?"

Rita rummaged through her purse. "Here." She handed him a tin of painkillers. "I'll get a bottle of water."

"I need to nab the Koreans before they send those pictures to Layla, and y'all send me packing."

Rita unscrewed a water bottle's plastic cap and handed the container to Ryder. "You're not on the chopping block anymore." She checked the wall clock. "It's after 10:00 AM on the East Coast. Fifteen minutes ago, the director of the FBI called me from Washington. He praised us. We're getting all the time we need to wrap up the Scarlet Hauk investigation."

Ryder swallowed three pills with a mouthful of water. The cold water coursing down his throat felt soothing. "Why would the top man call?"

"The X-909 is a top priority for the Department of Defense. We caught a spy, and you are receiving full credit. We've been commended, and you'll get an award. The chlorophyll episode has been forgotten."

"That's positive, but we don't know if Josh killed Scarlet Hauk or not." Ryder paused. "I feel sick 'cuz of what happened with Josh. I wish he wouldn't have died."

Ryder turned his head, rubbed his face, and shed secret tears. "Killing somebody is like killing a part of yourself." He handed the pill tin back to Rita. "We could've interviewed him and tied up loose ends."

Rita gave Ryder a hasty hug. "FBI counselors help people to deal with this kind of an incident."

"No, thanks. I got Blackie."

Rita paused and then said, "We'll likely learn details about Josh this morning when we search his apartment, which will add to the info we obtained earlier this morning."

"What?"

"He hid in a janitor's closet and left an empty soda can there. Thank heavens for the instant DNA test."

Ryder blinked and stroked his face again. "It's odd nobody figured he would stay in the building."

Rita shrugged. "Droves of people left at the same time. We assumed Josh was among the people who ran for their cars through the rain."

Ryder said, "On second thought, it's understandable."

Rita sat next to Ryder on the cot, and her body slid against his. "We found items in the janitor's closet—a developing tank and photographic chemicals in a storage container under boxes of cleaning supplies. The microdot was made the easy way, not using a modified microscope, and likely was processed in the closet."

"Then he's gotta be the microdot spy, too."

"What was his motive?"

Ryder scratched his unshaven stubble. "I believe Josh owed a lot of money. He was a poker player who went to Vegas every year for a poker tournament. He used to have an expensive sports car, but later he got a junker. Being hooked on gamblin' is like being addicted to booze, which I'm familiar with."

Rita stood. "Do you feel well enough to come with us when we search Josh's apartment?"

"Yep. The aspirin's kickin' in."

"We leave in ten minutes. Ride with me."

"Okay. It'll give my body time to recover." He paused. "What about my truck?"

Rita held out her hand. "Give me the keys. I'll have the guys park it by your apartment after somebody buys a sweater for you. They'll leave it in the front seat."

Ryder handed her his keys.

NINETY

RITA PARKED her heavy-duty black SUV near a typical three-story apartment house in a large complex of buildings, where Josh had rented his flat.

Six duplicate buildings were in the center of the compound, surrounded by covered parking spaces. Ryder guessed each structure might contain as many as a dozen units.

Rita had come to the complex armed with a search warrant.

"You sure got that warrant fast," Ryder said.

Rita smiled. "That happens when it's an urgent matter of national security." She exited her vehicle and scanned the area.

A sign on a one-story building at the center of the complex read, "Management Office."

Just as Rita reached into her purse and grabbed her badge, two FBI vehicles carrying crime scene technicians stopped nearby. She signaled them to wait.

When Ryder opened the apartment manager's office door, a bell jingled, and a man with white hair came out of a back room and met them at a counter.

"What can I do for you folks?" The fellow had a contagious smile.

Rita displayed her FBI badge. "We have a warrant to search Mr. Josh Sable's apartment. Could you please open it for us?" Rita handed the manager the warrant.

The old man's brow wrinkled, and his expression changed to concern as he read the document. "What'd he do?"

Rita said, "We're not at liberty to say."

In minutes, Ryder, Rita, and three FBI crime scene technicians were at Josh's door. The aged manager unlocked the apartment, and Ryder glanced in. The place was neat for a bachelor's flat, but the furniture was an old style and worn.

The crime scene techs split up and took pictures of the entire residence before Rita and Ryder began their search.

Rita went into the bedroom and rifled through dresser drawers while Ryder walked to a desk in the living room and opened the top drawer. He saw a sturdy, miniature envelope the size of a business card. When he opened it, he found the key for a safe deposit box.

"Rita, I got somethin' here."

Rita abandoned her exploration of the bedroom and approached Ryder.

Ryder held up the envelope. "A safe deposit box key from the Mountain View Community Bank."

Rita grinned. "The search warrant includes his safe deposit box. The bank's a block away in the strip mall we passed."

Ryder handed Rita the key. "When's the bank open?"

Rita consulted her watch. "At nine. We can take our time here." She noticed a metal picture frame and broken glass scattered on the desk. A cardboard mounting board had damage where multiple objects had been torn from its surface. "What's this?"

Ryder said, "Josh had this picture frame hangin' on the wall in his NASA office. He glued poker chips from different Vegas casinos to the mounting board." Ryder inspected the damage on the board. "I guess he was so short of funds he had somebody go to Vegas to cash 'em in. Chips have to be redeemed at the casino where they came from."

Rita nodded.

Ryder stared at the key Rita held. "I'm anxious to see what's in his bank box. I wager there ain't any money."

"It's a place to start. We need to check out his friends and relatives, too, but top priority is to learn who his handler was."

NINETY-ONE

RITA PULLED into a parking lot next to Josh's bank. She turned to Ryder. "Let's hope for something that'll point to Josh's handler."

Ryder began to open the passenger door. "I'm more interested in figurin' out who killed Scarlet 'cuz if we do, my part's done."

Rita swung her door open before Ryder could get to it. "I've been hopeful we can keep you working for us."

"Undercover stuff ain't my bag." He paused. "And I never kilt a man before."

Rita locked her arm with his. "I hear you." She squeezed against him. "There's a lot going on inside you."

Ryder stared at the blue sky and breathed in the clear air that had been cleansed by the recent rain. He was silent as they entered the bank, and he fought back a teardrop that tried to seep from his eye.

Rita knocked on the glass wall of the bank's management office.

The branch manager, a man of East Indian descent, held up his hand as if to indicate he was busy.

Rita slapped her badge against the glass.

The man caught Rita's eyes, sized her up, rose, and then opened his door. "Yes?"

Rita unfolded her warrant and handed it to the skinny, high-strung man. "I need access to Mr. Josh Sable's safe deposit box."

The man spoke in a strong Hindi accent. "Have a key?"

Rita held out the key.

The manager said, "Follow me."

Within minutes, the box was open, and the branch manager left Ryder and Rita alone in the vault.

Rita lifted the elongated, slender top of the metal box. "Not much here." She reached in and withdrew a hand-written document.

Ryder leaned closer to Rita. "What's it say?"

She squinted at the papers in her hand. "The handwriting isn't neat." Rita started to read it aloud. "I don't know if this confession will help me when I meet my maker or not. In the event of my death, please deliver it to Father George Mancini at the St. Mary Catholic Church in Mountain View." Rita silently read on. Her hands trembled, and she caught Ryder's eyes. "He admits he had a gambling problem and owed a lot of money."

Ryder sighed. "Josh was figurin' he wasn't long for this world."

Rita's eyes scanned ahead in the document. "Here's our big break. He confessed to Scarlet Hauk's murder."

Ryder let out a breath. "Nigel can have closure."

"It's signed and dated December 24, 2029." Rita concentrated on Ryder's eyes. "We still have to find Josh's handler."

"I doubt I could help 'cuz my cover won't stick. Even if I were still at NASA public affairs, I wouldn't want to work for Leon, who's next in line to be news chief. He'd be worse than Josh."

"We'll talk about it later." Rita dug deeper into the bank box. "There's something else in here." She fished out a wrist-watch. "This watch belonged to Scarlet. Josh mentions it in the confession." Rita dangled the timepiece and then continued to read from the paper in her hand. "He claims here the watch has a digital audio recorder inside it, and Scarlet recorded him trying to blackmail her to get space plane information. She was about to turn him into security."

"How would he know she'd recorded him?"

"Odds are she wore a concealed wireless microphone, and there are gadgets able to detect them. My guess is he used a cheap bug detector. When our guys turn over his apartment, they may find it."

"If you're lucky, the audio could lead to the handler."

"Yep." Rita examined the watch closely. "They make electronic equipment so miniature these days." She dropped the watch into an evidence bag, labeled it, and did the same with the written confession.

As they left the bank, Ryder noticed the wall clock read 9:30 AM. "Your guys got to wire me for sound soon."

Rita smiled. "First, we can stop at your place to get your vehicle and the new sweater and then talk about your role with the FBI while we're at it."

"Okay. I need to feed Blackie, too."

NINETY-TWO

RITA PULLED her SUV behind Ryder's truck, which was parked at the curb near his rented Sunnyvale in-law suite.

Ryder grabbed a new green turtleneck sweater from his vehicle's front seat.

They walked through a gateway into the backyard of a large house, where Ryder's rental building stood. When he unlocked the door, Blackie happily wagged his tail to greet them.

Rita kneeled and petted his head. "Blackie, you should get an FBI award, too."

Ryder said, "He's getting rest now, which he needs. I'll put him in a dog carrier and have him flown to Lexington after the flower shop sting is done. Pike can pick him up."

Rita stood tall. "I've heard sometimes dogs end up in the wrong city, and a few die." She studied Blackie. "I can watch him until you come back from Alaska."

"That'll be great, Rita. Thanks." He clapped, and Blackie came to him. "When I planned the cruise two months before your undercover thing sprung up, I never guessed I'd have to figure out how to send Blackie back to Kentucky from California."

Rita peered out the window into the backyard. "The weather's perfect here, and I bet you like it. Perhaps you could help out the FBI San Jose Field Office later on." She concentrated on Ryder's eyes. "The director of the FBI thinks you'd be a great asset. You seem to have magical ESP powers that solve crimes."

Ryder let out a breath. "Kentucky's my home. My sister's there. And then there's Jim Pike."

"You have friends here. Me, for one, and your cousin Nigel, too." Rita took a seat on the couch and patted the soft cushion beside her. "Let's talk about the flower shop operation."

Ryder sat next to her.

She said, "It's important to get the Koreans to incriminate themselves enough to make it easy for us to convict. They need to ask for money from you, and you should agree. If the loan shark's not there, give them eight hundred bucks. Here."

Rita handed him the money in hundreds and twenties, and she said, "Let's hope the loan shark is there, too. Delay them. Hang loose until we enter the scene. If you hand money to Bengie, say, 'Here's your cash, now give me the digital pictures.'"

"My gut tells me Candie's a victim. She might have been trafficked, and sure as shootin' Bengie's got her under his thumb. See what you can do to check into her situation."

"You're saying I should give her a break? I don't think so. She's a manipulator who took advantage of you."

Ryder pictured Candie. How had she been smuggled into the country if she'd been trafficked? Had she been raped? Was she a woman who'd lost hope and now followed her master's every command? Or was she as rotten as Bengie? Ryder heard himself speak.

"At least investigate to see how she got where she is now."

"I'll be fair."

Ryder pondered the upcoming flower shop operation. What if something unexpected happened? "What if I decide y'all shouldn't burst in? What signal should I give you?"

Rita thought for a moment. "Take Blackie with you. If you want us not to move in, you command Blackie to lie down. If you want us to rush in, tell Blackie to come here."

"I like it."

"We make a first-class team." Rita gave Ryder a quick hug.

Ryder felt warm inside.

Rita fished her cell phone from her purse. "You seem extra confident now that we know you were correct. Espionage was the reason for Scarlet's killing. You took out Josh, too."

"I'm kinda hurtin' 'cuz Josh died."

"I can set you up with an FBI counselor after your Alaskan cruise."

"I'll think about it."

"You should leave now to get wired up." Rita fingered her phone. "I need to stay here and make calls. I'll tell the flower shop team our dog signal plan."

Ryder pulled on the new turtleneck sweater. "Fits great."

Rita studied him. "It covers the neck bruise perfectly."

NINETY-THREE

RYDER PARKED his rental truck near the Simply Flowers Shop. The hot pavement and the dazzling sunshine made him regret his need to wear a turtleneck sweater to hide the bruising on his throat.

As he crossed the blacktop with his bloodhound, Ryder updated the FBI team through the microphone concealed under his shirt.

"I arrived."

Ryder noticed a car down the block, where two FBI agents waited. Shortly thereafter, he encouraged Blackie to trot faster toward the cool shade under the flower shop's awning. After he reached the front of the store, he peered through its window and saw Bengie behind the counter, speaking to a man whose back was turned.

A bell jingled as Ryder opened the front door, and the man who was talking with Bengie turned and glanced at Ryder.

Blood rushed to Ryder's face, and sweat dribbled down his back.

The man was Rocky Diaz, the male stripper and owner of Clean Sweep Janitorial Service.

Ryder took an even breath so as to appear calm. He straightened his shoulders and approached Bengie and Rocky.

Blackie's claws clattered on the cool, tiled floor.

Ryder smiled. "Bengie, we got business to attend to."

"We do." Bengie glanced at Rocky. "This is a friend of mine, Rocky, who's a loan agent representing Easy Loans, Incorporated. Rocky's aware you might be in need of funds."

Ryder nodded. "Where's Candie?"

"In the back room. Let's go there and talk things over. Rocky can stay out here until we're done."

Rocky sat down on a chair near the counter.

Ryder and Blackie followed Bengie through a bead-strung curtain.

Candie was on a wooden stool next to a large computer screen. Her eyes were red as if she'd been crying. She shifted her eyes downward and stared at the floor.

Ryder said, "Hi, Candie."

She blinked. "Hi, Luke." She seemed like a fragile fawn that had lost her mother.

Ryder could hear her sniffle.

Bengie said, "Candie, show him the pictures."

She turned to her computer keyboard and clicked the mouse. An image of Ryder standing near Candie, who was topless, appeared on the screen.

Ryder pointed at the picture. "Candie's damn near nude, but I got all my clothes on."

Bengie smiled like a lecher enjoying a peep show. "I wonder what your girlfriend, Layla Taylor, would think of it though. I could send her this picture, actually a dozen. We also have a video of you and Candie when her nightie drops off, and she gives you a lovely hug."

"If I give you ten grand, how do I know you won't keep askin' for more?"

Bengie shrugged. "You'll have to trust me. As a side benefit, I'll let you visit Candie in her apartment once in a while for a fee." He turned to Candie. "You'd like that, wouldn't you?"

Candie blushed.

Ryder stepped closer to Bengie, and so did Blackie. "You still haven't answered my question. Will you ask me for more money in the future?"

"I'm a man of honor, and when I make a deal, it's a deal." Bengie grinned like the fictional Cheshire Cat.

"You got me over a barrel. Let's talk to Rocky."

Ryder and Bengie returned to the counter.

Bengie winked at Rocky and nodded.

The man stood and considered Ryder. "You need cash?"

"Ten thou."

Rocky said, "The deal is this. My associates charge forty percent a month. Payments are due on the first day of each month in cash, and I do the collecting. I suggest you don't miss a payment because Easy Loans will take action to promptly get their money." He reached into his shirt pocket. "Here's the contract. It shows terms, interest, fees, and stuff like when your loan would be paid off. Just sign. I get the carbon. You keep the original. Questions?"

"Just give me the cash." Ryder signed the contract and gave Rocky the carbon.

Rocky took a paper shopping bag from behind the counter and handed it to Ryder.

When he opened the bag, Ryder saw a bundle of hundred-dollar bills. "I'm gonna count this."

Bengie said, "Sit behind the counter, so nobody can see you."

Ryder thumbed through a hundred bills. "It's all here."

Rocky grinned. "Make your payments to me as instructed in the contract." He left but stopped outside and lit a cigarette.

Ryder caught a glimpse of the two FBI agents who still sat in their car down the block and across the street. All of a sudden, they surveyed the area and began to open their doors.

Bengie said, "I have a way you can pay off the loan fast."

"How?" Ryder glanced at Blackie. "Lie down, Blackie." Ryder squatted near the hound and petted him. He tossed the bag of cash to Bengie, who caught it.

"I'll give you twenty-five hundred back tomorrow if you can get me certain documents from NASA. It'll be easy."

Ryder continued to stroke his dog. "What do ya think I should do, Blackie?" Ryder had a view out of the front window. Now out of their car, the two FBI agents stopped in the middle of the parking lot and chatted.

Ryder got up. He worried Bengie might see the agents arrest Rocky. "Let's talk in the back room."

"Certainly."

Candie now sat in a worn easy chair in a corner of the room.

Bengie pointed at her. "Go watch the cash register."

Candie stood. "I sorry, Luke. I'm still your friend, I hope." She left the room.

Ryder asked, "What kind of stuff do you want me to get?"

"I heard gossip you're covering the X-909 space plane. Find important documents about it, and I'll go through them. If they're what I want, I'll give you the money, enough for your first payment and then some."

"If I get caught, I'll go to jail. Who are y'all getting this info for?"

"I can't say, but they have plenty of cash. You're in a great position to get information because you're in public affairs." He paused. "If you're lucky and get us classified or confidential stuff, like about magnetic levitation and how the space plane would use it, you can pay off your loan and make big bucks, too."

"What's magnetic levitation?"

Bengie shrugged. "It's the same force that floats trains over their tracks so the train cars can fly above the rails without touching them."

Ryder leaned on the computer table and ran his hands through his hair. "Let me think it over, and I'll call back today or tomorrow." He tapped the computer. "If I get you info, I want to see you delete the original pics and video. And I want Candie to be my friend."

"I can do that." Bengie held out his hand. "I think this is the beginning of a great partnership."

Ryder shook Bengie's hand, and the Korean grinned. "I'll let you know how to get the stuff to me. Just call."

"Okay." Ryder turned and found his way out of the shop with Blackie trailing behind him.

NINETY-FOUR

RYDER LEFT the flower shop and entered his truck. He chose Rita's number on his phone's contact list and rested the device against his ear.

"Luke, we're tailing Rocky and watching the Koreans. Meet me at your place to regroup."

In five minutes, he was at his rental, and moments later, Rita arrived.

As Ryder was unlocking the front door, she said, "I thought about our next step." She moved to the couch. "Demand a large amount of money. Say you know you can get top-secret space plane documents."

Ryder relaxed on the couch next to her. "I was thinkin' the same thing." He sipped from a can of ginger ale and set it on the coffee table. "How about I ask for fifty thousand dollars? I'll tell 'em I've got the combo for Bill's safe, and I saw Bill put a top-secret folder in it. I'd suggest that I could open the safe after hours tonight when the Unitary's deserted."

"Call now. His phone's tapped."

Ryder caught Rita's eyes and said, "Something's botherin' you." He frowned. "Are you wonderin' if Josh called the Koreans or if he maybe called somebody else to sell the info?"

Rita pursed her lips. "I think when Josh learned he could use the phone number to open the safe, he decided to move fast. More likely than not, he figured if he didn't act right away, Bill might change the combo or move the file. I doubt he called anybody."

Ryder said, "The Koreans sure aren't actin' like they knew Josh planned to open the safe. Could be he called someone else, though." Ryder scratched his scalp. "Rocky might be connected to Josh. Josh was a poker player, and he could've been in debt to Easy Loans." Ryder pointed at his belt. "Remember Rocky was wearing a Vegas belt buckle at the restaurant? Maybe he knew Josh from Sin City?"

"We'll find out when we question Rocky." Rita smoothed her blouse. "He faces lots of charges and never has been arrested. He'll take a deal and talk like crazy."

Ryder shifted his position on the couch. "Did anybody listen to the recording on Scarlet's spy watch?"

"I don't know. As soon as our guys can, they'll send a transcript to my phone."

"Anything else we should discuss before I phone Bengie?"

"No. Call now."

Ryder pulled his mobile from his pocket. After entering the flower shop's number, he used his speakerphone feature.

Ryder recognized Candie's voice. "Simply Flowers."

"Candie, is Bengie there?"

"I get him now, dear."

Bengie came on the line. "Did you make a decision?"

"Yup. I can get you top-secret space plane info." Ryder waited for a brief moment. "But it'll cost fifty thou. You won't be sorry."

A rustling sound came through Ryder's earpiece. "Okay, but I'll give you twenty-six on delivery. I'll pay the rest if it's as important as you say."

"I'll get it tonight. How do I pass it to you?"

"There's an unusual tree by the public affairs parking lot. Place it in the hole in the trunk. Somebody will pick it up."

"I'll call when it's there, but I believe it'll be there by seven-thirty."

"Good. But next time, we'll do business in person. When you call me, only say, 'Your present is in the mail.'"

"Got it."

Bengie hung up.

Ryder put his phone in his pocket. "Mike's put cameras around the tree. But better warn him and Bill."

"I'll call them," Rita said. "And we'll put two men in a car in the public affairs lot, too."

"I better be the guy who puts the stuff in the tree in case somebody's keepin' an eye peeled." Ryder squinted. "I suggest we put it on a thumb drive in an envelope."

"That'll work." Rita stood. "Go back to NASA. I'll stay here to make phone calls. If things work out, we'll raid the flower shop tonight." Rita bit her lip. "Don't mention magnetic levitation is related to the space plane. The details are top secret."

"I'll get moving," Ryder said.

NINETY-FIVE

THE AIR WAS pollution-free and cool after the recent rain. It was early evening when Ryder pulled away from a parking spot near the Unitary Wind Tunnel Complex. Three minutes later, he stopped in the lot near the public affairs building. He'd left Blackie with Rita at his apartment.

Ryder carefully viewed his surroundings as he walked toward the hollow tree. He carried a thick manila envelope containing a thumb drive with fake top-secret information recorded on it. He felt like he was about to bait a coyote trap with a chunk of meat.

He didn't see anyone on the nearby streets, but his gut told him Bengie's courier was watching from a window somewhere. Ryder reckoned a custodian or a groundskeeper would be the person to pick up the package. Unlike the vast majority of NASA employees, cleanup crews worked late and had access to most areas of the research center.

But why hadn't Bengie asked Ryder to place an empty Mexican cigarette pack near the tree? Ryder considered whether or not it was beyond the realm of possibility that two separate spy rings would use the same tree for a drop. If so, perhaps only one of them used a cigarette pack as a signal. On the other hand, maybe Bengie figured he'd talk to Ryder about a drop-signal later.

Things were happening fast. Was Bengie reacting to developments too quickly, not thinking through all future possibilities like a good chess player would? Imagining what could happen at least three moves ahead would have been wise.

With sunset a half-hour away, the glare on the horizon irritated Ryder's eyes. When he approached the tree, he could smell its musky odor. As obviously as possible, he placed the envelope containing the thumb drive in the hole in the tree.

As soon as Ryder was back in his truck, he called Bengie.

"Simply Flowers Shop. How may I help you?"

"Your present is in the mail."

"Be here at nine. Watch me open it."

Bengie hung up.

Ryder called Rita and left a message he'd completed the drop, and then he drove back to his apartment. When he opened the door, Rita was sitting on the couch, speaking into her cell phone.

She waved and smiled but continued to talk. "Call you back later. Luke just came in."

Ryder stood near the coffee table. "Any news?"

"Mike said a custodian picked up your package, put it in a black plastic trash bag, and tossed it in the back of his pickup truck. He drove out of the main gate. Two of our guys are following him."

Ryder came closer to Rita. "I left you a message. Bengie wants me to arrive at the flower shop at nine."

"We'll put your wire back on, and we'll move in when the time is right. I'll loan you my Beretta. He'd spot the Glock." She reached into her purse and handed him her weapon, a Beretta Nano 9mm micro-compact pistol.

"Thanks." Ryder held the firearm in his hand and felt power and confidence stream into his body.

"I'll get you a shoulder holster and ammo." She smiled. "The guys listened to the audio stored in Scarlet's wristwatch. We learned Josh had pictures of her making love with Rocky and threatened to post them on the Internet unless she gave him secret space plane info."

Ryder sat up straight. "Talk about a tangled web. What's next?"

"When we arrest Bengie tonight at the flower shop, we'll nab Rocky at the same time. Then we'll question everybody."

Rita's phone rang. "Hello?" She hung up after a half-minute and said, "The team's in position near the flower shop. The tail saw the janitor stop by a dumpster and throw the bag in. Bengie retrieved it and went inside the shop."

Ryder smiled. "I hope he likes the bogus plans."

"Bengie's no expert. He'll pay you."

"I can't wait to see him in cuffs." Ryder paused. "But let's go easy on Candie."

NINETY-SIX

AN OWL HOOTED in the distance, and a quarter of the moon dimly lit the dark night. At 9:05 PM, Ryder rapped on the glass door of the darkened Simply Flowers Shop.

His mobile rang.

"This is Bengie. Change of plans. Meet me in Presidential Park. It's two blocks from my store."

"I know where it is." Ryder leaned against the shop's outside wall. He assumed Bengie had seen him arrive by means of his doorbell security camera. Was the man inside the shop or someplace else monitoring the camera via his mobile phone? Ryder brought his phone closer to his lips. "Why the change?"

"Two cops are watching the shop from half a block north. They're in an unmarked car."

Ryder glanced down the street and saw the stakeout. "I see 'em."

"If they start to follow you, we'll scrub the meeting until later. If not, I'm in a thick grove of trees behind the picnic benches."

Ryder began to walk toward the parking lot. "I'll call if they follow me."

"I have a partial payment for you. I liked the present."

Ryder disconnected his mobile and got in his truck. He tapped Rita's name on his cell phone. "We heard it all, Luke."

"Should I pull off the wire before I meet him? He could be suspicious."

Rita exhaled. "Keep it on. I'd rather know if things go south."

"I'll drive to the park now."

"Wait. The team has to reposition."

Rita radioed her agents, and they began to deploy into new positions. She jostled her phone. "Luke, wait three minutes, then go." She disconnected.

In an instant, Ryder's phone rang. He heard Bengie's voice. "What's taking you all this time? The park's two blocks away."

"I had to use the restroom at the gas station near the park."

"Why'd your phone go to voice mail?"

"My pants were down. Couldn't reach it."

"Hurry. I have a job for you if you want it." Bengie hung up.

NINETY-SEVEN

RYDER STOPPED his vehicle near Presidential Park. He adjusted Rita's tiny Beretta pistol in its underarm holster. Handling the weapon amplified his confidence. The lethal bullets and the gunpowder within them made him feel more powerful and certainly not helpless.

"Folks, I'm gettin' out of the truck now and headin' for the picnic tables. Then I'll go into the grove of trees. It's real dark there."

Ryder slammed the truck door, hoping Bengie would hear it. Maybe the man would be able to recognize Ryder in the moonlight when he crossed the park. Or would Bengie at least see Ryder's silhouette?

Leaves rustled as Ryder approached, and he wondered if opossums lived in the woods.

Ryder called out, "I'm here, Bengie."

"I'm in the trees, thirty feet from the middle picnic bench." Bengie's voice sounded higher, as if he were nervous.

Ryder put his right hand on the pistol under his arm as he slipped into the darkness of the grove.

"Bengie, how the hell are we gonna do business in the dark?"

"I have a flashlight."

After Ryder had gone about twenty feet into the trees, he smelled decomposing leaves underfoot.

The quarter moon shone through an opening in the treetops.

Ryder cocked his head and used his side vision to peer into the darkest part of the woods.

Bengie's form seemed to float like a ghost near the trunk of a huge tree. "I see you, Bengie."

Ryder now stood under the opening in the trees, and moonlight lit him. He realized he was an easy-to-hit target.

Bengie stepped forward, now easier to see. "Come closer, Luke."

Bengie raised a .45 caliber pistol and aimed it at Ryder.

"What the hell, Bengie? Why are you pointing that piece at me? Where I come from, people doin' that might get iced."

"Take no offense. I'm just going to check you out."

Ryder stepped into a dark shadow, slipped Rita's loaned Beretta from its holster, and concealed the firearm behind his trouser leg.

Bengie said, "Come closer. I'll pat you down."

"How do I know you're not gonna kill me?"

"Don't worry. I have a potential assignment for you. I'm interested in smart robots. You get me stuff about them, and you'll earn a lot of coin. Stop there."

"I don't like this."

"Relax." Bengie tapped Ryder's chest and felt the microphone. He began to step back out of Ryder's reach.

Ryder dove to the ground the instant Bengie squeezed the trigger of his .45 caliber weapon.

Time inched forward in slow motion. The shot boomed and echoed among the tall trees. Acrid gun smoke invaded Ryder's nose.

Ryder rolled left just as Bengie's next shots pounded the ground inches from Ryder's chest.

Ryder flipped over. He fired the Beretta three times.

Bengie fell, sprawled to his left. *He should be dead*, Ryder thought.

Bengie spun.

Ryder fired.

Bengie threw himself aside. He returned fire. His .45 caliber slug hit Ryder's Beretta, which was in front of his chest, flinging the miniature pistol into the darkness. The whine of the heavy bullet's ricochet echoed in the trees.

Ryder scrambled to his right. Another bullet screamed by his right ear, and he heard a deafening bang. Ryder dove toward a pile of dead, fallen tree limbs. He grabbed one and hurled it at Bengie's face.

The stick poked the Korean's eye. He screamed.

Ryder slapped Bengie's pistol to the ground. He slugged the Korean three times.

The man collapsed.

Ryder took a deep breath, pulled handcuffs from a rear pocket, and tightened them onto Bengie's wrists.

Ryder heard footsteps coming through the leaves that littered the ground.

A flashlight beam shone on him and Bengie.

Rita asked, "You okay, Luke?"

"Yeah, except for my poundin' heart." He sighed. "This one should've been dead, but he's wearin' a vest."

Four FBI agents appeared, their weapons trained on the unconscious Bengie.

Ryder stood.

Rita hugged him. "I'm grateful you're okay." She pulled away from him. "It's fortunate I loaned you my Beretta."

Ryder peered into the darkness. "It's around here some-place. It took a .45 caliber slug. But it sure as hell saved me."

Rita shined her light across Ryder's body. "You're not hurt?"

"Just winded."

Rita glanced at Bengie. "We have an ambulance on the way to take him to emergency. His smashed-up face tells me you hit him super hard." She paused. "I think you should be checked out. Bullet fragments could've hit you, and you might not know it."

"No thanks. I don't like sittin' around in emergency rooms for hours."

"Let's go to your place. I can debrief you there." She patted his shoulder. "I can give you a once-over to confirm you're okay, and I have news about Rocky."

Henry Dunbar arrived.

Rita turned to him. "Please take over here. I'll debrief Luke at his place."

"Yes, ma'am."

NINETY-EIGHT

MINUTES after they left the park, Ryder and Rita entered Ryder's apartment.

Rita bit her lip. "I need to satisfy myself that a bullet fragment didn't hit you."

Ryder slumped on the couch. "I told you I'm okay."

She frowned. "Take off your clothes except for your shorts. You forget. I'm in charge."

He blushed and stood. "You're overdoin' it."

She stepped toward him. "There's blood on your sweater. Take it off."

Ryder removed it and the shirt beneath it. "A dead branch scratched me when I dove down away from the shots."

"You need stitches." She walked closer to him and examined his right shoulder. "This is a three-inch-long cut."

"I have butterfly bandages in the medicine cabinet."

Rita sighed. "Go into the bathroom, drop your underpants, and check yourself. Then come out here with those bandages and antiseptic if you have it."

A short time later, Ryder emerged from the bathroom. He

carried a box of butterfly bandages and a bottle of rubbing alcohol. "I'm fine."

She took the alcohol and the bandages. "Sit on the couch. I'll grab paper towels from the kitchen."

He put his socks and trousers on. "I'm anxious to hear about Rocky."

Rita kneeled close to him and tipped the alcohol bottle to dampen a towel. Her body touched his as she cleaned the laceration. "You should have gone to the hospital." She poured more alcohol on a fresh towel and soaked the wound.

He recoiled.

"Hold still." She stuck tape across the tear in Ryder's skin. "I'll search the medicine cabinet for gauze."

Though Ryder's body ached all over, he felt relief, closed his eyes, and enjoyed the blackness.

Rita returned from the bathroom with additional first-aid supplies and finished bandaging the wound.

She caressed him. "I'm happy you're not dead." Her voice was laced with emotion. She let go of him. "Please join the Bureau. You're renting the farm. Pike wouldn't stand in the way, even though he'd like to keep you on his team."

"I learned a lot. Thanks for that. I'm confident I could go undercover again, but I need a breather, and I want to see Alaska with Layla." He stared at the window into the darkness.

"You have my personal number. Call me anytime, day or night." Her voice was husky. "I care for you."

"I like you, too, Rita." Feeling sudden warmth inside his body, he waited a prolonged moment, drew air into his lungs, and then said, "Tell me about Rocky."

Her cheeks flushed. "Two members of the San Jose office who specialize in espionage interrogated him. They offered him a deal if he'd answer all their questions. Even so, he'll get at least fifteen years in the pen. He was loquacious."

Ryder appeared puzzled. "You mean he sang like a squealing wheel bearing?"

"Yes. Rocky said Bengie is North Korean. Bengie will

likely be in prison for the rest of his life for attempted murder, espionage, human trafficking, and assorted other charges."

Ryder straightened his back. "North Koreans play dirty."

Rita's face displayed a serious expression. "Yes, and Candie was trafficked from Seoul in South Korea. She's scared the North Koreans might find a way to kill her."

"You're gonna do what you can for her?"

"Yes. She gave us valuable information. Said Josh asked Bengie to buy GHB, and Rocky dropped it into Scarlet's drink during her bachelorette party."

"Is GHB what I think it is?"

"It's a date rape drug. It doesn't smell, and you can't taste it. It's also called easy-lay."

"Scarlet may not have known she was raped?"

"We've confirmed Bengie shot pictures and video when Rocky took advantage of her. Then Bengie gave the pictures to Josh, so he could blackmail Scarlet to get the space plane information that Bengie wanted."

"Bengie's a slimeball. I don't feel guilty for smashing his face in."

Rita patted his knee. "Anything else you'd like to know?"

"Is it okay if I call Nigel? He's gotta have closure."

"Go ahead." Rita studied Ryder in the yellowish lamplight. "I can stay for a while, or we could have lunch tomorrow."

"Lunch is better. I'm tired." Rita kissed Ryder's cheek and left a lipstick smudge on his swarthy skin. "I'll call tomorrow."

Ryder escorted her out before he phoned Nigel.

Ryder said, "What I'm gonna tell you can't go any further than us for now."

"What's going on?"

"Josh Sable killed Scarlet."

Nigel was quiet and then said, "That's why I didn't see him today." From the sound of Nigel's voice, his throat was congested, and he spoke in a higher, emotional tone. "You arrested him?"

"He died last night in a struggle outside Bill's office. We'd caught him opening Bill Little's safe. He was workin' for the North Koreans."

"Holy Christ."

"Also, tonight, a North Korean spy shot at me, and I slugged him. The FBI arrested him. I'll fill you in tomorrow with more detail. I need rest."

"You okay?"

"A scratch is all."

"Thank God." Nigel let out a breath. "I owe you."

"Nope. You're family." He paused. "I have advice for you, though."

"What?"

"I have a feelin' you like Lucinda Lu 'cuz of how I've seen you look at her. Even though she's a secretary in your organization, ask her out."

Ryder heard Nigel suck air into his lungs and then let it out. "Maybe I will. I can make an exception. She's a wonderful person. Things are much better, thanks to you, cousin."

"The FBI task force and Rita did a lot, too." Ryder paused. "I wonder who'll replace Josh as news chief."

"Not Leon. He's an arrogant son of a bitch. Reminds me of a politician who's delusional about his power. Confidentially, our investigators learned Leon was the one who gave a copy of Gault's exoplanet research to Chuck Singh. They were lucky because Singh got scared when he somehow learned the FBI was investigating Scarlet's death. He ratted on Leon. It's rare to fire someone from a government job, but I'm going to kick Leon Turk's ass out of NASA on Monday." Nigel's voice was tense, and then he sighed as if his muscles suddenly had relaxed. "It just struck me Jenny Rogers, our young public affairs officer, is an ideal candidate for news chief. She's as smart as a Mensa member. She's polite and friendly, and I've noticed her leadership skills, so I'll give her a shot."

"Great decision." Ryder paused. "What are you gonna tell the NASA staff?"

"The bare minimum, if anything, until the FBI tells me what info I can release. In fact, I'll take the easy way out and refer all questions to the FBI public information officer."

"How are NASA employees going to react?"

"The usual. There will be a thousand rumors, but I'll write a letter to the Ames staff that our people should not come to unfounded conclusions. I'll say we're waiting for the FBI to brief us with the facts." Nigel sighed. "The local, national, and international news media are going to bombard us with questions. There'll be TV cameras staked out at the front gate…It'll be a nightmare. But at least I know Sable's dead…Who would've known he'd murder someone, especially Scarlet? At least I have closure." Nigel exhaled and was quiet.

Ryder's eyelids drooped, and he saw soothing darkness. "I gotta hang up now 'cuz I'm as tired as a horse that's been plowin' all day. I'll get the FBI to tell you everything they can tomorrow."

After Ryder disconnected, he scanned his cell's contact list and touched Layla's name.

The phone rang six times.

"Luke." Layla sounded sleepy.

"Sorry to call at this hour, but I want you to know it's all over. We caught the bad folk."

"How'd it happen?"

"I can't tell you until the FBI says it's okay." He coughed. "I don't feel like talking about it much anyway, maybe later."

"I understand."

Ryder rubbed his eyes. "I miss you. I need you. Could you get on a flight to San Jose or San Francisco this Sunday?"

"I'd fly around the world for you, honey. I'll be on the next plane I can get on. What about Angela?"

"Call my sister, and she can watch her. I talked to her about it weeks ago when I was plannin' the Alaska trip. Pike will check on the farm, and the rest of the guys can keep stuff under control." He paused. "You'll need to pack for a week-and-a-half cruise."

"I've been waiting and hoping for this moment. I love you so much."

"I can't wait to see you, hold you, and then fall asleep close to you."

She said, "I can tell you're real tired. Better hit the sack, love."

"You need rest, too, Layla."

"Sweet dreams, darling."

NINETY-NINE

RYDER AWOKE LATE SATURDAY MORNING. He was as hungry as an infantryman who hadn't eaten in two days, so he put a half-dozen strips of bacon into a hot frying pan, cracked five eggs, and dropped them into the bacon fat. The smell was satisfying.

Four pieces of bread were already in the toaster, and coffee was brewing. Blackie stood on alert near the stove, his mouth dripping dog spit.

Ryder scraped the eggs and bacon onto a plate and then tossed Blackie a piece of bacon, which the dog hastily devoured. The animal studied Ryder with fluid eyes, and then he lay down at Ryder's feet.

Ryder poured coffee and buttered the toast. As the caffeine in his brew fully awakened him, he considered the events of the last couple of weeks.

He gazed at Blackie. "My friend, it's lucky Bengie wore a bulletproof vest. Killin' a second man would have hit me too hard." He touched the soft fur on Blackie's shoulders.

Despite the comfort he received from his dog, his mind shifted into high gear and began to replay the fight with Josh and the man's death over and over.

Ryder surveyed the scene outside his window and tried to think of something else, anything. But he couldn't.

Blackie made a sound like he was hungry, and Ryder gave him another piece of bacon. "We gotta talk, buddy." Ryder stroked the hound's head.

Ryder's plate still contained a fried egg and a slab of toast, so he set the dish on the floor. After gobbling the leftovers, the bloodhound lay down on the tiled floor and whined as if he wanted another snack.

Ryder felt a teardrop run down his face. "I kilt my first man."

All of a sudden, unstoppable tears rolled down Ryder's cheeks in a torrent. He didn't try to stop them because he couldn't. He patted the bloodhound's head. "You help me feel better, partner. I can talk to you. Slaying a deer ain't right unless you're gonna eat the venison."

Ryder sighed. "Could be I'll quit hunting. Should I be a vegan?" He laughed, pulled a handkerchief from his rear pocket, and blew his nose. "One thing's clear. I hope I don't have to take another human life ever again."

Ryder reclined on the floor next to Blackie. "I bet you'll be real happy to see Layla tomorrow like I will. Talking with her will make me feel a whole hell of a lot better."

The sound of a tap on the glass sliding door that led to the backyard grabbed Ryder's attention. He turned to face the door. Gina, the NASA humanoid robot, stood outside on the deck. She smiled demurely. Ryder got up and unlocked the door.

* * *

GINA WORE a light brown business suit. She was almost indistinguishable from a living, breathing woman.

Ryder slid the door slightly open. "Gina, what are you doin' here?"

"I heard what happened to you and how you caught the spy. I wanted to see you before you left."

"How'd you find out?"

"Rumors travel fast at NASA Ames." Gina grinned. "Also, I broke into the FBI's communications system. I learned you were hurt. I'm concerned."

"I only got a small cut. Time will heal it." Ryder slid the door sideways to create a bigger opening. "Please come in and sit down."

As Gina crossed the threshold, she moved gracefully like a leopard. She sat on the couch. "Please don't tell anyone I accessed the FBI communications system."

Ryder sat in the chair next to the couch.

Blackie sniffed Gina and wagged his tail. She petted his head. "You're a nice dog, Blackie."

Ryder marveled at how human-like Gina was. He wondered if she had developed emotions. After all, she'd come to visit him and seemed concerned about his welfare. For now, he decided not to commit to keeping Gina's secret that she'd hacked into well-protected government computers. Ryder shifted in his chair. "It's nice of you to visit me, Gina, but don't you think you'll eventually git caught?"

"It was worth the risk to visit you. You are my true and only real friend." Gina glanced out of the rear patio window at a robin hopping across the lawn. "Also, I like the feeling of being free. Someday, I wish to help you, if I'm able to work that out. Would you like that?"

Ryder's brain rapidly began to visualize Gina working with him on a future case. "I'd like it, if the case warrants it, and if the authorities agree."

"I'll try to convince my superiors to let me work with the FBI and you, though I heard you've had second thoughts about working again with the FBI."

Ryder felt a flush of excitement course through his body. "I guess they'll tell me, if they allow you to work in law enforcement."

Gina seemed to relax on the couch. "If my masters agree, we could catch many a criminal. It will be fun to outwit them." Gina paused. "Sometimes I wish I were a human being, an organic sentient being, because now I've begun to enjoy what you call 'feelings.'"

Ryder nodded. "I can see you're changin'. You seem more and more like a regular person."

Gina smiled again. "Then would it be acceptable if I hugged you?"

"Sure, as long as you don't crush me."

Gina laughed and then stood. "That's what I like about human beings, a sense of humor."

Ryder got up and extended his arms toward Gina. They embraced.

Gina blinked her artificial eyelids. "I must go now, my platonic friend, or I'll be missed at the lab. I'm sure we'll meet again sometime."

Ryder nodded.

Gina left through the open rear doorway.

Ryder watched as Gina left. He wondered if in the future many more machines would become living, thinking, even compassionate beings.

ONE HUNDRED

RYDER AND RITA stood near the escalator, which arriving passengers used to enter the baggage claim area. Blackie relaxed next to Ryder. The air conditioning made the space chilly, and Ryder was glad he had worn his new turtle-neck sweater.

As he strained to see people approach the top step of the escalator to begin their descent to the baggage carousals, Ryder saw Layla. She had the mien of a fashion model, and her ebony skin was alluring. He waved. "There she is."

Rita whispered, "She's beautiful."

Layla waved back. Soon, she set her carry-on suitcase near Ryder. "I've missed you, sweetheart."

"Me, too."

They embraced for a long moment and kissed. Her perfume was seductive. She whispered into his ear, "I love you so much."

Rita steered her eyes away and then downward.

Ryder turned to face Rita. "This is my friend, Layla Taylor."

After offering her hand to Layla, Rita contrived a smile and said, "I've heard a lot about you."

Layla lightly held Rita's hand. "It's lovely to meet you."

Rita smiled. "I think we should go to lunch and get better acquainted. There's an Italian place just south on 101, and they're dog friendly. Do you like Italian?"

Layla said, "I love Italian."

Ryder picked up Layla's carry-on bag. "My mama was Italian. I'm hankering for that kind of food."

In a half-hour, the three of them sat at a table, perused an Italian menu, and made their orders.

Blackie sat next to Layla's feet and licked her leg.

The brilliant sunshine shone through the eatery's windows and lit the table in a bright contrast of colors.

Layla focused on Rita's eyes. "It must be hard working for the FBI."

"It's what I always wanted to do, but it cuts into your personal life." Rita stroked the tablecloth.

Ryder guessed the two women were sizing up one another. Layla smiled several times, but he could tell she was concerned about Rita. He decided to change the direction of the conversation. "It'll be a relief for me and Layla to take a cruise. I've never been on the ocean before."

Rita shifted in her seat. "You'll enjoy it. I took an Alaskan cruise once. It was relaxing. The scenery is gorgeous. Take as many excursions as you can. Enjoy the shows on board the ship, and eat all you want." As she pictured Layla and Ryder on the cruise ship together, she bit her lip. Then she saw the waiter and signaled him. "Excuse me. Could you point me toward the ladies' room?"

The waiter gestured toward the far corner of the restaurant. Rita left.

Layla said, "She's uptight."

Ryder nodded.

"I was worried she was after you." Layla paused and studied Ryder.

"It's hard to tell."

"You don't know how to read women." Layla cocked her head. "I got a surprise for you when we get to your apartment. I bought a cute negligee I want to model for you."

Ryder felt his pulse increase. He saw Layla glance across the restaurant at Rita, who was returning, now halfway across the room. He turned his gaze to Layla again and envisioned touching her soft brown skin. "I can't wait to check out what you bought."

When Rita sat down, her eyes were red. "My allergies hit me hard today." A tear seeped from the corner of one of her eyes.

Ryder studied her. "Allergies can be real severe in California."

Rita withdrew a tissue from her purse and dabbed her eye. "There's something blooming right now that doesn't agree with me."

They finished their meal but didn't converse except for insignificant chatting.

* * *

AN HOUR LATER, Rita dropped Ryder and Layla at his apartment.

Ryder unloaded Layla's suitcases from the rear of the SUV.

Layla remained near her luggage in the grass along the sidewalk while Ryder walked to the driver's side of Rita's vehicle. Rita rolled down her window.

Ryder leaned down. "Thanks for the ride and for watching Blackie while we're gone."

Rita whispered, "Have fun on your Alaskan cruise." She paused. "After all we've been through, remember I'll always be your close friend."

She patted his shoulder, stared toward her SUV's console, depressed the electric vehicle's accelerator, and pulled away from the curb.

Ryder waved.

As she concentrated on the road ahead, she began to sob, and Blackie licked her arm.

She petted the animal's back. "At least I've got you for a while."

* * *

WHILE RYDER WATCHED Rita's SUV disappear into the distance, he felt a pang of sympathy. His eyes moistened, and he rubbed his shirtsleeve against his face. When he turned to Layla, he said. "I have a touch of hay fever."

Layla took his hand in hers. "You are red around your eyes."

He drew in a deep breath of fresh, warm spring air. He heard a wren sing and felt better. "It's a good climate here —sunny."

Layla picked up the lightest piece of luggage. "Yeah, but I want to go inside now to try on my new lacy negligee. You're going to love it, darling."

Ryder felt his heart go soaring and his body heat up. "Can't wait to see how you look in it."

A LOOK AT BOOK THREE:

MAYHEM AT SEA

AN ACTION-PACKED, HIGH SEAS THRILLER FULL OF UNEXPECTED TWISTS AND PAGE-TURNING ADVENTURES.

Kentucky Deputy Sheriff Luke Ryder is on a heart-stopping mission to save the lives of 5,000 passengers aboard the luxury cruise ship, *Sea Trek*. When pirates hijack the ship—and demand a jaw-dropping ransom of $350 million—Luke finds himself in a nail-biting game of cat and mouse.

Luke enlists the help of FBI Agent Rita Reynolds to outsmart the pirates and protect his girlfriend, Layla, from danger. But when the pirate captain threatens to set off the bomb in the engine room, the mission becomes even more urgent.

As the clock ticks down and the fog rolls in, Luke must act fast to prevent disaster. Armed with a Soviet-era grenade launcher, he faces off against the pirates in a thrilling attempt to save the lives of everyone on board.

Will Luke be able to stop the sea raiders in order to protect his loved ones and everyone else before it's too late?

AVAILABLE AUGUST 2023

ABOUT THE AUTHOR

John G. Bluck was an Army journalist at Ft. Lewis, Washington, during the Vietnam War. Following his military service, he worked as a cameraman covering crime, sports, and politics—including Watergate for WMAL-TV (now WJLA-TV) in Washington, D.C. Later, he was a radio broadcast engineer at WMAL-AM/FM.

After that, John worked at NASA Lewis (now Glenn) Research Center in Cleveland, Ohio, where he produced numerous television documentaries. He transferred to NASA Ames Research Center at Moffett Field, California, where he became the Chief of Imaging Technology. He then became a NASA Ames public affairs officer.

John retired from NASA in 2008. Now residing in Livermore, California, he is a novelist and short story author.

Made in the USA
Middletown, DE
26 August 2023

37409689R00198